"With all the suspense of a finely wrought mystery, this remarkably assured first novel tells the story of a marriage unexpectedly—and unwittingly—revisited, testing the boundaries of love and memory—and it does so with prose exquisitely calibrated to reflect the subtleties of these two characters' thoughts and feelings in all their strangeness and familiarity."

—Ellen Akins, author of *Hometown Brew, Public Life, Little Woman* and *World Like a Knife*

"[E]ach word that is spoken or left unsaid becomes important in a cat-and-mouse mind game that gives this pensive story some elements of a thriller. The love that's described is always on thin ice ('But the moment he touches her, the spell will break, and they'll just be two people in bed together, without any enchantments'). Hausler's ability to describe the precarious state of the emotions involved is consistently convincing. . . . A strongly written tale about resurrecting a marriage under the most unusual and mysterious of circumstances."

—*Kirkus Reviews*

"This disturbing, haunting and powerful story explores the minutiae of the relationship between the couple as they start to live together again . . . [T]he ending was a masterpiece of the power of 'less is more' in storytelling—but if you want to know what it is, then you will have to read this wonderful novel."

—Linda Hepworth, *Nudge Books*

"Hausler's debut novel was an incredibly beautiful look at love put through the test of time. *Retrograde* is very much about the nature of love as it features many of the ups and downs of a difficult relationship. From touching dates and admiration to petty fights and full blown arguments, Hausler's breakout has it all."

—Melissa Ratcliff, *Paperback Paris*

RETROGRADE

A NOVEL

KAT HAUSLER

Meerkat Press
Atlanta

ISBN-13 - 978-1-946154-02-6 (Paperback)
ISBN-13 - 978-1-946154-03-3 (eBook)

Library of Congress Control Number: 2017911522

Cover art front cover, "The Disappearing," and back cover, "Love,"
© 2017 by Laurel Hausler

Book design by Tricia Reeks
Cover design by Tricia Reeks

Printed in the United States of America

Published in the United States of America by
Meerkat Press, LLC, Atlanta, Georgia
www.meerkatpress.com

"That awful thing, a woman's memory!"

—Oscar Wilde, *The Picture of Dorian Gray*

JOACHIM

Leila left Joachim when she found out he was married. It wasn't the only reason, but it was *a* reason. There's always enough resentment between two people for a separation; all it takes is a catalyst. That's what Joachim tells himself, anyway.

In this case, he'd made an innocent remark about his wife. He can't remember afterward what he and Leila were talking about, what caused him to say: "My ex-wife always used to say that."

He must've said it a million times. But this time, the million-and-first time, Leila had a rare moment of curiosity about his past and asked, "How long ago did you actually get divorced?"

"Well," he said, "the thing is."

The thing is that they aren't divorced. Not because there's any lingering chance of reconciliation, but for the simple reason that Joachim can't reach his wife. For almost three years, he hasn't had any idea where she is. Not only did she change her number after she moved out, but all of his emails were either returned automatically or never answered, whether he sent them to her, her parents, or the friends—and that had been most of them—who sided with her. No one he called would admit to knowing where she was, and that got embarrassing fast. Her parents had his number blocked, and at the time, he was too ashamed to call from another phone. What would he have said?

After all, he doesn't really want to talk to Helena. He just feels that he should be able to if he needs to. To divorce her, for example.

It's not that he's in any hurry to get married again; he's just tired of being married to someone he never sees. It's like one of his arms up and pulled itself free of him, and is out there now, shaking hands and signing documents in his name. He doesn't like knowing there's a part of him out there without him.

But Leila wasn't convinced. She said it was just like him not to have said anything and that he was always keeping important things from her.

"Yeah, that's what my ex-wife—" he started to say, out of habit.

Leila piled her dark, bouncing curls into a bun on top of her head, always a sign that she was about to leave. He reached up to stroke her hair and she slapped him hard enough to leave a mark.

"For heaven's sake, darling, I haven't heard from her in years. I could probably have her declared legally dead."

"I'm leaving," she said.

He managed to keep himself from repeating his fatal remark a third time. Unlike his wife, the first time Leila said she was leaving, she actually did.

• • •

He's surprised at how abrupt the break is. Leila comes once to pick up her things and leave his spare key in the mailbox. She had astonishingly little at his place, for a relationship of almost a year. He cleans the apartment twice after she leaves but finds nothing more than a few stray hairs on the bathroom floor. And no teary phone calls, no one ringing his doorbell at 3:00 a.m. to say "I didn't mean it." He calls her after two weeks, and she says she'd appreciate if he didn't call anymore. So he doesn't.

• • •

Leila wasn't the first woman in Joachim's life post-marriage, just the first to stick around this long. Careful experimentation after Helena packed her things and slipped below the radar has shown that "my ex-wife" meets with more favorable reactions than phrases like "my estranged spouse" or "married but separated." He doesn't consider it lying, because it's true that they're no longer husband and wife. But it would be a lie to refer to her simply as "my ex," and try to play down the most important event in his twenty-some years of romantic experience.

He doesn't miss Helena and he isn't still in love with her. In fact, he rarely thinks of her, except to identify a certain period of his life—*When I was married*—or when something specific reminds him of her.

He doesn't think of her after his breakup, except as the cause of it. Just after the door closed behind Leila, there was an instant in which his mind leapt toward the memory of his separation from Helena, but fell short of it. He didn't want to remember. It wasn't a clean break like this one, but a state of almost unbearable misery that lasted for months.

The week after Leila told Joachim not to call, he has a big assignment that takes up most of his attention. A major client complained that the campaign he designed for their new line of granola bars wasn't catchy enough. The result is that he has to redo a month's work in four days, and do it better than the first time around.

Although he clocks about twelve hours of overtime and is exhausted by the time he turns in the new proposal Friday evening, he can't bring himself to go straight home.

Instead of hurrying to the U-Bahn station as usual, he strolls toward the Landwehr Canal. Once he's crossed the bridge over it, he stops abruptly, no longer knowing what to do. A bicyclist swerves to avoid him, rings his bell, and curses. Joachim responds with an embarrassed smile. He follows the trail along the bank of the canal and sits down on the first unoccupied bench. He feels like he's waiting for something, or someone. A pair of joggers gallops by, leaving behind snatches of conversation about the Eurozone Crisis.

Although the water is just a few meters away, he can't see

it from where he's sitting because of the thick undergrowth and tufts of yellow weeds. It's late July, but doesn't feel like it; all in all, it's been a disappointingly cool summer.

He sits a while beside the invisible water, thinking empty thoughts about the weather. He's aware that he and Leila walked along this canal together the month before, that Helena was living in this part of Kreuzberg when they first met, but it's no use thinking about these things, trying to find a meaning that isn't there. Just a couple more memories to clutter up the back of his mind with all the other irrelevant debris that's accumulated over the years: choruses of songs he listened to in his youth, illustrations from *Shockheaded Peter* that gave him nightmares as a boy, the dates of the Thirty Years' War.

He begins to feel weak. *I must be hungry*, he tells himself. *And tired. Have to make an early night of it.* But he doesn't move until the first stars have appeared at the edge of the sky. Someone—who was it? Helena, trying to make up for his thoroughly unmagical childhood?—told him you could make a wish on the first star you saw each night. But he can't remember which he saw first, or decide what to wish for.

Walking to the station, he decides it must've been Helena who told him that, but he can't be quite sure and that bothers him, though neither the silly superstition, nor the memory of being told about it, ever held any significance for him. *I'm getting old*, he thinks.

• • •

The feeling of weariness remains when he wakes the next morning, and everything seems to take longer than usual. Shaving in front of the bathroom mirror, he counts a few more gray hairs on his chin. The pouches under his puffy brown eyes are like two deflated balloons, and he feels nervous combing the thin, ash blond hair at his temples, as if he might startle his skittish hairline into retreating further uphill.

HELENA

Exactly 3.24 kilometers away, Helena is looking into her bathroom mirror, weighing pros against cons. Her cheeks, so flushed with anxiety she doesn't need blush, make her gray-blue eyes shine despite the faint circles below them. She's painting on a glistening layer of lip gloss and wondering whether blue eye shadow is too much for a first date.

It's not, she decides, and smooths moisturizer onto her eyelids to keep the powder from collecting in the fine lines running through her skin. On the whole, she thinks she looks pretty good, though her wavy, copper-colored hair was so uncooperative she had to confine it to a tight knot at the back of her head.

No, the eye shadow *is* too much for so early in the day, and it draws attention to the shadows under her eyes. Tobias has already seen a picture of her, but she wants him to say she's prettier in person.

She washes off the eye shadow and puts on too much perfume, telling herself it will wear off before her date. She doesn't want to seem like she's trying too hard.

She leaves the bathroom and, not knowing what else to do, begins to clean her already clean studio apartment. She wants to laugh at her absurd anxiety, but she's too anxious even for that. How long has it been since she kissed a man, or even went on a date?

Much too long. At thirty-three, she hardly has the time to spare. She washes the few dishes in the sink, washes her hands and rubs lotion into them. It isn't that she avoided dating after her separation from Joachim; it just didn't happen.

There was even a time, a few months after, when she began answering personals ads. Her friends said it would help her move on. She would've preferred to meet men in some more conventional way, say at a bar or party, but no one approached her. There must've been—maybe there still is—some subtle signal in her body language telling them to keep away. Which, on a certain level, was what she wanted.

Back then, about three years ago now, she went home and sobbed after each date. Home was with her best friend Magdalena, and once she'd cried herself out, the two of them would take a walk around the block. Helena felt like an invalid who couldn't be let out on her own.

She sits down on the sofa and sighs. She's doing it again: hoping too much. It'll make it that much harder when nothing comes of it. But then that attitude is just as bad—she shouldn't give up on Tobias before she's even met him.

Tobias is the divorced cousin of one of Helena's coworker's husband's friends, putting enough distance between them for it not to be awkward if things don't work out. None of Helena's coworkers at this agency know she was married—or that she still is. It isn't relevant. At the same time, many were surprised to learn that she was single.

"But you're so pretty!" Doro, who sits next to Helena, burst out when the subject first came up in the office kitchen. Doro is in her forties with Helena-can-never-remember-how-many children and a pleasant husband who stays home to tend to them. Children are a subject Helena avoids bringing up, because discussing them somehow always gives her a sudden, suffocating pain in her throat, like swallowing something large and sharp.

Like all happily married women with inexplicably single friends, Doro searched all seven degrees of her acquaintances until she came up with a possible match. Helena demurred, but only briefly. She trusts Doro's judgment. She has older and better friends, but sometimes it's hard to be around them. They always want to talk about the past, and even if they don't, it's there, the elephant in every room. Sometimes she feels ungrateful for seeing so little of them, all those mutual friends she won in a kind of custody battle after leaving Joachim. She's known Magdalena since they were girls, but that time is overshadowed by more recent memories. She met Sepp, Susi, and Susi's husband, Thomas, through her old job, and they were always her *and* Joachim's friends, even if they took her side in the end. Maybe it's natural; maybe they just belong to another part of her life. Anyway, why think about that now, when everything's so strange and exciting? She's so used to feeling alien to the world of romance that the mere thought of becoming involved with someone has an exotic, thrilling appeal.

When she can't stand waiting around anymore, she goes up a floor to see whether Julie is home. Julie's a sloppy, lovable, and fearless strawberry blonde from England who befriended Helena by force one day when she came to pick up a package Helena had signed for. Julie will know the right way to look, the right things to say.

But Julie doesn't answer, even when Helena rings her doorbell a second time. Was this the week she was going to visit her parents? Julie's the kind of person who barely knows her own vacation plans until she gets on a plane, and Helena can't remember. She can't bring herself to go back into her apartment, but the thought of telling Julie about the date later on reassures her. Or Doro, if Julie's out of town, though she can't say anything too harsh about someone Doro knows, so maybe Magdalena or Susi, if she can get herself to call them. It's hard to keep up with old friends, harder still when they're part of a time you don't want to remember.

JOACHIM

The selection at the bakery is disappointing—after all, it's quite late for breakfast—but Joachim is too embarrassed to leave again after he walks in, so he buys a stale-looking Berliner pastry, a cup of coffee, and a copy of the *Tagespiegel* to read while he eats.

Because it's a warm day and the bakery sells ice cream, a procession of parents and small children files in and out, bickering and cajoling and dripping on the floor, some taking seats to raise the ambient noise a few decibels.

Usually, Joachim overlooks children the way a wild animal overlooks street signs: they have no meaning for him. But in the strange mood that he's in, they catch his attention, and an even heavier weariness settles over him despite his long sleep.

He feels old. Not in comparison to the children, but to their parents, perky young couples who still hold hands. Having children, he realizes, is something he didn't do. Never before has it been so clear to him that the part of his life in which he might have done so is over.

How ridiculous, he thinks. I never wanted children that badly. He forces down his doughnut—soggy on the inside where the jelly soaked in, and dry on the outside, with enough powdered sugar to choke on—and washes it down with coffee. When he wipes his mouth, it feels raw, as if the doughnut had been powdered with sand.

There's nothing to get so sentimental about. He must've

slept poorly. Opening the newspaper between himself and the laughing, crying, slurping, chattering families, he struggles to focus on the articles in front of him: "Completion of Airport Postponed Again," "CDU Politician Accused of Bribery," "UN to Send More Troops."

But why has it been so long since he had thoughts like these? Maybe he hasn't allowed himself to. Helena wasn't able to have children, and although they sometimes mentioned adopting, it was always something they might do down the road, when they were ready. Which they never were, because there was always some other difficulty, something to fight over, an impossible issue that had to be worked out. When the time came that Joachim could've had a child, becoming a father was the furthest thing from his mind.

For the first time, he allows himself to look back on what must've been the ugliest period of his life.

It was the year a local paper ran the headline: "Cheating: Berlin's National Pastime." Helena was particularly jealous and irrational, though he'd never given her a reason to be. In their calm moments, they both knew this had more to do with her insecurity and the many other problems in their marriage than any actual suspicions, but their relationship was swept from storm to storm, and calms were few and far between. Her office was laying off staff, and he wasn't getting enough freelance work to support both of them. There were nights he couldn't sleep for worrying. Not about any one thing in particular, but about how things could possibly go on the way they were. Outside of his home, he felt ashamed and dishonest, because he played the good husband when, again and again, his evenings ended with Helena crying until she wretched in the bathroom sink, and him on the living room sofa, sniffling, terrified, but never crying loud enough for her to hear. It seemed to him that these were strange, inexplicable problems no one else had, peculiar blights that reflected on his character. Things he somehow deserved. His parents had certainly thought so when he alluded to the situation, but they were the wrong people to confide in. Even if he'd found the right person, he wouldn't have known what to say.

Staring blindly at his Saturday morning—or now afternoon—paper, he remembers what a relief it was when they
finally decided to take some time off. "A break," they called
it, as if their exhaustion were merely physical, and they could
carry on as soon as they'd stopped to catch their breath.

Helena's childhood friend Magdalena offered up her spare
room, and he stayed behind in the apartment. It was remark-
able how civil they were, once the decision was made. Maybe
because they were up against something larger than themselves,
a darkness against which all their petty squabbles paled to a
muted, funereal respect. He helped her carry her bags to the
cab waiting downstairs and kissed her on the cheek. They
hadn't set a definite time frame, but she said she'd let him
know when she was ready.

He didn't call for the first few days; then he called every
day. She rarely picked up. Sometimes she'd send a message
saying she was busy, but not with what or whom; other times
he went without any answer at all.

Still, he didn't feel the gutting sorrow he knew he would
if their separation were permanent. Helena wasn't gone from
his life; she was merely absent, as if out of town. Once she'd
been called away unexpectedly to help with a photo spread
and been similarly unavailable, albeit only for five days. There
was nothing to do but keep busy, so he did it, avoiding their
mutual friends and spending more time on assignments, job
applications, and drinking with colleagues from his part-time
corporate design gig. He was always among the last to leave
the office or the bar. The apartment was so quiet in those
first days.

He stopped calling Helena, and she began to call him
once every week or two, never for more than a few minutes
at a time. She sounded happy and very far away. After she
hung up he held onto the phone a moment too long, lonely
as an exile to the ends of the earth. But they didn't fight on
the phone.

On one particularly grim Saturday in November, he
dragged himself to a coworker's going-away party. He wasn't
close to the man but felt the need to be among people, away

from the stillness that burned in his ears, and all the surfaces in his home that were cold to the touch.

The party was a drag and broke up early; his coworker had movers coming in the morning. But some of the guests moved on to another bar and then another, and after all, no one was waiting up for Joachim.

Vague and dizzy at the third bar, he found himself talking to a girl with dark hair and bare legs that glistened like silk stockings under her short skirt. He felt so virtuous letting her know he was married, in that way that always sounds so forced: "Ah, Provence? My wife and I always . . ." And he never took off his wedding ring.

There was nothing special about the girl, and that made him feel safe. She was short, curvy without being fat, with a bland, pleasant face. Red lipstick. He felt the blood flowing below his waist when he looked at her, but when he left the dance floor to get her a drink, he immediately forgot what she looked like. Besides, she knew he had a wife. Even if he was taking time off and free to do as he pleased, he knew and she knew that he had a wife.

Still, her attention was pleasant, therapeutic after months of fighting with Helena, and weeks of being ignored by her. When they'd agreed to take a break, he'd had no intention of seeing anyone else. Wherever their marriage might be headed, he had his hands full with Helena. Getting involved with someone else would've been like taking a break from a marathon to swim a few dozen kilometers.

But it was easier than he'd thought. He didn't decide to go home with Ester based on the current status of his marriage; rather, upon finding himself in a loft bed in her filthy apartment, he recalled this "time off" with relief, clutching it like an amulet to ward off guilt.

The sex was mediocre. They were both drunk and Helena was better in bed. But since this sex didn't come at the price of recriminations, tears, and fights over the pettiest issues, since there was no pathos and no panicked, urgent need to solve all the problems in their two-person universe before he fell asleep, he saw Ester a few more times in the next couple months. He made his situation as clear as he could: despite the bleak outlook of his marriage, it was still his top priority.

Ester didn't seem to mind, maybe because she didn't believe him. He noticed this and felt somehow at fault for not convincing her. But he reminded himself that he'd told her nothing but the truth from day one.

A few weeks into the new year, Helena called and said she missed him but she needed a little more time. She asked how he was, and they talked a while without saying anything. Another month passed and she said she was ready if he was.

It had been a couple weeks since he'd slept with Ester, and he hadn't heard from her in the meantime. Although he knew it was cowardly, he called her to break it off. He told himself he didn't trust himself to see her, but really he just wanted to avoid an inevitably unpleasant situation.

She didn't sound too upset, and he was relieved, though on some level also offended. She must have many other Joachims lined up, he thought. After all, they'd only seen each other a handful of times. He was happy to have the whole thing behind him.

Helena returned looking cheerful and well-rested. She came in, dropped the handle of her suitcase, and wrapped her arms around him for a good five minutes without speaking. He felt so secure in her warmth he could've wept like a child.

"Hey," she said. "I think we're gonna be okay."

But they weren't.

Three weeks after Helena's return, Ester called. She needed to see him, she said. It was urgent. He refused. He hadn't told Helena about the affair because it had taken place outside of time, because it was irrelevant. He wouldn't see Ester again.

To his surprise, she insisted. Gone was the flippant girl who didn't mind about his wife. When he told her it was absolutely impossible, she hung up but turned up at his door that evening. He didn't know where she'd gotten his address, since they'd always been at her place. She must've looked through his wallet at some point. Miraculously, Helena wasn't home from work.

He took Ester by the arm and led her downstairs, away

from his home. It was drizzling and chilly, but he didn't stop to zip his coat. He took her into a dingy old men's bar around the corner, where the air smelled like stale smoke, stale beer, and staler flesh. He wanted to push her in and leave her there, as if removing her from his life could be that simple. Afterward, maybe even at the time, it seemed to him that he already knew what she was going to say.

"Joachim, we're having a baby."

And of course it was right to say it that way, right that it was their problem and not just hers. In fact, he was probably at fault—after years of sleeping with his infertile wife, he might've been careless. Besides, he'd been drinking every time he met up with Ester. Remembering whether he could've made a mistake was as impossible as recalling the details of brushing his teeth that morning. It had all been so automatic, rolled along so smoothly, until now.

The grizzled old bartender asked what they wanted, then brought the two cups of mineral water Joachim ordered, probably after spitting in them. One of his eyes didn't quite follow the other, and Joachim watched it covertly, unsure whether it was real. He felt like the old man was trying to pull one over on him, like life was.

"When?" he asked, because that was the kind of question people asked, and because he had to say something.

It was a stupid question because they'd been sleeping together such a short amount of time, and when she told him, the date meant nothing to him. He couldn't even begin to think about the possibility of having a baby with the scared, half-unknown girl across from him; all he could think about was Helena getting back to the apartment—hopefully she'd stopped for groceries or some other errand—and wondering where he was. A feverish sweat soaked his skin, and his head ached as he forced himself to focus.

"What are you—I mean, what are we going to do?" he asked.

"That's what I came to ask you."

Focus, focus, he urged himself. There's a solution to every problem, an answer to every question. Once in Gymnasium, he'd come down with a stomach virus in the middle of a history exam and bravely sat out all three hours of it before handing in the papers and vomiting at his teacher's feet. He'd known how furious his parents would be if he didn't finish it. Vividly, he recalled the dizzy nausea pressing against him like a stiff headwind, and the answers squirming on the pages, mingling with the questions, interchangeable. Everything equally true; everything equally false. He had to relearn to read, to understand German, with every line; had to create the lecture hall around him over and over again through sheer strength of will, like a dreamer trying not to wake up. If he succumbed to the black pounding in his brain, it would all disappear.

But he had not, and he would not now succumb to it. There was a question, and there were possible answers to it. Either she'd keep the baby, or she wouldn't. If she didn't plan to, there was little he could do. Accompany her to a clinic, maybe. Talk her through it. Pay. But if that were all she wanted, she would've asked him right away. And she would've said it differently. "I'm pregnant" was a condition, a potentially transitory state. "We're having a baby" was a binding plan.

"So you want to keep it?"

She didn't nod, didn't shake her head or speak, but in the way she looked at him he knew that she did. There was a softness to the look on her round, childish face, a touching vulnerability. And yet they'd never said *I love you* or talked about a future together. He couldn't remember her last name, or whether he'd ever known it. Still, there was no denying his part in this baby. So there was another question, and now he had to focus on choosing from another set of answers.

"You know I'm married," he said, and with an extreme, almost painful effort, added, "but . . ." He didn't know where to go from there. Instead of dealing with the situation at hand, his brain wrestled with the question of whether he could conceal this from Helena, and by what means. Could he justify keeping this secret? The pregnancy might've come about during a temporary separation, but he and Helena were back together now. What would he tell her when he came in?

"I know," she said. "But."

Neither of them seemed able to say anything else. Perhaps she wanted to but couldn't, and he wanted nothing more than to leave as soon as possible, to collapse in Helena's arms and awake as if from a nightmare. But it was no use being melodramatic.

"Well, about the baby, if you need anything . . ." Yes, that was it; of course she'd need something. Babies were complicated. And expensive. "I'll certainly help you out . . . financially." The last word came into his mouth with a sour foretaste of sickness.

She paled still further, which he wouldn't have thought possible. He was as ashamed as if he'd hit her, and wanted more than ever to flee.

She swallowed loudly. "Are you going to tell your wife?"

HELENA

Helena arrives at the café a quarter of an hour early and takes a table in the nearly empty interior, with a slight cross-breeze from the open door. There are still a couple of tables left on the sidewalk, but she prefers to retreat to the dim, stifling atmosphere of summer indoors, to hide somewhere she'll have to be found. This is the advantage of arriving early. She doesn't have to approach the other tables, asking all the solitary men if they're Tobias; she doesn't have to make questioning, hopeful, pathetic eye contact with every passing male. She's early enough to reasonably assume that she's the first one here. All she has to do is read her book and try to get her pulse down to a normal level.

She should've asked Doro for a picture. She didn't want to, didn't even want to send her own with its too broad smile, looking like an applicant who's been out of work a long time. But it might've helped to know what he looks like.

Only two other tables inside the café are occupied: one by a mother and her extensive collection of children, sharing rapidly melting sundaes and speaking a language Helena can't identify, and one next to the newspaper rack by a generic male form behind a spread paper. That would really have been the thing to do. Why bother with her tiny little novel when she could hide her entire body behind a sprawling issue of *Die Zeit*? Already, she wishes she hadn't come. She knows just how he'll be, and how she will. He'll say things that got a laugh from other women, and she'll pretend to find him charming. She'll keep nodding and smiling through three dates or so, then snap at him under the pressure. He won't like the real her, whatever that's supposed to mean. Nor will she like him. But they'll sit across from each other a few times, each hoping against hope for a ticket out of solitude. Each willing to forgive, to overlook flaws, to swallow the medicine with the sugar, and try to believe that a life with this person wouldn't be too unbearable.

The man abruptly lowers his paper, and their eyes meet. She looks down at her book. She wasn't staring at him, really, just into the vague expanse of headlines she can't quite read from here. But he won't see it that way. He's what she'd call pleasant-looking rather than actually handsome—slightly too broad in the jaw with a short beard, overgrown blond hair, and thick eyebrows that would give him a leonine appearance if not for the deep laugh lines in his face and his bashful, puzzled expression. As it is, he better resembles a sheepdog.

In spite of herself, she smiles. It doesn't matter; Tobias will arrive in a few minutes, and the bearded man will see his mistake and retreat behind his paper again. She looks just to the left of the newspaper man, out the door. She wasn't watching him; she just happened to pass over him as she turned to look for someone else. For added emphasis, she checks her phone.

One of the first things she did after she and Joachim broke up—after I left, she reminds herself—was to buy a new SIM card. It was the only way she could keep herself under control. Not that she would've called him. When she makes a decision, she sticks to it. But there was no other way to stop herself from constantly checking to see whether he'd called, from incessantly, permanently, and pathologically waiting for something she didn't even really want.

Hearing the crinkle of newsprint, she looks up to see the bearded man standing over her, his paper folded under one arm.

"Tobi," he says, offering her his hand. "In case you happen to be Helena."

She nods, briefly at a loss for words.

"Should we get a table outside?"

When they sit down again in the sunlight, they're two new people: she's no longer the wary stranger eyeing him through his newspaper, and there's no longer anything ironic about his smile. For the first time in years, conversation is so easy she doesn't have to think about it. When her phone rings with the bail call she set up—Doro pretending to be locked out so Helena can rush to her rescue—she doesn't even pick up. They get through the basics in a few minutes, maybe because this is a set-up and they already know a rough outline of each other: he's an architect from Bavaria and she's a graphic designer from the Rhineland. He has two brothers and she's an only child; neither of them smokes. And then they talk about anything and everything, and she's astonished that three hours could pass so quickly.

He doesn't seem to have expected the afternoon to go so quickly, either. He apologizes for having to rush to a fitting—his cousin is having a big wedding and he's the witness—but they exchange numbers and he says, "I want to see you again. Very, very soon," before getting their check. When he kisses her on both cheeks, her heart shudders with fear and happiness. She stands a moment watching as he heads toward the S-Bahn station to catch his train, then starts toward Warschauer Strasse for a tram.

But when she reaches the stop in the middle of the road, the airy, pulsing feeling within her won't allow her to stand still, so she decides to walk home. It's a long way but she can always catch a train later, once she can think clearly again. A few slugabed songbirds are chirping and the traffic sounds distant, as if she were floating above it. She's distinctly aware of the red glimmer across from her as she crosses Warschauer Strasse again, but the light seems insignificant, part of a world she's left behind. She hears the blare of horns honking but something hits her before she has time to turn and look. Her only sensation is shock. She's out before the pain comes, a butterfly after the windshield, falling lightly to the ground.

Joachim

The red light flashing on his answering machine catches Joachim's eye as he comes in; he almost never gets a message. It must be his mother. Everyone else has heard of call ID by now.

Before he can play back the message, the phone rings again.

"Mr. Schmidt?" a strange woman's voice asks. She sounds official; maybe it's something to do with this year's taxes.

"Yes?"

"Vivantes Hospital. It's about your wife."

If he'd ever pictured this scenario to himself, if he'd imagined his next words, he would've expected to ask: *What wife?* But he feels no such confusion. In the immediacy of the moment, their separation vanishes, as if she'd only just stepped out.

"Is she all right?" She can't be dead, he reminds himself, or it would be the police and not the hospital. She can't be dead or they'd come in person.

"You'd better come in."

HELENA

Helena wakes with a general sense of nausea. She doesn't feel like she's going to vomit, but like each individual part of her body is about to heave its entire contents into the white glare surrounding her. Then the light takes shape and becomes a narrow room with two beds—the one she's lying in, and one to her right, in which a shriveled old woman is either sleeping or dead. Helena shifts her arms and legs, just to make sure she can. Her right arm feels strangely heavy and the white sheet spread taut over her legs resists her, but she can control her body. There's some kind of cast from her right wrist to her elbow. Her mouth tastes like metal and soap. There's a window to her left with the blinds down, and when she turns to examine the strange feeling in her left arm, she discovers a tube clamped to the inside of her elbow, pumping an unidentified fluid into her. She winces and swallows hard, more nauseous than ever.

Gingerly, she leans forward and explores her face with her left hand. Most of it is bandaged. She can feel something hard on her right leg that could be another cast, and something firm is holding her torso in place. She wants to yell for help or simply an explanation, but is afraid of disturbing the old woman. Something is terribly wrong, but she can't think what. She must've had an accident—did she fall down the stairs? It must be the medicine in her arm making her groggy. She'll remember when she's more awake.

She finds the call button on the wall and presses it firmly, like an insistent visitor ringing a doorbell.

The nurse who comes in is young, just out of school, with thin blonde hair and a blotchy complexion. She looks first at the old woman, as if she'd long expected an emergency call from that bed, then approaches Helena.

"So, you're awake. How are you feeling?" She uses the formal *you*, but Helena still notices and resents something condescending in her tone. She may have just regained consciousness but she isn't a child.

"Where am I?" she snaps.

"The hospital—"

"I know that! I mean . . ." She feels angry, helpless, helpless to direct her anger toward anyone. She wants to shout at this young woman, stand up and shake the answers out of her. What hospital? What's happened? She doesn't even know what day it is. Or, she realizes to her horror, what year. Has she been here for long? She can't breathe and a wave of dizziness washes over her so that she falls back against the stiff pillow behind her.

"Calm down, ma'am. Everything's fine. You've had an accident, but you're going to be okay. Your husband will be back in a moment; he just stepped out to get some coffee."

"I see." Helena struggles to remain calm, to act with dignity. But already tears of relief are rolling down her face. *Just like Joachim*, she thinks. *Stepping out for coffee right when I need him.* But the thought of his presence reassures her, takes away all her confusion. Joachim will be here any minute, and he'll explain. It can't be as bad as she thinks.

He comes through the door and the young nurse dashes out as if chased.

"Oh, darling, I was so scared!" She doesn't want him to think she's blaming him for stepping out, but she can't help herself.

"Hi, Helena. I'm glad to see you up." Something about him is different, though she can't quite place it. His hair's longer, for one thing.

"How long have I been here? What happened? What day is it?"

"There, there." He walks over to her bed and places his hand on hers. "It's all right. You're going to be all right now."

They must've had a fight, she thinks. That's why his manner is so strange. They must've had a fight before whatever happened to her happened, and now he feels awkward because of that. He shouldn't bother. She can't remember the fight, whatever it was. She wants to tell him that but he begins to answer her questions in that measured, soothing tone he uses when he knows she's upset. Like she's a bundle of explosives he's taking care not to ignite.

"Today's Tuesday. You've been here for three days now," he says. "Don't worry, I let your work know what was up. Do you remember what happened?"

"Of course not! Why else would I have asked? Nobody around here wants to tell me a thing!" She presses his hand so he won't be angry with her. The drip in her arm pulls taut. He hates when she raises her voice.

"You were crossing the street and you got hit by a truck. The driver braked, but you still got knocked down, broke a couple ribs, your arm, and your ankle. The doctor said none of it will leave major damage, and you'll be on crutches in a couple days. That's pretty lucky, right?"

Yeah, lucky. A few broken bones and who knows how much work piled up when she gets back to the office. And who's going to be cleaning the apartment while she hobbles around on crutches? He sure isn't.

"Where was I?" she asks. It's not important, but it bothers her that she can't remember. Something isn't right here, and it's not just the nausea coursing through her body and keeping her from thinking straight.

"They said you were in Friedrichshain, crossing Warschauer Strasse."

"But Joachim, weren't you with me?"

He doesn't answer, and she doesn't blame him. He must feel guilty for not having been there. As if he could've known. He squeezes both of her hands and mumbles something about speaking to the doctor. When she looks up, he has tears in his eyes.

"What's wrong, darling?"

"Nothing, nothing. I was just so worried." He kisses her forehead and steps out of the room.

Joachim

At the nurses' station, Joachim demands to speak to a doctor. "The one responsible for . . . my wife," he adds.

"Dr. Hofstaedter is just finishing her rounds," the lanky young man resting his elbows on the counter says. "She'll be here any minute now."

Any minute turns out to be twenty-three minutes later by the clock hanging above the nurses' station. He thinks of returning to Helena, who's awake and alone all this time, but is afraid of missing the doctor. And afraid of being alone with Helena, not knowing what to say to her. The way she spoke to him! It was as if no time had passed. As if *less* than no time had passed, as if they'd gone back to before the end of things. She called him *darling*, not once but twice. Does that mean she's reconsidered? There are plenty of cases like that, people's whole lives flashing before their eyes and making them into different people afterward. If only it were that. But the way she spoke to him, it almost seemed like—

"Mr. Schmidt?" A short woman with a dark, lined face and white hair offers him her hand and a mirthless, professional smile. "I'm Dr. Hofstaedter. Perhaps you could join me in my consultation room?"

The lights in the consultation room are dimmer, and sitting in a comfortable chair opposite the doctor, he feels foolish for nearing hysterics a few minutes before. It'll be all right. It's probably nothing.

"Doctor, have you seen my wife?"

She nods and waits for him to continue. She probably doesn't have time for this.

"And you noticed . . . Did you notice something strange about her?"

"Mrs. Schmidt doesn't—"

"Excuse me, it's Ms. Bachlein. She kept her name when we married." As if that were important now.

"Of course, of course. Now, you're probably concerned because Ms. Bachlein doesn't remember what happened the day of the accident, right? It's perfectly ordinary for patients with head trauma to forget things like that. She may regain the memory later, or she may not. After all, it must've happened very quickly. Most likely she didn't even have time to realize she'd been hit."

He nods slowly. He is, perhaps, the only one who knows. He could leave now and they'd let Helena walk out of here years behind on things. "And the other things?"

"Pardon?"

"What about the other things? Will she remember everything later?"

"What other things?"

"Dr. Hofstaedter, my wife just asked me where I was when she got hit."

"And?"

"And we're not together anymore."

The doctor exhales loudly through her nose. "Did you separate recently? She came in unconscious so the police pulled up her registration record, and you were listed as her spouse. Otherwise we would've asked Ms. Bachlein herself."

He has the impression that she's missing the point, assuming he or Helena is offended by this forced encounter, and making sure the blame lands squarely on the police rather than her staff. He'd be a lot less worried if Helena *were* offended. "No, we just never got divorced." No need to explain why right now. "This is the first time I've spoken to her in three years."

"I see." For the first time, Dr. Hofstaedter sinks back into her chair. The V-shaped crease between her eyebrows deepens.

See? he wants to say. *I wasn't getting hysterical; there really is something wrong.* But this slight satisfaction is overwhelmed by concern for Helena.

"Does this mean she has brain damage?"

"Yes, most likely, but don't be alarmed." She waves her hand downward to indicate that he should stay in his seat, though he made no indication of getting up. "As I said, this kind of amnesia can happen after an injury to the head. She will, most likely, remember everything within a day, except perhaps the accident itself. I'm sure she knows exactly who she is, where she grew up and so on. Our older memories are more firmly embedded in the brain."

He nods again. "But . . ." He knows what amnesia is; everybody knows that. So what is it now, a big farce, some comedy where he has to pretend it's a different year? "But do I have to keep it secret from her?"

Dr. Hofstaedter cocks her head. "Keep what secret?"

"You know—everything she's forgotten."

The doctor laughs once, and her thick eyebrows go up like a cartoon exclamation point above her head. "Of course not! Reminding her of these things is the best way to help her. If she doesn't start remembering them herself within a couple days, she should certainly see a specialist."

He smiles and nods a few times. Why is he disappointed instead of relieved? It might've been nice to pretend. And how perfectly they could've pretended. After all, it was always Helena who couldn't let go of the past.

"We'll run a few tests over the next couple days to make sure there's nothing else wrong with her, but she could be out of here by the end of the week."

"Great."

"My only concern is . . . Frankly, Mr. Schmidt, I'd prefer to release a patient like this into someone's care, at least until she's a little clearer in the head. Does she have any family in Berlin?"

He shakes his head without even processing the question. "I'll look after her."

"That's very generous of you, Mr. Schmidt, and you are

technically her next of kin, but considering your estrangement—does Ms. Bachlein have any close friends you know of?"

"Not off the top of my head," he says, though of course
Magdalena is the first who comes to mind. Helena's parents
live about five hours from Berlin and would certainly come get
her if they knew. Still, the lie seems somehow safer. "Maybe I
have an old address book lying around somewhere," he adds,
though every trace of Helena was eliminated years before.
The only thing she left behind was her wedding ring, and he
keeps that in the cellar, out of sight, out of mind. But he feels
that it will reassure the doctor to know he's not trying to iso-
late Helena or prevent other people from taking care of her.
They gave him her things the first time he came to see her;
he could look through the numbers in her phone. It makes
more sense for him to look after her, though. He's right here
and willing to do it, and she already knows her way around
the apartment. She'll feel at home. And maybe they'll finally
really be able to talk.

Dr. Hofstaedter continues to watch him. He can't tell
whether she's considering his proposal, or at a loss for words.

"I think it would be best if I discussed the matter with
Helena and let her decide," he says. Looking at her watch, Dr.
Hofstaedter is quick to agree.

• • •

At home that evening, he flops down on the sofa, exhausted.
He spent longer than he expected at the hospital and he'll
have tons of work to make up tomorrow, but that isn't the
only thing hanging over him.

He meant to tell Helena after he spoke to the doctor. He
was going to break the news gently, say they'd had a fight and
decided to separate for a while but he wanted to look after her
until she was well again. At least until then. He wasn't going
to mention how long they'd been separated, not right away.
He was going to let her get used to the fact of their separation
first, before he mentioned the time that had passed.

He was going to do all those things, but he didn't.

He thought, at first, that she was sleeping. But when he came closer, he saw that she was just staring up at the ceiling, wide awake.

"Oh, it's you," she said when she saw him. And she watched him with those wide, unblinking pewter eyes that were like a grip he couldn't shake free of. He'd forgotten the matching, slightly asymmetrical beauty marks she has, one between the corner of each eye and her reddish brown hair. He focused on first one and then the other to keep from seeing the swollen right side of her face, divided in two by a little black fence of stitches.

"I was talking to the doctor," he said. And he told her she was going to be all right and it was normal not to remember about the accident right now and she was going to be out in a couple of days. He thought that would be the moment to bring up where she'd go when she got out, but she looked so helpless lying there, and when he left, she'd be all alone. So he talked a little bit about other things, about work and the weather and what was in the paper, just to keep her company a while.

Then there was an instant, one brief moment, in which he thought she must know.

She said, "I'm so glad you're here, Joachim. Whatever happened before."

But when he asked what she meant, she only said that he was looking at her so strangely; they must've had a fight. "Or did you push me?" she asked, with that mischievous twist of her lips he'd forgotten how much he adored.

"I'll always be here," he said, because it sounded like the right thing. "No matter what happens before or after." He meant he'd always be there for her at a time like this, when crisis knocked down the barriers between them and eliminated normal social behavior. But seconds later, he hated himself for saying it. She was confused now, and wouldn't understand how he'd meant it.

He left in an awkward hurry, promising to bring her some books. Recalling that, he looks at his watch. The stores will be closed now, but he can get some in the morning. There's that fitness studio campaign he needs to brainstorm, but he can bring his laptop to the hospital. They'll understand. When he told his boss that his wife had been hit by a car, Mr. Braun said, "Oh, I didn't realize you'd gotten married," and Joachim knew he must be thinking of Leila, who'd come to the last office Christmas party, but didn't bother to correct him.

Word got around pretty fast, and Jean and Max, the colleagues he sees the most of outside of work, stopped by his desk to ask whether everything was all right. Jean is a talented French designer who speaks such abominable German that Joachim could've pretended the whole wife thing was a misunderstanding if Max hadn't been there. Max is from Baden-Württemberg like Joachim, and has a nervous stutter that causes him to listen more than talk. Both of them were fleetingly aware of Leila as a female presence in Joachim's life, someone stopping by to pick him up from after-work drinks or calling to see when he'd be home. Still, who was going to come tell him he wasn't married, especially at a time like this? He mumbled something about a stable condition and thanked them for their concern. It was too much effort to explain everything to everyone. Even he didn't really know what was going on.

He was telling the truth when he told Helena he'd called her office. The first day at the hospital when they'd given him her shoes, purse, and stained clothing, he didn't have the heart to say he wasn't the one to take her things, that she wouldn't want him to have them. Instead, he unlocked her phone with the same old PIN, the year she was born—it was just like her never to change it—and scrolled through her contacts. When he called the last place she'd worked, he was told she hadn't been there in years, and hung up without giving his name. The entry "CuttingEdge Medien" was the only other one that sounded like a company, so he confidently reported the accident to the first person who picked up. When the woman on the other end asked who he was, he said he was her cousin, because Helena wouldn't have said she was married. He knew that much about her, anyway. Even if she always accused him of not understanding her. The woman asked which hospital and what the visiting hours were; Joachim told her the hospital but added that they were only letting in family members.

It was strange how you could lie without expecting to. When he'd tried to keep things from Helena in the past, he'd agonized over each word that came out of his mouth, analyzed how far it was from the truth and how likely she was to believe it. Whether he'd be able to take it back later, to circle around the truth at a distance, gradually spiraling toward it. But now that lies come out more naturally, he doesn't regret having lied so clumsily to Helena; instead, he wishes he'd told her the truth after seeing Ester in that decrepit bar.

He considers now what he would've said. That it had meant absolutely nothing, just been a few nights, because he was so hurt and lonely and depressed. That he'd felt guilty and regretted it. And now this. She would've had to forgive him because he had the courage to be honest with her, to face her certain wrath. She would've told him what to do about Ester. And she would've held him in her arms through all the years, protected him from his own failings and indecision, and from the loss of her.

He sits up with a start. He was starting to drift off on the sofa, dreaming of a chance he missed so long ago it's not even worth thinking about. The fact is that he went back to the apartment with a stupid excuse about wanting to pick something up from the store but not making it in time. With Helena's wide, storm cloud-colored eyes on him, knowing he was lying, but not how or why. She always knew.

But not anymore, he realizes. She doesn't know a thing about it. As far as she knows, they're still just bickering, without any serious issues to fight about. A small voice at the back of his mind tells him that now would be the opportunity to act differently, to protect himself from future regrets. To be honest when it's easier to lie, be honest now like he wishes he was then. But the voice isn't loud enough to stop him from picking up Helena's phone again.

She has a few new messages. He skips through the ones from colleagues asking whether she's okay, and focuses on two from a certain Tobi. The first says: *Hey, was great getting to know you, would love to take you out tomorrow if you're free.* Dated Saturday. Well, she's already missed that appointment. The next one, from yesterday, says, *Hey, haven't heard from you. Busy or not interested? Hope you're just busy!* With a stupid smiley at the end. Letting his mind go blank, Joachim opens the back of Helena's phone and removes the SIM card. Then he puts the phone on the floor and stomps on it, over and over again. He puts the pieces in the bag with her things and throws out the SIM card. It could just as easily have gotten crushed in the accident. As an afterthought, he throws her bloodied clothing in the washing machine. He'll have to buy her a few more things before she gets out.

HELENA

Helena wakes feeling clearheaded and optimistic. Joachim said she'd be out in a few days, and she's seeing him again today. There's nothing seriously wrong with her and she is lucky, like he said. They've already taken the drip out of her arm, and when the heavyset orderly brings her a tray with a stale muffin, weak coffee, and a heavy dose of oral painkillers, she asks him calmly for the date.

"July thirty-first," he tells her after a moment's consideration, then leaves the room. The old woman is awake today, staring blankly at the small muted TV set opposite her bed. She probably doesn't know the date, either. Even the orderly had to think about it. But now Helena knows and things are okay again. A blow to the head will do that to you, knock a few odd facts out. It's just a matter of starting over. Today is Tuesday, July thirty-first; yesterday was Monday, July thirtieth, and tomorrow will be Wednesday, August first. From now on, she'll know exactly what's going on. It was stupid to get so upset. A few days unconscious and she felt like she hadn't seen Joachim in years, couldn't bear to see him leave. He should be here soon. He said he'd come.

And soon he'll take her away from here, and she'll spend a few weeks working from home while her bones heal, and then it'll all be okay again. Some physical therapy sessions, probably. She never broke a bone as a kid and didn't expect to as an adult. But life's always good for a surprise or two.

The orderly comes in to clear her tray and wipe up where she spilled. It's hard to drink coffee with a cast on when you can't sit up properly. At least Joachim didn't see her eating so sloppily.

Some time later, he comes in. Funny how she can't tell how long it's been, how much time later. That's the way things are in here, one big unbroken blur. You doze on and off throughout the day and stare at the dark ceiling half the night, so there's not even really sleep to break things up. But soon she'll be out of here, moving, living, each moment a fixed point in time, each fact firm and sure in her mind.

After he kisses her, her eyes move greedily to the daily paper under his arm. 2013. So there's that. It's later than she thought, not that she had a specific year in mind. The way you sometimes get busy during the day, and then look at your watch and find it's already evening. Or like in early January, when you keep writing the wrong year because the change isn't yet fixed in your mind.

Joachim opens his briefcase. He sets his laptop on the chair between Helena's bed and the window, and then hands her four hardback books. She doesn't recognize any of them; he must've just gone to the new releases table and stocked up. As if she'll have time to read that much in just a couple of days. It's touching, though. She almost expected him to forget.

"Thank you. These should be enough to keep me company for a while."

"Well, you won't be needing company for a few hours, but I thought they'd keep you busy while I catch up on the last few days of work." He plugs his laptop into a spare outlet and starts it up.

"You're staying?" She can't believe her good fortune. But she shouldn't show it. He's always offended if she acts surprised at a time like this. As if she couldn't believe he'd do something nice for her.

But he just settles into the chair with his laptop and says, "Of course." Doesn't even sound annoyed. So she picks up one of the books—a thriller set in the Weimar Republic—and begins to read, pausing every few pages to look over at Joachim, who's wrinkling his forehead in concentration, clicking and typing in short sporadic bursts. He looks tired, and somehow older. Poor Joachim. This accident must've really taken it out of him. But it's good that he's here, and maybe, in some strange way, all this is good for them. He's so gentle toward her now; they're both so careful with each other. They never realized they could lose each other. He meets her wandering eyes over the edge of his screen and smiles. Whatever else, this is good, right now.

JOACHIM

Joachim leaves the hospital in the evening. He tells Helena he's exhausted, and this is true, but he has another stop to make before he goes home. According to the labels in the clothing Helena was wearing when she got hit, she's a size 38 and a B cup. He stops in a couple stores at the mall and in a thrift shop—because it's not plausible that she'd own just two brands of clothing—and buys pants, skirts, dresses, t-shirts, blouses, tights, socks, and underwear. He's on his way out when he realizes he's forgotten shoes.

At home, he takes the tags out of all the clothing and puts a load in the washing machine. He'll have to come up with an explanation for what happened to her other things. Not that he isn't going to give her the real explanation, the truth, but he wants to do that in his own time. At the right moment. If she comes in and asks too many questions right away, he'll be forced to say it at the wrong time. He doesn't want to startle her; she needs to ease back into things, as if the here-and-now were a pool of cold water. She'll need time to get used to it. And he will.

When he opens her purse again to get her ID, there's none of the saving unconsciousness he experienced destroying her phone. His eyes burn as his shaking fingers peel the most recent address label off her ID to reveal his address. He can feel sweat tracing his hairline and the path of his part. He's certain that the door to his apartment will open at any moment, that someone—maybe, impossibly, Helena herself—will catch him in the act. But once he's finished, he returns the card to her wallet and the wallet to her purse, and everything is still and safe. He takes a deep breath and relaxes his clenched fingers, dropping the crumpled label. The address on it isn't far from his own; he'll need about twenty minutes to get there. That she lived so close all this time and never crossed his path! That she lived so close, and as if on another planet, in another universe with no connection to his own. He finds her keys at the bottom of her purse, weighed down by key chains like he remembers them, but the charms are different, and the keys lead to a different home.

Does she live alone? There's no one he can ask, no way to find out without going there. He puts the keys in his pocket with the address label, picks up his own keys and leaves. He's doing this for her as much as himself. They both need this time together, need to end things properly after all these years. Or not end them. They need to finally take all the possibilities into account. He'll be fair to her this time; he'll tell her the truth and let her decide, not wait for some letter to break the news to her.

In the train his mind goes blank again, as if he were on his way to work or running some errand. For a moment, he feels certain that she lives alone. It would be like her. Even when they lived together, she was always slipping off, hiding, disappearing for hours at a time. She could disappear even when they were in the same room, buried in inscrutable silence—him wanting to know what was wrong, and her saying "nothing" until he learned not to ask.

And if there is someone? If he unlocks the door and walks into a room full of people? How will he explain himself? He'll simply say that Helena's in the hospital, and he's come to get some of her things. The crisis situation will explain away any strangeness. The train reaches his stop—her stop—and he leaves the station.

Outside, it's cooler than before, the air fresh like after a storm, though there wasn't any rain. The street lights have come on. He feels weary and wishes he were returning to his own home, not the one he just left, but a shared one, one that's safe and warm and requires no dishonesty. One where nothing needs to be forgotten.

There's only one name on her doorbell, a relief. While he can't imagine her with roommates, he realizes in the silent, dim stairwell of her home that he could very well imagine a partner living there with her. After all, why shouldn't she have one? After all these years. Helena's a beautiful, intelligent woman. More beautiful than he remembered, even with the bruises. Odd, yes, at times maddening, but ultimately endearing, finally, after all, loveable. It bothers him that she should be alone. And it bothers him more that he's happy she lives alone. He has no right to be. Then he remembers that Tobi who wrote to her twice since her accident, and that bothers him most of all.

The lights are out, the windows are closed and the apartment is cool, everything holding its breath. He waits a moment in silence, a burglar getting his bearings, honing his sixth sense to be sure he won't be surprised by his victim's righteous anger. But there isn't even a breath of wind or the creak of a floorboard. She really and truly lives alone.

It's a simple studio apartment with a single bed in one corner, a sofa, a small kitchen table in a little nook with that Mauritian painting that used to be theirs, dressers lining the walls. He finds some grocery bags under the kitchen sink and grabs a few items from each of her drawers. As he packs her clothing, he sees how far off he was with his earlier purchases. He thought it would be enough to have the right size, when each of these garments is so uniquely Helena's he could've entered this apartment blindfolded and known it was hers just by opening a drawer.

Always that same limpid softness; everything she owns fits like a favorite t-shirt she's been wearing for years, even if she just bought it. Then there are her colors: red, pink and black, the occasional kelly green or royal blue, but never gray, never white, never neutral. The flawless outward appearance of the apartment, not a speck of dust on the dressers, and yet a chaotic jumble within the drawers. She still hasn't learned to fold. He recalls that she never wears anything that needs ironing, and lets her blouses drip dry to get rid of the wrinkles.

He fills another bag with her shoes, then takes a third into the bathroom for her cosmetics. Here, he realizes he's been fooling himself: he couldn't have said what brand of toothpaste she likes or how she puts up her hair. It could be anyone's bathroom; the mirror could've held anyone's reflection day after day. He doesn't know her anymore.

He feels an overwhelming, painful weariness, an ache in his shoulders as he picks up the bulging plastic bags. He no longer wants to do what he's doing, but he's like a powerful machine running down, and can only slowly coast to a standstill. When he reaches his apartment again, he leaves the bags by the entrance to the cellar, goes down the moldering steps and opens the wooden gate of his compartment by the flickering light of the bare bulb overhead. He squirms through old furniture, rusted tools, and cardboard boxes to get to the shelf at the back, where he finds a creased envelope stuffed into a box of old books and papers. He puts it in his pocket, feeling the two hard, cool pieces of metal in one corner without opening it to look.

Upstairs, he sets the bags down by the sofa and sleeps for an hour, then gets up again to unpack them. They're letting him bring Helena home tomorrow.

HELENA

Helena wakes ecstatic, with the blind, instinctive joy a child feels just before recalling that it's Christmas morning. She's going home today. She's getting out of this place in a few hours. Joachim will be here to take her.

She had an awful dream the night before. It must be the painkillers. She and Joachim fought and he left her in the middle of some dark, eerie forest where she could feel slimy hands with long fingers groping at her ankles. She wandered, exhausted, for hours, and then abruptly found herself in the apartment with Joachim, who was on the sofa reading a newspaper. He kept telling her everything was fine and she'd only dreamt the part about the forest, and she began to believe him. But just as she sat down next to him, she heard a baby crying in another room and leapt to her feet. Yet how no matter how many doors she opened—and there were so many doors in their apartment now, one after the other, dozens, hundreds, millions—she could neither find the crying infant, nor return to Joachim. The last door opened onto perfect, impossible, unbroken darkness, and she was in the forest again, and she was in the hospital again, and she was hoarse as if she'd been screaming, but she must not have, or someone would've come.

Medication can have side effects like that. Magdalena's sister Sara told her that, when she used to take sleeping pills, she could feel a dark, shadowy form standing over her bed every night, bending down to her, but never quite touching her.

So there are all kinds of things like that. The dream doesn't bother her anymore; only, it's strange that she can remember all that about the shadow over Sara's bed. Why something so trivial, a stray conversation, and so little of the past few years?

Her pulse speeds up and she feels slightly nauseous. She has to stay calm and take deep breaths. She still has a lot of recovering to do and panicking won't help. Joachim said the doctor said she'd be better soon. That the blanks in her mind would fill in again. So none of it matters, now that she's getting out of here. Soon she won't even need the painkillers, and that will be the end of nightmares like this. She'll tell Joachim about it later, and he'll tell her some crazy dream he had and they'll laugh together. She knows seeing him will reassure her. As much as the medicine, that's probably what was messing up her sleep—being alone here, spending so much time away from her husband.

When he comes in later that morning with a tired smile and bags under his eyes, she knows she was right. It's hard on him, too, being away from her.

Joachim

Someone catches Joachim's arm as he comes into the hospital, and he looks down into Dr. Hofstaedter's lined face, which seems a little kinder now. She smells like she's just back from a cigarette break.

"Here to see your wife again, Mr. Schmidt?"

"I am." He presses his lips together lest a single extra syllable slip out and betray him. It was foolish to be so open with Dr. Hofstaedter; she's the only one who could give him away now. He holds the glass door and waits for her to enter. She smiles over her shoulder. After all, they both have Helena's best interests at heart. Dr. Hofstaedter wants Helena well, and he wants Helena well, happy, and where she belongs. Wherever that turns out to be.

Dr. Hofstaedter walks quickly for a woman of her height, but she holds the door of the elevator for him.

"She's doing better? Your wife."

He can't tell whether this is a statement or a question he's meant to answer. He can feel sweat appearing in the armpits of his dress shirt. "Yes, she seems better." With an awkward attempt at a laugh, he adds, "But then, I'm not a doctor."

"And yet, we doctors see so little of our patients." The elevator comes to a halt, the doors open, and an orderly wheels in a miserable-looking old man. "If you hadn't told me," the doctor continues, "it's possible I wouldn't even have noticed her amnesia."

The doors open again to let out the old man and the orderly, and then they're on Helena's floor.

"Well, my rounds await me," Dr. Hofstaedter says. But just as Joachim starts to glow and sweat more than ever with relief, she turns back to ask, "You did tell her that you'd been separated, didn't you? How long did you say again? A year? You're very dedicated, after all that time."

"About three." He speaks the words as if expelling something lodged in his throat, and then coughs drily into one hand. "I was just on my way to discuss it with her."

"Glad to hear it." Dr. Hofstaedter is out of hearing range before he can manage another word.

He doesn't know what to say when he comes into Helena's room. He needs to say something, to keep at least a little of his promise to Dr. Hofstaedter, but it's hard because Helena isn't expecting any bad news. She's smiling and watching him fixedly, as if he were about to do a magic trick. Or maybe just taking her away from here is enough to impress her now. He has to say something. He felt this way after Ester told him she was pregnant, back in the apartment with Helena, who'd had a good day at work and was making dinner. He knew he had to say something, but she wasn't expecting anything, so there was no signal, no cue to prompt a confession. She believed him when he said he'd had a long day and was tired, and then, to his surprise, the evening passed without his telling her. He was just as surprised not to tell her the next day, but the day after, he began to realize he wasn't going to.

"I had this crazy dream," Helena says. "I'm so glad you're here."

This isn't going to be like that time. He's going to start telling her the truth now, little by little. He'll do it slowly and carefully, make sure he says it all the right way so as not to hurt or frighten her, but he'll do it.

"There's something I need to tell you."

She looks hurt and a little surprised. She must've been expecting him to ask what she dreamt. He can see her lips slipping into a pout, but at least she's listening.

"We had this fight before your accident," he begins. Just

a fight, not a breakup. One step at a time. "We both said a lot of things we didn't mean, I guess. We'd been having a lot of issues anyway. What I'm trying to say, Helena, is that we decided to separate . . . for a while."

She inhales sharply and he wants to stop speaking, but this is the very sign he needs; this is what the truth sounds like. Still, everything in moderation. She needs to recover.

"We had decided that," he corrects himself, "but I changed my mind. I want to stick it out no matter what, spend this time with you now. I want you to come home with me and rethink all of it. What do you say?"

"Me, too," she says. "Let's just forget about it." And then they both laugh, and it's a little painful and a little hollow, because they both know she already has.

"Oh," he says, "I almost forgot." He takes the torn envelope out of his pocket and lets the thin gold band fall into his cupped hand. Hopefully she didn't notice that he didn't have his on the day before. "Your fingers were too swollen, and they had to take it off." He slides the ring onto Helena's third finger, and if it feels out of place, if the sensation of wearing a wedding ring is strange for her, she doesn't say anything.

His heart still pounding, he helps her into the folding wheelchair the nurse left beside the door, and wheels her to the nurse's station so they can sign her release forms and pick up her crutches. She seems happy to be leaving with him, but then, what choice does she have?

• • •

Joachim carefully places Helena on the last step, where she sits a moment looking uncomfortable, but not complaining. His back aches and it takes him longer than he expected to catch his breath, but even after he feels the heat of exhaustion melting out of his pores, he waits a moment longer. He isn't quite ready. But he isn't going to be ready for this, so he wipes his palms on the front of his pants and takes out his keys.

He helps her to stand. He would've helped her more, swung her legs over his arm and carried her over the threshold all over again, but she shakes her head and limps after him on her crutches. She must be weak from lying in bed because she looks as sweaty and worn-out as he feels.

He pulls out a chair at the table but she hobbles over to the sofa. He doesn't know whether the gesture is deliberate. You never know with Helena. She falls more than sits on the sofa. For a moment, for several long moments, neither of them speaks. He comes and stands across from her, as if waiting to take her order.

She wrinkles her nose slightly and quirks the right side of her mouth as she looks around. Does she notice anything? He can't for the life of him remember what's changed about the apartment in the past few years. Except, of course, for her absence. But she makes her lips into a thin, flat line and looks just over his shoulder, so he knows something's bothering her. He knows and hates that look but loves that she's here, loves that she's here looking like that, for him to know and love and hate. It's a wonderful thing, an unbelievable thing, a chance most people don't have in their entire lives. It's time travel and reincarnation and something Helena herself will appreciate when she can.

"What's the matter? Are you feeling okay?" Stupid question, but rude of her not to answer. He tries again. "Do you want something to drink?"

"I'll get it." She starts to stand, winces and remains on sofa. He pours her a glass of water. It's a relief to have his back to her, to let his face relax. Only these few moments are impossible; then everything will be okay. And once he's told her, everything really will be okay, once and for all. He hands her the glass with a forced smile. She drinks too eagerly and chokes a little; he brings her a napkin before pouring himself a glass.

He sits down beside her. He can't tell her now because it wouldn't mean anything. She's been gone so long he barely remembers what it was like to be with her, and whatever she remembers is outdated anyway. She probably remembers how their relationship was, with all the fighting, crying and accusations, the problems that never got solved. But he'll give her new memories: He'll show her how good it can be, how happy they can be together. And then she can decide. Not everyone is lucky enough to have a chance like that.

She clears her throat and takes a smaller sip of water. "Something's different. Isn't—aren't some things missing? Where are the plants, and the painting of Port Louis?"

Leave it to her to pick out details like that. He doesn't remember what plants she had in which windows, and it didn't occur to him to take that painting from her apartment. But of course, she remembers all that like it was yesterday. For her, it is.

"I didn't want to tell you while you were in the hospital, but some pipes burst upstairs. The neighbors were out of town, and tons of water came through the ceiling while I was on a business trip and you were visiting your parents. The repairmen have been in and out fixing everything up, but not everything could be saved." He's practiced this lie so many times that it seems true; his memories of imagining the soaked apartment, the crumbling plaster of the ceiling, the repairmen's dirty footprints and the smells of mildew and fresh paint are as vivid as real experiences.

As an afterthought, he adds, "I'm having the painting restored. I should be able to pick it up next week."

"Oh, that old thing? It's hardly worth the trouble."

But he can tell she's pleased. They picked the painting up from a local artist selling on a table near their hotel in Mauritius, so it took on a kind of sentimental charm, though the picture isn't especially well-done. A boat, roughly daubed waves, some kind of hut in the background. It was the only real vacation they took together after they got married.

"It's good to be back," she says.

"It's good to have you here." He strokes her hand, tentative at first, then, remembering his role, puts his arm around her shoulders and kisses her on the cheek, avoiding her stitches.

She smiles, but a moment later she's restless, fidgeting in his grasp. "I wonder when I'll be able to go back to work."

"I bet you can work from home," he says, improvising. It didn't occur to him that she'd want to fly the nest so soon after he picked her up from the ground. "I'll stop by your office tomorrow and see what you need. You'll have to remind me of the address, though."

"Where's my laptop? I can work on that."

"I'm still waiting to hear whether they were able to recover the hard drive. The flood, you know. But you can use mine. I had it with me when the flooding happened, so it's still in good shape, and I've got a couple design programs installed for when I work from home. I'll take it by your office tomorrow and have them put on everything you need."

"Thanks, Joachim."

He wishes she'd said "darling." They only used each other's names when they were fighting. But that's over now.

"Let me know if there's anything else you need."

Helena

Helena lies awake a long time the first night. All that time in the hospital has thrown her off schedule. Dozing around the clock, always half-sedated. When you're indoors all the time, there isn't much difference between night and day. Your allotted portion of light comes from the window, or it comes from a fluorescent lamp.

To make matters worse, she can't help feeling acutely aware of each of her injuries, running over the list in her head, feeling her blood pulse past twisted muscles and fractured bones. When she puts her hand to her face, she can feel the throbbing warmth of her bruises, the peculiar rigidity of her skin and the crooked seam across one cheek she isn't supposed to touch.

And her brain, too, is supposed to be bruised. It must've knocked against her skull when she fell, like a piece of fruit rolling against the side of a crate.

Retrograde amnesia. Both Dr. Hofstaedter and Joachim told her. As if she'd forget, ha ha. But would she have known if they hadn't? How do you know what you don't know? She feels the blank space between her and the world now, but if she didn't know, maybe it would all seem okay. After all, what's she missing? She and Joachim decided to separate for a while. But that's no surprise; they were always fighting. That could be just the decision of a moment, something said in the heat of a particularly bad fight. Besides, that's over now, no longer relevant. Well, there's her new job, still graphic design, still advertising, but in a different office with different people.

And what else? At least they still live in the same apartment. Not much has changed here, though a few things are missing because of the flooding. She suspects that he lost track of where all her things are, which are getting dry-cleaned and which are getting repaired and so on. Either that or he had to throw out a lot more than he's admitting, and doesn't want to tell her right away.

Something clicks into place with this thought. Something he doesn't want to tell her. But what? It's nothing she knows for certain, only a feeling . . . There's been something off about him these past few days. At first, she thought he was just worried about her, being particularly attentive, but now, listening to the peaceful sighs of his breath at the very opposite edge of the bed, she's sure there's more to it. There's something *cautious* about him; that's it. As if he were taking great care to avoid a certain subject.

But what could it be? Is it something she knew already and has forgotten, or something that just happened? Maybe he's waiting to tell her when she's better. Or planning never to say anything. As if she were too stupid to notice. On the other hand, how can she confront him about it? Joachim, I know you're hiding something from me. And then what? If he says she's imagining it, what evidence does she have? She drifts off in the great void of this question.

Joachim

At Joachim's office, everyone is careful and kind to him. Since word got around that his wife was hit by a truck and is now an invalid, deadlines are extended, everyone's willing to help out, and any strange behavior on his part, any lack of concentration, is perfectly understandable.

He appreciates their kindness but feels guilty accepting it. It's true that Helena's an invalid at the moment, but is she really his wife? As soon as he left his apartment, the absurdity of the whole situation became clear to him. It can't go on this way. He has to tell her. It was ridiculous to think he could keep this up for more than a couple days.

Sitting at his desk, staring blankly at the InDesign file in front of him, he considers all the aspects of her life that didn't occur to him before. He thought of her work, fine, and her clothing and shoes, but what about her friends and family, all her connections to the world, and what about her secret life, the world within her he's never known anything about? How can he restore that to her?

He should tell her when he gets home. Should he have told her before? But it would've been kicking her when she was down to tell her at the hospital. What if she remembers now and hates him for keeping it from her? That would be even worse than if she'd remembered all along. Dr. Hofstaedter said that telling her about the past is the best way to help her. Does that mean she won't remember as long as no one tells her? Or will her brain just reset automatically one morning? Will she wake up and push him out of bed? Either way, it's not fair of him to do anything that could slow down her recovery.

Even the night before, he began to have his doubts. She was quiet, not bubbly and cheerful as he expected her to be after leaving the hospital. She spent most of the evening staring into space as they ate the dinner he prepared and had a few drinks—wine for him, grape juice for her, since she can't mix alcohol with her painkillers—and he couldn't begin to guess what she was thinking about. It occurred to him that the awkwardness he felt was not estrangement from a partner after a fight, but rather the distance between two strangers. Somehow, in spite of everything, she must feel that, too.

In the morning, he helped her to bathe, dress and eat breakfast, but still felt like he was abandoning her. She has books and movies, but no one to talk to. And he's the one who made sure of that, by unplugging the wireless router and the phone line while she was in the bathroom. It was a close call, because she wanted to call her parents a little while later. He blamed the flooding. But he felt bad leaving her alone like that.

At the same time, it would've been worse to tell her the truth and then leave her, helpless, trapped, alone with all those thoughts and questions. First things first: He'll go to her office during his lunch break and get her something to do during the day. Then, when they have a lot of time together, when he can break it to her gently, he'll tell her.

Why is the truth so difficult? Why do lies come out as smoothly as lines from a well-written script, while the truth sticks in your throat until you could choke on it? And when you finally say it, it never sounds true, never relieves you or conveys the meaning you really wanted.

That's how it was when Helena got the letter from Ester. Half of it was lies, hysterical accusations. Ester wrote about her affair with Joachim that "lasted for months and never really ended properly," implying that this was just one of his many affairs, and then, far worse, about his refusing to help her when she was pregnant and coercing her into an abortion she didn't want. Then some graphic details about related health problems, and finally, the wish that Helena find out what the man she was married to was really like. Ester had included her address and phone number in case Helena wanted to learn even more.

He doesn't know whether Helena ever contacted Ester, or whether she already knew as much as she wanted to. When he came home that evening, cheerful, planning to take her out to dinner, she started to ask him a few things, then simply handed him the letter. Her gaze was excruciating; he couldn't get it off of his face. So he told the truth with downcast eyes and a catch in his voice, and it sounded like a bunch of lies and excuses and the hateful piece of paper in her hand must've read like gospel, and that was all there was. There was no way to make the truth sound true.

Realizing he's been looking at the same file for half an hour without absorbing anything, he decides to take an early lunch. He looks up the address of Helena's company and logs out of his computer. It won't be that way this time. He won't wait until he's caught out. She'll have to believe him then, if he tells her when he has no reason to, when he has nothing to gain by it, and it can only hurt both of them. That's how she'll know it's true.

• • •

He tries to approach her office with the confidence of a man who knows all about his wife's work, her daily struggles and routines, the dull office gossip. As if she'd been coming home to him every evening all along. When he buzzes to be let into the building, he simply says his name and that he's there on behalf of Helena Bachlein. No relationship necessary.

A tough-looking woman with short, spiky maroon hair meets him at the door and takes him back to the HR office. He doesn't catch her name—Annika? Ulrike? She's wearing a casual, sporty outfit but has such an authoritative walk that he feels like he's being led to a cell.

"I called up about Helena's accident last week," he begins, once he's seated opposite her in a small glass-walled office.

He fumbles in his briefcase for the papers from the hospital; Dr. Hofstaedter recommended that Helena not come in for at least four weeks. He watches in anxious silence as the woman opposite him reads over the papers with a fine wrinkle forming between her dark, overplucked eyebrows.

"But she'd like to work from home," he adds, when she looks up.

And then the very thing he was afraid of happens. "And you are?" the woman asks with unapologetic curiosity, its frankness bordering on accusation.

"Her husband—that is, her cousin's husband," he says, feeling the onset of a cold sweat all over him. This woman works in HR; Helena's tax status is enough to let her colleague know that she's either single or permanently separated. "Helena's staying with us while she recuperates," he adds. "So we can look after her. She lives alone, you know."

"Of course."

So there's always a right answer, even if it isn't the true one. You have to say things that make sense to people. The kind of things they expect. So maybe Helena always expected to hear something awful about him, was waiting, all along, for a letter like the one Ester finally sent. But that's not fair.

"The thing is," he continues, getting the ball rolling now, sure of his performance, "we had some flooding in the apartment recently, so our Internet connection's practically nonexistent. What with her broken leg, Helena can't really leave, so it would be a big help if you—that is if her colleagues were able to load the things she needs onto a flash drive." He pulls one out of his pocket, but then the line is back between the woman's eyebrows so maybe he brought it out too soon; maybe it looks like he's trying too hard.

"That's all very well and good for getting her an assignment now, but what then? How do we get her work, or give her a new project?"

So it's just a matter of practicalities. In a way, all this is easier than you'd think. People ask you questions and you answer and keep answering until they have nothing left to ask. He'll have to tell Helena about this later, all he's learning about people now. Maybe they'll laugh at his pathetic tricks together, or just marvel at the strangeness of it all.

"I was planning to bring the drive back once she's finished."

"Mr.—"

"Schmidt," he reminds her, wondering what suddenly made the situation so formal.

"Mr. Schmidt, Helena usually has at least two or three major projects a week. Are you really planning to come here that often, for weeks?"

"Yes." And then, because this isn't enough, he adds, "It's on the way to my office." Actually, it's quite a detour to stop by Pankow on his way to Kreuzberg, but she doesn't need to know that. It wouldn't make sense to her. You have to say things that people understand.

"Well, that's a relief. Helena's a big hit with one of our most important clients—I don't know if she mentioned the FuTur36 account to you?—and things have been piling up since she's been away. No one else has the same design competencies here."

He smiles vaguely. After all, he's just her cousin's husband. No need to know the finer details.

"I suppose you're in a hurry." She leads him out of her small glass room and around a corner into an open-plan office, where she shows him Helena's empty desk between a pale palm tree and a woman with a round, childish face but gray streaks in her brown hair, who watches him closely through thick-lensed glasses. Joachim feels not only her eyes, but all the eyes in the room on him. The feeling is similar to that of starting a new job, being led around the office to meet everyone, not quite managing to note any of the names or job descriptions, and giving out one clammy handshake after another. But his reason for being here is even more tenuous.

"Doro, this is Helena's cousin Mr. Schmidt." Suddenly in a hurry—maybe she hasn't had her lunch break yet—the woman tells Doro to download everything Helena will need for her next project onto the flash drive, and heads back to her office.

"We were worried," Doro says when the woman from HR is out of sight. "Helena hasn't been answering her phone or any of the emails we sent. How is she?"

He gives a brisk summary of her condition, trying to play it down enough for her colleagues not to worry and up enough for them to understand why she's fallen out of touch. To round things out, he explains about the Internet connection and that her cell phone got smashed up in the accident. "The drivers here are crazy," he concludes.

"Well, I'm relieved to hear that she's out of the hospital," Doro says. But there's a certain disconnect between the quizzical look in her eyes and her calm, conversational tone of voice. He feels nervous and wishes he could leave, but the progress bar shows that only 64% of Helena's work has been transferred to the drive. "Oh," Doro adds, with an I-just-remembered tone that doesn't quite ring true, "give her this, would you?"

She hands him a greeting card. On the cover is a picture of a puppy with a bandaged paw; on the inside "Get well soon" and the signatures of all her coworkers. He reaches for it but Doro takes it back at the last second.

"I almost forgot to sign it myself."

HELENA

Having the work is a relief, and Helena's grateful to Joachim for that. More grateful than she is when he helps her dress and makes her breakfast. Those things only matter for half an hour or so, but this is something to occupy her all day, to keep her time from going to waste and keep her from going crazy in this apartment. And keep away the strange, morbid thoughts running through her head all night.

What seemed certain in the darkness is now equally possible and impossible. What could he be hiding from her? After all, he came right out and told her they'd decided to separate. It couldn't be much worse than that. Could it? Maybe he really is just handling her with kid gloves because she's injured, because he almost lost her and got scared. Or even because they had such a bad fight, and he's trying to make it up to her. Not that she can remember what it was about.

But isn't that just it? What could they have fought about that was serious enough for them to separate over, but not serious enough for him to mention? Maybe it was nothing; maybe it was all the little fights over all the years that wore them down. But maybe it *was* something. She'll ask him when he gets home tonight. He may think he's clever, but she'll know whether he's telling the truth.

Once she's made this decision, she feels a weight lifted from her, almost as if she were suddenly able to walk without crutches. Almost, but not quite. She hobbles over to the table where he set up his laptop with the flash drive. Even taking a deep breath hurts. There's a get-well card from her coworkers next to the laptop, but since she doesn't remember any of them, she simply glances at the picture of the puppy and sets it aside. Thoughtful of them, anyway.

There are a lot of old ad campaigns from some urban planning company called FuTur36 on the drive as reference material. All the file names have "Bachlein" in them, so these must be her ideas, her work. She examines the print ads and layouts one after the other until she begins to feel like she remembers them, but maybe she's only fooling herself. As it is, no matter how hard she tries, she still only remembers them as if she'd passed them on the street, not as if she'd spent hours designing and perfecting them.

But she did this work before, and she's the same person she was then, plus or minus a few experiences. At least she's still working in the same field. What if she'd become an engineer or a surgeon in the past few years, and could only remember working in advertising? Would she still have the skills she'd learned, even if she couldn't remember acquiring them? Or would all of that be gone, too? She doesn't know enough, has no way of finding out more about this condition. And Joachim hardly seems concerned. Fine, he's careful of her broken bones, but what about her brain damage? Shouldn't they be more worried about that? Shouldn't she see a specialist? But there's no one there to answer her questions and no way for her to call anyone and ask, so she gets to work illustrating the advantages of an innovative new cloud solution for architects in a series of two-page spreads. After all, you have to make it through the day.

Joachim

Helena's working on his laptop when Joachim comes in, her crutches propped against the wall. She gives him a weary, distracted smile that's both a greeting and a warning—she's welcoming him back, but forbidding him to distract her. He nods as if she'd spoken aloud and goes into the kitchen to make dinner. That won't bother her. It's never noise that bothers her, only people speaking to her, demanding her attention. If you leave her alone, she's perfectly content. Helena never needs to leave a room to be alone; she carries her solitude around with her.

But that's fine; he's not a child and he doesn't need her constant attention. He begins looking around the kitchen and finds that the refrigerator's almost empty. Not much in the cabinets, either. For a moment, an absurd resentment fills him: Why does he have to do everything? Then he looks across the room at Helena typing, her long adroit fingers extending past the end of her cast like the fur in that picture of the puppy, and doesn't know whether he wants most to laugh or cry. Of course she couldn't go grocery shopping; of course she couldn't do anything, not without someone to carry her down the stairs. It's his own fault for not thinking to pick up some groceries on his way back from work.

What upsets him is the realization that it's always been like this, that maybe he can't help being like this, and she can't either. The pettiness, the irrational resentment, the fights so stupid you'd be ashamed to tell anyone about them. They're not fighting. Yet. But there's still that anger within him, that animosity toward her coiled and ready to spring. What is it about the two of them?

He never fought this way with Leila. Making another tour of the kitchen, he comes across a forgotten jar of pasta sauce and half a box of spaghetti. So it'll be okay for tonight; he doesn't have to go out again. Tomorrow he'll buy some nice things. With her trapped here all day, it's the least he can do to make something nice for dinner. But the thought is insincere, like words you say aloud while thinking something else. He fills a pot with water, shakes in some salt and puts it on the stove. It's strange to think of Leila now, strange to think how important she seemed—how important she was—just a few weeks before. He covers the pot and rummages in the cabinet for a saucepan, feeling a strange guilt, as if it were Leila he betrayed Helena with. Not that he betrayed her, not on purpose. But more and more he finds himself falling into Helena's reality, seeing things the way she does. Or the way she used to.

It shouldn't be hard to keep track. He remembers all the years without her, remembers the way Leila's hair curled in the night from the damp heat of their bodies, and before that, how it was to look at women on the street with polite but open interest, suddenly allowed. He can't remember exactly what it was like after Helena left, because he's had the apartment to himself so much since then. Just a few vague details, the way the quiet rang in his ears when he lay in bed, not hearing her breathing, not even hearing his own. When he tries to picture himself mourning her absence, he recalls the days after Leila left, when he felt dull and bluntly bewildered, looking at the phone without intending to call her, sometimes doing it, but then mostly and finally always not.

Leila's face is mixed up with Ester's, and he feels a creeping pressure down his neck and shoulders, as if Helena were standing just behind him, not only watching him closely, but looking right into his thoughts. But he hears her shutting his laptop, and when he looks over, she's getting up, no accusation in her eyes, only the satisfaction of having finished her work. It's strange how ordinary it is to have her here—no great transition, no awkward collisions between his bachelor life and her constant presence, only a few minor details to explain away. He remembers the painting, her laptop, all the things he claimed were being cleaned or repaired. The thought of going to her apartment to get them exhausts him, not because of the physical journey there, but because of the confrontation he'll face. The glaring fact of her life without him, their separation writ large.

"Na? How are you?" She moves awkwardly, her crutches scraping against the tiles of the kitchenette, and he takes her left arm to steady her.

"I'm beat," he says. Because he is and because that's what you say when you can't think what else to tell someone, when you need a catchall explanation for wandering thoughts and silence.

"Me, too. But it was good to get back to work. I feel almost like I'm part of society again."

He notes the "almost" and presses his hands to the small of her back, but holds himself a little away from her stomach, afraid of shifting her broken ribs out of place just by brushing against them. He feels a certain melting softness between them, her breathing slowing as her heart rate picks up. She presses her face to his chest, and for a moment, he's terrified of her vulnerability. If everything were different, this would be the moment to make love, to take her in his arms and carry her to the bed or the sofa, not hearing the water boiling over, not knowing anything but each other.

This is her feeling as much as it is his; he can feel it moving through her skin into his. But he's afraid of breaking her. It isn't just her injuries. It would be wrong. What he's doing now is wrong, but this would be a whole new level of wrong. At least he's taking care of her now, feeding her and helping her dress. Who would do that, if not him? Some friend from the office? Some new fling? Hardly. But that would be using her sickness, taking advantage of her helplessness and ignorance. And yet it's what she wants. In spite of himself, he counts in his head how long it will be until her ribs are healed.

Still a couple of weeks to go. He'll have told her by then. Once he's told her, everything will be fair and honest, no more tricks between them. Just this softness and safety. The desire he feels for her is so different from attraction to a stranger; right now, if they could, they'd make love with their souls.

He feels her look up and bends down to kiss her on the mouth, then the beauty mark beside her right eye and the top of her head. Leila was tall and he'd forgotten how small Helena feels in his arms. "Dinner's almost ready," he says, and they shuffle to the stove together so he can turn down the heat, save the noodles from sticking to the bottom of the pot. He wants to tell her everything now, give it to her like an offering, the worst or at least strangest sides of himself. And the compliment of letting her know he still wants her after all this time, wants her like there never was and never could be anyone else. But he waits a few seconds too long, and her words come out faster.

"Joachim, I'm worried."

"What about?"

He feels her tense, holding something in, probably anger.

"How long did the doctor say it would take me to remember things?"

He thinks for a moment. "She didn't exactly." This is close to the truth, but it isn't enough; it isn't an answer.

"Joachim," she says again, and then inhales, and he realizes it's tears that she's holding back. The words tumble over the catch in her throat like a bump in an ill-paved road. "I want to see a specialist. Not some general practitioner rushing around the hospital—someone who really knows about this kind of thing. I'm worried," she says again, and this time there's a slight accusation to it, the emphasis on "I'm," asking him why he isn't.

"Of course." He knows he should be worried. But when he's in the apartment with her, he barely notices her condition. Is she really missing anything of value? It isn't fair for him to make that decision. But it also seems to him that her memory is like the rest of her, bruised and broken but slowly on the mend. He realizes he's been thinking of the moment he tells her the truth as the moment that she'll recover, as if her memory were in his keeping, his to give back. "I'll ask Dr. Hofstaedter if she can recommend anyone."

"Thanks."

"Here, come back to the table. I'll bring the food over." He can tell by the fixed way she's watching him that there's something else she wants to say. But he can tell by the trouble she's having saying it that it's something he doesn't want to hear.

She moves back to the table, compliant or helpless. He drains the pasta, pours the sauce into the pot with it, and sets the whole thing on a trivet on the table. He's relieved to get up again for plates and silverware, and then another time for napkins. He's sure that the moment they start eating, she'll come out with whatever she has to say.

"Thank you for cooking," is the first thing she says, but even this feels like a preface. He remembers to get each of them a glass of water.

"I need to get to the store tomorrow," he says. "We're out of almost everything. Is there anything special you want?" The question sounds strange after he's asked it—shouldn't he know what she wants? Haven't they ostensibly been living in the same household for years now, sharing the same kitchen, the same meals? It's the sort of question he'd ask a guest, someone whose tastes he doesn't know. But maybe she'll just see this as thoughtlessness, a sign that she's been doing most of the grocery shopping. He can't remember whether that was the case; only the way it was toward the end, cooking separate meals in the same kitchen. The small, petty hatefulness of it.

"Yeah, I can't remember when I last got my period," she says. "I didn't see anything in the bathroom so I must be all out."

Stupid of him not to think of that. He brought her toothpaste and two kinds of face cream, but didn't even check for a box of pads. Or does she use tampons? What else has he forgotten, what other stupid mistakes has he made?

"Do you want tampons or pads?" he asks. He's just a man after all, so why should he notice that kind of thing? Even if it's supposed to have been sitting in his bathroom for years.

"I guess pads would be easier until my leg's better."

So the question made sense; she didn't think anything of it. He's just being thoughtful, making sure he gets the right thing.

"Anything else?"

"Not that I can think of."

He feels her resignation now, her decision not to say whatever she was going to. He knows he should coax it out of her, ask concerned questions and listen thoughtfully to whatever it is, but he can't bring himself to. Whatever it is won't be nice, and the nasty things always end up getting said anyway.

HELENA

Sitting on the toilet lid as she brushes her teeth the next morning, Helena feels guilty, complicit in whatever Joachim's keeping from her. Why didn't she ask him what caused them to separate? It might be unpleasant to remember, but she's got the advantage there—she won't remember it any more vividly than whatever's in today's paper. Will it really be that bad? But why should it be? She knows the kind of things they fought about, the banal arguments, the stray remarks flung like lit matches into a pool of gasoline, erupting into fury. Why should this have been anything special?

Separating was something they always talked about, usually after the fight rather than during it. While the wounds were still raw and they weren't sure they'd ever heal. But a few days later, they were happy again, happy enough to pretend there had never been any problems between them, though not happy enough to forget. But it was just something they talked about. Something must've changed that.

He helps her up to spit into the sink, turns on the tap for her to rinse. Whose decision was it? Did she want to leave or did he? It's hard to interpret his kindness to her now. Of course he feels bad about her accident and all that. But beyond physically caring for her, there's a gentleness in his speech and attitude toward her—careful not to offend, not to start a fight. Is he regretting having told her to get out, or trying to keep her from deciding to leave again? She's missing some minor crucial detail, the key piece that would allow her to put the whole puzzle together.

He looks at his watch. He must be running late, and it doesn't help that he has to stop by her office again.

"Don't worry about getting me dressed," she says. "I can do that on my own. I mean, I've got all day." She tries and fails to laugh.

"Okay, if you're sure." He doesn't quite manage to hide his relief.

"I'm sure." The small sentence echoes with dishonesty, referring to everything and nothing, all the things she no longer knows and maybe never did. When he closes the door, she waits to see whether the apartment will fall to pieces in the resounding silence he leaves behind, but everything remains still. The ceiling doesn't cave in; the walls and windows don't crack or crumble. Everything is okay. As long as she makes it through this day, through each of these days, everything will be okay.

• • •

Every morning is the same. Helena wakes sore and a little sweaty, feeling like she's had a wild night out. Then she becomes aware of herself, of her broken bones and damaged flesh. Today, Joachim's already gone. He hasn't left her a note like he did the past few days. She picks up her crutches from beside the bed and hobbles into the bathroom. Her armpits ache from bearing her weight, even over the short distances she travels in the apartment. It will be hard to get in shape again later, but she tries not to think about that now.

He's left the drive by the computer, another assignment. She can't believe their Internet connection and the landline are still out. Isn't there someone they can complain to? She'll work all day, seeing no one, speaking to no one, and then he'll take the flash drive with him. Carefully preserving the vacuum around her.

Her face looks greasy in the streaked bathroom mirror, and the bruising on the right side of it is still a grotesque array of colors: blue, green, yellow, purple, and the red-brown of scabs about to fall off. The dark little stitches have already dissolved. She didn't like to look in the mirror while they were there. She can take the bruising, but there was something so horrifying about those small, dark marks, foreign objects threaded into her skin. She splashes water on her face and almost falls down when the cold of it startles her. This has been her routine for days now. She tries but can't figure out how many. She started and finished her period, and there were weekends she spent sleeping and playing cards with Joachim, watching whatever was on TV. Even a few days are an eternity when you can't remember what the last thing you can remember is. She'd like to take a shower but it's too dangerous—she could slip and break something else. Joachim will help her into the tub when he gets home.

When he gets home. Patting her face dry, she feels resentment welling up in her for this dependence. She can't work, can't bathe, can hardly get herself something to eat without him. It'll take her another twenty minutes of sweating and struggling to get dressed, and what for? She's not going to see anyone.

The thought is so dispiriting that she simply brushes her teeth and hobbles out of the bathroom in her pajamas. She stubs her left toe on the threshold of the room, as if she didn't have enough pain already.

In the kitchen, he's left the coffee machine on, two pieces of bread in the toaster. Well, that was thoughtful. She's supposed to keep eating even when the painkillers make her nauseous. At least the bottle's almost empty, so she can switch to ibuprofen soon. She makes her way to the computer, switches it on, and leans against the wall to rest before going back to the toaster. She eats the toast leaning against the counter because it would be too much effort to carry it to the table. He didn't leave butter or jam out, and she can't be bothered to get it herself. The dryness of the toast scrapes her throat, and she hurries to swallow it down.

By holding the cup against one crutch, she manages to

make it back to the table with half a cup of coffee. The rest splatters on her pajama pants and the floor.

She inserts the flash drive and waits for it to load. At least Joachim's laptop already had all the software she needs. It might've been better if it didn't, though, if he were forced to figure out something with the Internet connection. Loneliness fills her abruptly, as if she'd swallowed it with her coffee. If only she could check her emails, let her parents know how she's doing, or catch up with the people at work. She can't remember any of her coworkers, but all that will come back with time. If she asks Joachim tonight, she'll remember. Just one piece at a time, and she'll put the puzzle back together. The rest will come by itself. Hoping against hope, she checks the network connection on the computer. But there's nothing coming from their apartment, and all the neighbors' connections are password-protected.

Well, so what. It isn't the only Internet connection in the world. If she gets the laptop into a backpack, she's pretty sure she could carry it. She'll go slowly, even if it takes an hour just to get to that coffee shop down the street—what's it called again?—and she'll get connected there. Joachim's acting like she's a cripple, but won't he be surprised when he comes back to an empty apartment, finds a note saying she's gone out. Of course she'll tell him where she's going. It would be good if he came to pick her up. If he carried her things back into the apartment tonight.

This plan keeps her in good spirits all morning and into the afternoon as she finishes a corporate presentation for new and prospective employees. The date in the corner of each slide still looks strange to her, though she's known what year it is for a while now. She wonders about the past few years, wonders what became of them as if they were items of clothing that vanished in the wash or got left in a hotel. Like the things she remembers wearing but can't find now. Sometimes, when she describes these things, Joachim says she hasn't owned them for years; other times he says a lot of things got damaged when the apartment flooded and had to be taken to the dry cleaner's. Or thrown away. She doesn't really believe she'll see her things again, and when she gets into one of her strange moods, she doesn't really believe she'll get those years back, either. Did she really live them, if she can't remember a thing about them? How would her life be different now, if she had those years?

She's hungry, but decides to work through it. It's so much effort to get things out of the refrigerator, and she can just buy something when she goes out. Getting there will be so much of a struggle that she'd rather not wrestle with anything in the apartment first. It's just like Joachim not to think of any of these things. On the one hand, he babies her when he's here, does everything for her. When she got back from the hospital, he carried her crutches up the stairs and then came back for her. On the other hand, he doesn't think of how it is when he's at work all day and there's no one here to help her, to hold open the door of the refrigerator or pull the arm of a sleeve she can't get off. It's just a matter of time, though. It's been good between them these past few days. It seems to her that they were always fighting, but it's been calm between them, not even any bickering. The accident must've scared them more than they know. Or maybe they fixed things in their marriage before that, and she just can't remember. Maybe all that fighting was years ago, already a thing of the past. But then why the separation?

She forces her mind back to the task at hand, finishes the project and copies it onto the flash drive, heavy with the satisfying weariness of a job well done. She feels that she's good at her job, respected at her office, but maybe that was another office, another job. There's no point making her head ache now, trying to figure all that out. Her energy surges briefly as she shuts down the computer, and she manages to make it to the hall closet, pull Joachim's hiking backpack down from the top shelf with one crutch, and then pack the computer into it. Using her left hand, she pulls the straps over her shoulders. Her purse is on the sofa, and she rests a moment there as she moves it into the backpack. She won't need her keys as long as he comes to get her. She hasn't seen them lately, anyway; maybe they got destroyed in the accident, like her phone.

They'll have to have a new set made. She pulls a pen and an old bus ticket out of her purse, writes a note on the back. She can't remember the name of that café, but she knows it's to the left as you come out the door of their apartment, a couple of blocks away. He'll know the one she means.

Outside the apartment, she pauses to take stock. Twelve steps to the landing between here and the floor below, then another twelve steps to actually reach that floor. All that multiplied by four. Funny how you never notice things like that, the number of steps in your building. You just walk up and down, day after day, oblivious. Until you can't.

But she can. With the straps of the backpack cutting into her shoulders, she moves to the top of the staircase. A wave of dizziness comes over her and she grabs for the railing. Her left crutch slips out and crashes to the floor, then slides down the first couple of steps. Steady, steady. She'll just reach down and pick it up, no need to panic. Leaning against the wall, she clutches her right crutch in her left hand and tries to sweep the fallen crutch back onto the landing. She makes solid, promising contact with it, but then something about the angle's wrong and she loses control, watches in sweaty dismay as it tumbles down the rest of the steps. Steady, stea—

The door behind her opens, and her heart tumbles down some staircase within her, all hard angles and clatter. It's a bearded young man in boxer shorts and a wifebeater; he looks like he just woke up. She doesn't recognize him, but that doesn't mean they haven't met.

"Evening," she says.

He looks at her for a few beats, trying to understand the situation.

"Everything okay?" he asks. "I heard something fall."

"Yes, everything's fine. I just stepped out and then . . ."

Both of them look down at the crutch.

"I'll get that." He disappears into his apartment, comes back with flip-flops on, and hurries down the stairs after her crutch as if it were running away from him.

"There you go."

He stands in his doorway, looking at her. She must look

terrible, unfit to be outside. She realizes that she never even got dressed this morning, didn't wash herself or put on deodorant. She must look crazy. What was she thinking, trying to go out when it was too much effort even to put on a pair of clean underwear? But she just has to smile and act normal; accidents can happen to anybody. She never asked for this.

"I got hit by a car a couple weeks ago."

"Oh." He looks both relieved and embarrassed. He was probably afraid to ask. Maybe he thought Joachim pushed her down the stairs. How ridiculous. Things were never *that* bad. Maybe this neighbor knows Joachim. He might even know her. She feels dizzy and wishes she were resting on the sofa now, wishes she'd never had this stupid plan and come out here. She's so impatient to get better she risked hurting herself all over again. What would Joachim say if he knew?

"Do you want me to help you? I mean, were you trying to get downstairs?"

"Yes. Well, no, not exactly. I just needed some fresh air."

"If you need to get downstairs—"

"I think I'd better not. But thanks anyway."

"No problem. Let me know if you need anything."

"Thanks."

Smile, move away from the staircase, end the encounter. The friendly neighbor from across the hall who just stepped out for some air. It occurs to her as she hobbles back to the door that she doesn't have her keys, but luckily the man has already gone back in and closed his door.

Careful not to make a sound, not to attract his attention again, she props her crutches in the corner. Holding the doorknob with her left hand, she slowly lowers herself to the ground and leans against the door, exhausted.

It seems like an eternity before she hears Joachim's heavy tread coming up the stairs, but it may only have been a few minutes. After all, it was already evening when she left. She tries to stand up as he approaches, to laugh the whole thing off, but of course she can't stand, and pain shoots through her, ricocheting across her abdomen into her appendages and finally settling somewhere in her forehead. She cries out in spite of herself as he runs up the last few steps to help her. It's not until he bends to lift her that she bursts into tears.

"I didn't have my keys." She has to say this a few times before he understands. She's ashamed of herself, even after he's gotten her back inside the apartment and closed the door; she's ashamed to have him see her like this, letting herself go all to pieces. But he doesn't know what it's like to be trapped here every day, helpless, cut off from everyone. Well, not everyone—she has him, of course—but it isn't enough.

• • •

The worst part is that it's always fine again in the evenings, or fine enough. He's there, and the exhausting, claustrophobic despair of the day seems almost imagined. But then she wakes the next morning and it starts again.

Besides, there's still something off about Joachim, but she's too close to him to know what. She needs distance, perspective, advice from family and friends. She needs to know what the world looks like outside of this apartment, right now. It seems to her that she no longer has any idea what's out there, or who.

The next day, over her lunch of dry bread—he keeps saying she needs to eat—she reaches for the card from her company again, the cuddly puppy with its sad eyes and tufts of fur protruding from a pretend cast.

She opens the card, but none of the names jumps out at her. She swallows a hard chunk of disappointment. She was so sure she'd recognize one or two, her best friends at the office, or the colleagues she can't stand. So sure that she didn't even need to look. Or was afraid to. She scans the mass of names, trying to pick a face out of the crowd.

The effort is exhausting and fruitless. The only name that stands out is "Doro." Whoever this woman is has printed her phone number below her name, in a different color of ink. Why? Are they friends? Maybe Joachim told her Helena was lonely. But if he told her to write her number, why didn't he mention it? And why would he tell this woman to put in her number, knowing Helena's trapped here all day without a phone, no way to call anyone? If she were going to call someone, it would be her parents, not some random person she can't remember having met.

So that means it wasn't Joachim's idea. He must not know that she did it, or he would've said something. Does this woman have something to tell her, or was it just a meaningless afterthought? It's impossible to guess the motives of a person she might as well never have seen. For all she knows, she hasn't. Then again, all she knows doesn't mean very much right now. The point is that this woman wrote down her number for a reason. And whatever other factors might be involved, the main reason for giving someone your number is so that person can call you.

She struggles to her feet then stands still a moment, propping herself up on her desk with her sweating left hand. Deciding to call still doesn't give her any way of doing it.

She could wait until Joachim gets home and ask to use his phone. She borrowed it the other night to call her parents, but then it ran out of credit after just a minute or two, so she only had time to say she was okay, and hear that they were. His battery was dying, too, and he'd forgotten his charger at work. If her parents called back, it was after the phone died. And that was it. No mention of how she was getting along since the accident, or her decision not to separate from Joachim.

Did her parents know they'd decided to separate? She must've discussed the decision with them, with someone. And yet they hadn't mentioned it, not even with a quick "How are things with Joachim?".

There's something strange about that. There's something strange about a lot of things lately. Why is it so hard to make sense of everything? It can't all be the amnesia. It's the past she's forgotten, but the present that she can't figure out.

She feels dizzy from the strain of thinking and standing without her crutches. She picks them up and leans against the wall. Another aching breath. The room moves around her. Not quickly, but in sly, subtle ways, always glimpsed out of the corner of her eye. She can't keep track of anything.

Again, she wants to escape from the apartment by any

means necessary, wants to get down all those stairs, even if she has to ask her neighbor for help.

And then she has an idea. Why ask him to help an invalid down four flights of stairs when she can ask for a much simpler favor?

She starts for the door again, then thinks better of it. Better to put on some clean clothes first, brush her hair and wash her face. She doesn't want to look like a crazy person. She's just a neighbor who was in an accident, whose phone line is down. Not someone who's escaped from somewhere. Even if that's what this feels like.

Once she's made herself presentable, she spritzes on some perfume, picks up the get-well card and hobbles out of the apartment. This time, she remembers to leave the door open.

She takes a deep breath before ringing the doorbell, although he probably already heard her clattering across the landing. She forces her face into a smile and gets all her explanations ready, the things to say so he won't look at her funny or refuse to let her use his phone.

She's so anxious about the impression she'll make that it takes her a moment to notice that no one's coming to the door. How long has it been? Two minutes maybe, certainly not as long as it feels like. She holds her breath a few heartbeats, then rings again. Maybe he'll still come. Maybe he's in the shower or having a nap. Maybe he's on the phone himself. Never mind, she can wait.

She goes over the phone call in her mind. Joachim must've told everyone about her health problems. But how do you put that into words? Hello, this Helena; you must be Doro but I can't remember who you are. Hi, how are you; can you tell me whether we were friends?

She feels the heaviness of time passing, its slow weight accumulating on her shoulders, pressing her flesh into the unyielding pads of her crutches. He's probably out, will probably be out for a while. It's a weekday afternoon, no guarantee that anyone would be home. Just because he was home once doesn't mean he's home every day. And if he is home, he's not answering the door.

She feels something sinking in her, so low and heavy she'd like to lie down on this floor, not move until her neighbor comes home. And maybe not even then.

She doesn't even know his name. Silly to pin all this hope on a stranger. So many people are strangers now, strangers to her, and yet they must still know her.

It's not the end of the world, even if it feels like it. She moves back toward her apartment, pausing in the doorway with a last-ditch kind of hope. But no one's coming up the stairs.

All afternoon she works with the door ajar, listening for the sound of footsteps. Twice more she makes her way into the hallway, rings the doorbell and waits. Like she wouldn't have heard him coming in. When she finishes her work, she doesn't even try to distract herself, but sits on the sofa, listening. It's evening now; he has to come soon. Everyone has to come home sooner or later.

When she finally hears footsteps on the stairs, each one pounds within her louder than her own heart. She gets to her feet again, makes her way to the door and pulls it open, feeling that sad, fake, socially acceptable smile on her face again.

"Well, hello," Joachim says. "Look at you all dolled up." He's holding a bouquet of pink and yellow roses in one hand.

It takes her a moment to understand. First she looks over his shoulder, as if the neighbor might be behind him; then she checks whether there's any light coming through the bottom of his door. She let it get dark in her own apartment, she realizes; the sun went down but she never turned on the lights.

"These are for you." He starts to hand her the flowers, then thinks better of it and steps past her into the apartment, closing the door and switching on the light.

The paper around the flowers crinkles as he unwraps them so it takes him, and Helena herself, a moment to hear that she's weeping.

JOACHIM

Half an hour later, Joachim and Helena are in a cab, inching through the traffic of Charlottenburg toward Halensee. He called the cab, offered to take her out to a romantic dinner on the water, and carried her down the stairs, trying not to feel that she'd gotten lighter since he carried her up them. He feels miserable and more than a little afraid, but he can't let her see.

"How'd your work go today, darling?"

She mumbles something he can't understand, but at least she's stopped crying. It was horrible, seeing her like that. Not the way that seeing someone you love in pain is horrible, but the way you feel if you see some miserable stranger in the street: guilty, sorry, moved to help but not knowing how, more than anything hoping someone else will take responsibility so you don't have to. But he was at home and Helena was his wife again, and there was no one else.

He strokes the copper silk of her hair from the crown to the tips, gently, like she's an animal that might bite. Was he always this afraid of her?

He tells her about his day in a light tone of voice that sounds false even to him, stretches insignificant events into anecdotes to fill the ride across town. He feels ashamed in front of the cabbie, as if the silent man weaving through the West Berlin traffic knew all about them, knew the reason for her mournful silence, and despised his desperately cheerful prattle. When they finally get out, he tips the cabbie to excess, buying his thanks if not his approval.

At least she pulls herself together when they get there. She's still quiet as he takes her arm and helps her through the half-empty restaurant to the terrace overlooking the dark water, but her silence is no longer ominous. The danger—whatever it was—has passed.

"How nice," she says, sounding almost surprised to find herself there.

"Let's try to get something close to the water." They were here together a few years ago—he can't be sure quite how many—not to eat but just to explore the lake. It was something of a failed excursion, because the only swimming area was already chock-full of nudists and the path around the lake was chopped up by fences surrounding private villas. Toward sundown, they'd seen the lights of this restaurant twinkling across the lake, and he hoped to rescue the day by bringing her here. But when they finally reached the other side, they saw that it was closed for a private party. She teased him for the rest of the evening about his failed attempt to take her on a date. It was good when they could laugh about things. They could just as easily have fought. They always could have.

It's the kind of memory he hasn't thought about in years. Not that he'd forgotten, just that the thought never came up. There were so many things he could've remembered about her, it was better not to start in the first place. A wave of alarm passes over him, and he pauses a moment to regain his balance, as if the wooden boards of the terrace were moving under his feet.

"Well, you finally got us a table," she says when he pulls out her chair.

He laughs, but there's something uncanny about her now, the candlelight playing on her unreadable face. Does she really remember that evening the way he does, or did she simply pluck the thought out of his head? The light in her eyes is alarming; it's unclear whether they're reflecting the candlelight flickering between her and him, or being reflected by it.

"Do you remember?" she asks. "It was closed and we ended up eating currywurst at a bus stop on the way back."

She touches his hand and he relaxes. So this is real, after all.

HELENA

Helena manages not to cry, that Saturday, when Joachim shows her the collapsible wheelchair like a surprise he's brought home for her. Well, he did bring it home for her, at least on loan. And it certainly was a surprise when he called from the doorway that he had something for her.

But it is more practical than flowers or some bijou from the jewelry store. So, after the first moment, she resolves to enjoy the day, to savor it as the first foretaste of good times to come. After all, how else did she think she was going to get around? This is an improvement over the drowsy tedium of the last couple of weekends, anyway. And it's certainly an improvement over the weekend she woke up in the hospital. She can't remember how that one started, but getting run over definitely put a damper on things.

He helps her down the stairs, then goes back up for the chair. They stop at a bakery for sandwiches, and he wheels her toward the tram to Volkspark Friedrichshain so they can have a picnic. For the first few minutes, the sunlight dazzles her eyes the way it used to when she came out of a matinee movie as a child. They get out and she feels a lonely kind of longing for him as he pushes her along, so close and yet barely within reach, impossible to hold or be held by. She can't stand on her toes to kiss him, can only wait for him to bend and kiss her. She feels him as a warm blur in her consciousness, behind her, above her, but never quite with her. Trying to see him without seeing him takes so much focus that she can barely keep up with the meaningless conversation he makes along the way. But it's good to get out.

And to be out with him. She laughs aloud and the laugh has a painful feel to it, like a cough.

"What?"

"I was just thinking"—she gives another wracking laugh— "that I can't remember the last time we spent a day together like this."

He laughs, but it takes him a minute to get started, so she knows it hurts him, too. Knows that things didn't really get better between them, not enough for them to be able to laugh at the bad times.

She feels lonelier than ever, but when they reach the park, it's only a few bumpy meters down the dirt path, then he's parked her chair next to a bench and sat down, and they're together, still and at last. She takes his hand, urgently, as if she needed to tell him something, then drops it again. A magpie is shrieking at a hooded crow over something the two of them found in the tall grass, probably something dead. Joachim unwraps her sandwich and hands it to her.

The day is long and short. Long because they stay out until evening, rolling through an indifferent but—for Helena—fascinating world of strange faces, dogs off their leashes, and toddlers on wooden bicycles.

They stop at a few sidewalk cafes because she doesn't want to go in anywhere. And that makes the day short, one continuous shot, no cuts, no fade-outs to rest the viewers' eyes. She tries not to notice a certain residual sense of isolation, like a persistent ringing in her ears so quiet it seems imagined.

Dinner at another outdoor table, sushi she eats with her hands because the chopsticks keep getting caught in her cast. She wants to interrupt every conversation they have, take him by the arm and shout: *Know me! Come close to me!* But all this is absurd. It's only her pent-up energy, the overstimulation of being out after so long. After all, who knows her better than he does? Who could be closer to her?

They decide to have one more drink after dinner, though

it's clear that neither of them wants to. She isn't sure why they can't admit this, why they can't just go home and go to bed. Somehow, that would be admitting defeat. So she tells herself she doesn't want to disappoint him, that he went to all this effort to take her out, and she has to show him what a good time she's having. And maybe he's afraid of disappointing her by cutting things short.

A haphazard turn off of Boxhagener Platz brings them to a café they've never been to before. All the tables outside are taken, but for some reason she insists on being rolled into the stuffy interior instead of looking for another place, and he agrees. Maybe they've already given up on something.

The inside is lightly populated with a few stray couples who give Helena sympathetic looks but don't make eye contact. Something about the wooden newspaper rack near the bar catches her eye. Something familiar. But what? Her eyes move to the empty table nearest it, and she's certain that she's been here before. When? And doing what? Reading a newspaper? There's something about the juxtaposition of the two, that wooden rack bursting with newspapers and the heavy wooden table, big enough for two, but small enough that you could get away with sitting there on your own, taking up the whole table with a newspaper. But there was something else—

Joachim stops talking abruptly. He and Helena realize in the same moment that she wasn't listening.

"I've been here before," she says apologetically. "I was trying to remember when."

"Search me." At least he doesn't look angry. It's understandable—isn't it?—that she should try to remember, when she gets the chance.

"Maybe it was a long time ago, while I was in college or something." She's lost her grip on whatever fine thread connected her to that rack with the crumpled papers drooping on it. But she doesn't believe what she just said. The interiors of cafes, the cafes themselves, change too quickly for that. Besides, the feeling was so immediate, a matter of weeks rather than years. So she was in this café without him. What does that prove?

She keeps nodding and agreeing with whatever he's saying while her mind wrestles with itself, trying to get out of the impossible knot it's bound up in. It seems sometimes that if she'd just try hard enough, she could remember. But the superhuman effort it would take terrifies her: she might not withstand it. It can't last forever, can it? The specialist will let her know, when she goes to see one. The café loses the mysterious familiarity it had when they came in and begins to take on the mundane feel of an evening winding down. When he asks whether she's tired, she nods gratefully, somehow close to tears.

JOACHIM

On Monday, Joachim calls the hospital from his office kitchen. It takes him a few tries to get through to Dr. Hofstaedter, and when he does, he's almost sorry he called.

"You remember," he tells the doctor. "My wife was having problems with amnesia after the accident?" He can feel Dr. Hofstaedter judging him as he asks about a specialist, judging him for having waited weeks to call. And for not really wanting his wife to recover. Is that love?

The thought strikes him like a blow to the head, and he has to ask Dr. Hofstaedter to repeat the names she's just given him. After he's thanked her and hung up, he feels nauseous with fear, helplessly aware that the doctor could call his wife right now and tell her everything. He told Dr. Hofstaedter when he took Helena home that they'd discussed the situation, but he's never been a good liar, no matter what Helena thinks. He wants to hurry home to be with her, to intercept the call and tell her the news himself. Then he remembers that he disconnected the phone, that no one can possibly get through to her.

He leans against the wall opposite the coffeemaker, feeling a sickly breeze from the one small window. But what if something happens to her? How can he bring himself to leave her there, day after day, with no way of reaching him in an emergency? What if she fell down and hit her head again, or the apartment caught fire? He can hardly breathe for thinking of it. How many days has he left her there like that? It can't go on this way. He'll buy her a cell phone after work, one of those prepaid ones you can use right away. He'll put in his number, and if anything happens, she'll be able to reach him. He forces breath into his lungs and tries to regain his balance. This isn't how he pictured it. But then again, it wasn't the first time around, either. Somehow, he never knows what to expect of Helena—or himself when he's with her.

HELENA

Helena finishes her project early and feels a momentary thrill. Free! She can leave work early! And then reality sinks in. Leave work and do what? What, should she go home early?

She shuts down the laptop, becoming aware all at once of how warm the apartment is, how stifling the air. But she's always covered in sweat nowadays; what difference does it make? Everything is so much effort.

A walk around the block in the fresh air would be just the thing. Or sitting on a park bench and letting her mind wander, watching the passersby. Funny how humble your wishes can get. She was always so discontent before. That was different, though. A different kind of trapped. Better not to think about that now. Better not to think about stupid wishes, either. If wishes were elevators, she'd ride one out of this apartment. Ha, ha. Except it's not funny. She gets to her feet, first balancing her weight on the tabletop, pressing the blood out of her left hand, and then on the crutches, whose soiled pads press her sweat back into her skin.

She makes it across the room to the window and pulls the entire panel open. She props her crutches against the wall, presses her left hand to the windowsill and leans her head out. And thinks, just for a moment, of going all the way. Everyone would think it was an accident—she was injured, trying to get some fresh air and she slipped. It could happen that way. Even now it could. Everyone would think it was an accident, except maybe Joachim, and he'd tell himself it was. He'd have to.

There's something unsavory about the relish this thought offers her, and she moves away from the window.

What now? She could get herself something to eat, but she doesn't have much appetite. Eating almost never seems worth the effort now. A cup of coffee, then. The machine's still on; she can manage that.

But in spite of the absurd, disproportionate effort this takes her, by the time she's on the sofa with a somewhat full cup of milky, stale coffee, there's still at least an hour, more likely two, until Joachim gets home.

She could go to the bedroom and get a book, but she's tired of the books he bought her, tired of words that move without taking her with them. She isn't a big fan of TV—not on weekday afternoons, anyway—but she wants to treat herself to something and her options are limited.

She spends almost as much time flipping channels as actually watching anything—low-budget documentaries, poorly acted soaps, dubbed Hollywood movies. She finally settles on a vapid romantic comedy about a woman trying to win back her ex. In spite of herself, she buys into it, hoping for the woman's success, watching her dress to impress as if looking into a mirror, and bitterly disappointed by minor setbacks meant to provide comic relief.

When the film's predictable style makes it clear that the woman is unlikely to succeed, Helena is panic-stricken. She considers turning off the TV but can't even bring herself to change the channel.

In one of the later scenes, the woman packs a box full of things that remind her of her ex, holding up each one to examine it, sometimes with a flashback for the benefit of her audience—a moonlit picnic, a giddy joyride, a stolen kiss. Then, suddenly, she's weeping, violently, bitterly, with childlike despair. Helena joins her and keeps sobbing long after the woman on TV, long after she's turned off the set. What's going on? What's wrong with her? She can't think, can't breathe. But she knows this weeping, this desperate weeping after you've given up on everything, and it's the last thing you can do, a thing without hope.

Who was weeping like that? Why did that scene feel so familiar? Maybe she'd seen the movie and forgotten it. But that wouldn't be so gutting.

She dries her face on the hem of her shirt and slowly, slowly manages to stop. The irrational feeling of despair, of utter abandonment, stays with her, but she fights to keep it at a distance. She could swear the weeping she remembers is her own.

But why? She doesn't remember ever weeping like that. She often cried after a fight with Joachim, but never so achingly. And she never felt that alone in her misery—he was always there with her. It isn't a memory she has of weeping like that or feeling like that; it's just the familiarity of it. As if she'd tried some exotic delicacy in a far-off land, only to find that she knew the taste.

• • •

By the time Joachim gets home, she's cleaned herself up and pasted a smile across her face. Because people are unhappy enough on their own; they don't want to be married to someone who makes them miserable. But her happiness is sincere when he shows her the contents of a small shopping bag from Media Markt. A phone! Her own phone, to call anyone she wants! She could talk on it all day if she liked.

"Thank you!" she says. But a moment later she's reining in her delight. Why did he wait this long? Is there someone he doesn't want her to contact? Or was it just the usual thoughtlessness? Maybe she's in denial now, trying to come up with conspiracy theories to cover for the fact that he can be so inconsiderate. This is her marriage, not a spy movie.

She can't help testing the waters. "I'm really glad to have a phone again," she says. "I've been so lonely this whole time."

And then the conversation is like watching a play she wrote herself, except that it's too late to go back and change her lines. Were they always this predictable?

"You should've said something. I would've gotten you a phone sooner. I just didn't think—"

"You didn't think I might be lonely, not leaving the house for days, with no Internet and no phone? I haven't seen anybody in weeks!" Best not to mention that neighbor now. He hardly counts. It would be best not to mention any of it, now that he's finally gotten around to solving this problem, but she can't help herself. She may have to suffer, but she doesn't have to do it in silence.

"So I'm nobody? Guess it was nobody who carried you down the stairs and wheeled you all over Berlin this weekend. Guess nobody's been taking care of you all this time."

There's something unnatural about the way he's speaking: she can't tell whether he's acting angrier than he actually is, or whether he's even more furious than he seems, and holding it in. The thought frightens her. Maybe it frightens him, too. She props her crutches against the end of the sofa and slowly settles onto it.

"You know I didn't mean that." They can only allow themselves to get so angry. They can't take it too far. At least she can't. What would they do, separate when she can't even leave the building by herself? Or remember what happened last year? If they let it get ugly enough, he won't care. If he cares about anything, it'll be what people would say if he kicked her out in her condition. "I'm grateful to you for looking after me like this." At the same time, she runs over the alternatives in her head. He'd have to take her to her parents' house. It's a bit of a drive from Berlin, but she's doing home office anyway. And her dad's carpentry shop is right next door, so there'd always be someone nearby.

"You don't have to thank me for it," he says, and the sudden change in his tone disrupts her vision of escape. "I'm your husband. Of course I'm looking after you."

"Thank you," she says, for lack of anything else. It wouldn't be a real escape, anyway. She'd just dwell on their problems even more than she is here. And if they left it that way, if they ended things before she recovered, there'd be no going back. This is a kind of test, an extreme situation that swept in and turned everything on its head, and if they can't get it together now, they're never going to. If she can't count on him now, there's no point. The finality of that kind of ending scares her, but in a way she's just as scared of the alternative: the two of them walking around this apartment on eggshells, cautiously dodging fights and choking down their resentment, determined to keep the peace long enough for her bones to set. Knowing it's over but unable to leave, acting out an awkward epilogue that should never have been written.

He sighs and sits down next to her, strokes her hair. She wants to cry and cry until she's washed something out of herself, until she stops choking on it. But he wouldn't understand; he'd only see her tears as a trap for him, a ploy to force him to pity. The tension is unbearable, her awareness—and his—that they can't afford to fight right now, and of the violence they'll be capable of when this is over. Each knowing the other knows.

"I'm sorry," he says. "I should've thought of it sooner. I was so caught up in worrying about how you were physically, and I didn't think how lonely you must feel. I'm sorry."

Love fills her, and resignation that is its own kind of affection: This man, with all his failings, all his flaws, is her husband, her own imperfect partner for life. She loves him in spite of himself, she loves him for himself, and she loves him for his sacrifice now, swallowing the pride that was keeping them apart.

"Oh, I almost forgot to tell you, Dr. Hofstaedter gave me the names of some specialists. I'm going to call up tomorrow and find out who can see you soonest."

"Thank you." And now she is crying, but only passively. She's not weeping; something's just crying itself out of her, moving over her face like rain on a closed window through which she watches, safe and dry. And it's okay, this time, because he isn't angry.

"Shhh, shhh." He moves his thumb through the hollows under her eyes, sweeping out the tears, and kisses the corners of her eyelids. She lifts her head to kiss him on the mouth. Just mentioning the specialist seems to work magic. Doesn't she remember more already? Not that any concrete facts have come back to her, but a certain obstacle has been removed, whatever it was separating them, making them act like strangers: too polite to fight, but also too polite to really get close. She lies down slowly, moving her weight onto her left arm, and nudges him with her cast until he lies down facing her on the narrow space of the sofa, kissing her like this is the first night they've ever spent together: that passion, and that restraint.

His caution and gentleness remind Helena of losing her virginity. Her first lover was finishing his degree as she started hers, and far more experienced. Like Joachim now, he moved so slowly, so carefully, like she'd break if he dropped her, and kept asking whether he was hurting her. Because of her injuries and Joachim's nervousness, there's a strange stillness to their lovemaking, but also a kind of wonder, as if neither had believed it would really work. She can't remember it ever having been this intimate.

JOACHIM

Joachim wakes a few hours later and considers carrying Helena to bed, but she's so peaceful he doesn't want to risk waking her, so he simply covers her with a blanket and goes to bed himself. He expects confusion, racing thoughts, panic at what's just happened, but he only feels the same peace with which her slender chest rises and falls. He wakes just before his alarm with an absurd happiness, knowing before he knows anything else that there's something special about today, about life in general.

Helena

Joachim is already gone when she gets up. Long gone, judging by the light coming through the window, the sun already nearing its zenith. You get used to looking out the window when you never go outside. And guessing the hour when you have to start up your laptop to tell the time.

But this thought reminds her of her new phone, and she picks it up from the coffee table with a feeling of sublime happiness. For a moment, she can't think of anything really wrong in her world. The hard, cool feel of the cheap phone in her hand summons up the soft warmth of last night, of Joachim beside her, around her, within her. The lightness she feels isn't happiness about any individual fact, but the removal of some burden, the dread that's been weighing on her. She must never have believed it was going to work out.

She plays with the phone for a few minutes before getting up, figuring out where everything is. Joachim put his office and his own cell phone under the contacts, two lonely entries, barely enough to keep each other company. She tries not to let that loneliness pass into her, not this morning. She isn't lonely; it's just another thing she'll have to start over on.

She was lying so comfortably that the usual aches surprise her as she sits up and slowly gets to her feet. But they're only temporary, have no bearing on the strange bliss she woke to. Just a little longer, and she'll be walking normally, using both hands, able to put weight on her abdomen again. A bit of physical therapy and she'll be good as new.

In the bathroom mirror, she's surprised to see that her face is puffy and still lightly scarred, that her hair is matted greasily on one side. She feels so glowing. Brushing her teeth, she avoids eye contact with herself, as if this were just a reflection someone else forgot here, nothing to do with her.

Her stomach growls like a machine starting up, and immediately her hunger is ravenous. She feels like she hasn't eaten in days. Still, she forces herself to wash her face, brush her hair, put on clean clothes. She can't afford to let herself go, not when things are going so well with Joachim. She can't afford it anyway—that's the way people go crazy, sitting in their apartments day after day until they start to wonder who's going to care whether they get dressed.

She only notices when she comes out of the bathroom how full the living room is with the aroma of coffee. The machine must've been on for hours. Joachim has left two pieces of bread in the toaster, and today he remembered to leave out the jam and the butter dish. The jam jar is holding down a torn piece of paper with half the logo of what must be Joachim's employer.

I LOVE YOU!! the note says in large letters.

She reads it again, turns the paper over. Somehow, it seems like there must be something more. But there's just that big, frantically scrawled *I LOVE YOU!!* She puts the paper down again, pins it in place with the jam jar and presses the button on the toaster. So what? What's so strange about that? It's a nice thing to have done. He's her husband and he should love her; in a way it goes without saying, but it's still nice of him to say so.

She loves him, too, doesn't she? It takes a few milliseconds for the voice in her head to reply, of course you love him. What is it that bothers her about this note? The toast pops up and she extends her fingertips so her cast won't come into contact with the hot surface. She has to make a few trips to bring her breakfast to the computer, but she's getting better at it. Doesn't spill so much anymore. For some reason, she makes a last trip after she starts up the computer, and brings the note back with her.

She looks at it again. What more does she expect to see? But that's just what bothers her about it: that there *is* nothing else. It would be an ordinary thing to write at the end of a note, rounding out the contents with a well-placed reminder. Above or below the signature. But this isn't an afterthought or a postscript; it's a declaration. As if he'd never said it, as if he'd never even thought it before. As if he'd just realized it for the first time. And thrilling as it must be for him to love his wife like he only just fell for her, there's something not quite right about it. Not quite right for him, anyway. He never liked to get carried away—or to see her do it—whether it was in love or a fight. What brought on this sudden change?

The antivirus appears on the screen, then disappears. She inserts the flash drive. Maybe she's overthinking things. Whatever the reason, she should be happy about it. Not borrow trouble. That's what he always accused her of, never being able to let anything go, always picking at things. At the same time, it's only by picking at things that you get to the bottom of them, find out the truth.

But what truth? She's less and less sure that he's hiding anything from her. If he is, why did he find the specialist she asked for and buy her a phone, which she could use to contact anyone she liked? Well, not quite anyone. She can call him at two different numbers, or she can call someone whose number she has memorized. Which narrows it down quite a bit. The only numbers she has memorized are his cell, which she has anyway, her old phone number, and the number her parents used to have. She didn't memorize their new one; she just replaced the old one in her phone. So, basically, she's where she was before.

Except for one thing. There is one number that she has, and she retrieves her phone from the coffee table to dial it, consulting the get-well card from her office. To her surprise, once she's entered the first three digits, she finds that she knows the rest by memory after all. Did she know it before the accident, or has she simply looked at this card so many times that she memorized an unknown number?

It doesn't matter. She's done enough thinking and agonizing about things. She needs to talk to someone from outside this apartment, outside this marriage. She presses the call button and listens to the phone ringing over and over again, as if it never planned to stop.

She can't tell if she's disappointed or relieved when the voicemail picks up and she ends the call. What could she possibly say in a message? Before she can decide how to feel, Doro is calling her back, the sound of the generic ringtone echoing through the silent apartment.

"Bachlein, hallo."

"That you, Hel?"

"Doro?"

"How are you, Hel? We've all been so worried."

"I'm as good as can be expected, I guess." She forces a laugh. There's something so awkward about having no idea what the person on the phone looks like, and listening to her take such an intimate tone. Helena can't remember anyone having called her "Hel," and yet it sounds right as Doro says it, so it must be something she went by for the past couple years, maybe just at work or maybe just with this particular friend. Because she's sure now that she and Doro were friends. Or still are, of course. There's no reason that should've changed.

"Listen, Doro," she interrupts the other woman in the middle of an update on office gossip, "can you come by sometime? I need to talk to . . . you." She decides not to say *I need to talk to someone*, in case such a general statement would offend Doro. They may be quite close friends.

"Of course, do you need anything? I could go by the store or—"

"No, thanks."

"Oh, right, your cousin's taking care of you. He was at the office so early last time I didn't see him."

Cousin? Doro must've gotten her stories mixed up. "No, no, Joachim is looking after me," she says. "Would you be able to come by today? It's important."

She hears the sound of a door closing, maybe Doro making

sure no one can hear what she's saying. "What's the matter, Hel? Are you all right?"

"Of course. Of course I am." She can tell Doro doesn't believe her, and realizes she doesn't want her to.

"I'll be over in an hour."

Helena's about to end the call when Doro asks for Joachim's address. Helena gives it to her but has a sickly feeling in the pit of her stomach: If they're such good friends, why doesn't Doro know where she lives? Why did she ask where Joachim lives, pronouncing his name like a foreign word?

• • •

By sheer strength of will, Helena manages to work for the next hour and a half. She's only able to force the thought of Doro's visit from her mind because, on a certain level, she doesn't believe it will really take place. Then the doorbell tears through the silence like the shriek of a fire alarm. It takes her a long time to get to the door, not just because of her crutches, but because it's that hard to believe someone actually rang.

She buzzes Doro in and listens to her slow, uncertain steps in the stairwell, the steps, Helena is sure, of someone who's never been here before.

Then there's a rosy-cheeked, middle-aged woman in a bulky turtleneck on her doorstep.

Doro doesn't look the way she pictured her, though the moment she sees her, Helena can no longer remember what she expected. Perhaps someone stronger, more authoritative. Or just someone with a familiar face.

"Well," she says, opening her arms to embrace Helena, "how are you?" She uses the familiar *you* again, so this must really be Helena's friend. Helena retreats from the hug, stumbling awkwardly against the frame of the door and mumbling something about her broken ribs.

"Come in," she adds, trying to keep the reluctance out of her voice. She regrets calling Doro, regrets summoning a stranger into the close air of this apartment, where she'll have to entertain her and pretend to have some recollection of their time together. Surely Joachim must've explained, but she can already tell that Doro is the kind of woman who'll expect an exception, as if Helena should've forgotten everything but their friendship.

"Please sit down," Doro says. "I'll get the door."

Helena returns to the sofa, then remembers to offer her guest a drink. "Would you like tea or coffee?" Does Doro expect her to remember what she drinks?

"I'll make us some tea," Doro says. Her confident tone reassures Helena until she hears Doro rummaging in the kitchen cupboards, clearly unsure of where they keep the mugs and tea. Helena's afraid to ask about her unfamiliarity with the apartment. Maybe, like the wolf when Little Red Riding Hood remarks on his long teeth, Doro will become dangerous the moment Helena says something.

Then she's setting two cups of black tea on the coffee table and sitting down beside Helena, who thanks her and sips at her tea. Milky and sweet, the way she likes it. But maybe that was a lucky guess. Joachim keeps making her coffee, though. What does she usually drink in the morning?

"I told them I wasn't feeling well," Doro says into the silence that starts to grow between them. "Things are a bit slow this week, anyway, so they didn't mind sending me home."

"It was nice of you to come so quickly," Helena says. It takes great effort not to use the formal *you*.

"No problem, of course I came. Everybody's so worried about you and we've barely heard anything. Tell me, what exactly happened? Uli said something about a car accident? But you don't drive."

"Apparently I was crossing the street when I got hit."

"Apparently?"

"That's what they told me at the hospital."

"You don't remember?"

So she doesn't know. It seems impossible, but she really doesn't. "I can't remember you, either," she says. "Or anything about the last few years. I have amnesia from the impact. The doctor at the hospital seemed to think it would pass, but

Joachim's supposed to be getting me an appointment with a specialist." Suddenly, she doesn't know what else to say. Maybe that's all there is.

"Really, nothing at all?"

Helena shakes her head. "I know everything I knew a few years ago, but at a certain point, I can't figure out exactly when, it all becomes a blank. Not blank like I forgot something, but like it didn't happen yet."

Doro's silence makes her nervous. She seems to be considering something that has nothing to do with what Helena just said. Finally, she asks, "But you said your cousin was going to take you to a specialist?"

"No, Joachim is. What cousin do you keep talking about?" It seems almost like Doro doesn't know her, either, like she's only guessing the facts of Helena's life. She doesn't have any relatives in Berlin, let alone some cousin to take her to the doctor.

"Joachim? Is that this Mr. Schmidt who's been picking up and dropping off your assignments?"

Something about Doro's tone infuriates Helena, the way she moves the name out of her pursed lips carefully, like an overfull cup of tea she doesn't want to spill. Yes, of course Joachim, who else? She must've told Doro that she and her husband were having problems, and that's why Doro's surprised. Doesn't she understand that this was an emergency, the kind that wipes out all the petty fights? Of course Joachim's looking after her.

"Of course," she says, trying not to raise her voice. Brain damage sounds like one step away from crazy, and she doesn't want Doro to get any ideas. Not that it matters what she thinks. Let her sit there, drinking Helena and Joachim's tea, thinking about how their marriage was on the rocks. If she and Helena are such good friends, where's she been all this time?

"But . . ." Doro pauses for a long moment, maybe trying to come up with the answer to some riddle. "Who is he, if he's not your cousin?"

"What?"

The two women stare at each other a moment, mouths

slightly open, holding their cups of tea with both hands, like children mirroring one another.

"I asked who Joachim is," Doro finally says, putting her cup on the coffee table.

Helena's pulse jumps and she glances toward the door. What if this isn't really Doro? Does she actually know this woman, or did she somehow find out about Helena's amnesia, and decide to use it to her advantage? Con her way into an apartment where only a defenseless invalid is home. "I heard you," she says slowly. She puts down her cup of tea, slips one hand into her pocket and dials 1-1-0 on her cell phone. Now the police are just one button away. Will they trace the call if she isn't able to give them her address? How can she keep this woman from knowing? Stay calm, stay calm; maybe it isn't as bad as it seems. "Joachim," she says, watching Doro's blank face for any hint of recognition or guilt. "My husband, Joachim."

Doro's eyes widen but her mouth remains set in a firm, flat line. This is it, Helena thinks. She's going to attack me now, give up the pretense of knowing me.

When Doro speaks, her words come out even more slowly than Helena's, as if she were trying to coax a dangerous criminal into dropping his gun. "Hel, you don't *have* a husband. I've never once heard you mention anybody named Joachim. As far as I know, you don't even *know* anyone with that name."

"Don't be ridiculous." Helena can't figure out what this woman's game is. If she wants to con her, shouldn't she pretend to know all about Joachim? "Joachim and I have been married since before I started at CuttingEdge. If you don't believe me, just wait here a few hours and you can ask him yourself. I may have gotten knocked down, but I certainly know whether I have a husband or not. And now," Helena puts out her right arm, keeping her other hand in her pocket, ready to press the call button, "I'd like to see your ID."

"What?"

"You heard me."

"What do you need my ID for?"

Stalling, of course. "How could you be a close friend of

mine and not know I'm married? Give me your ID right now or I'll scream for the neighbors to call the police." Better not mention the phone. She can't move quickly, so she has to maintain the element of surprise. Her throat is painfully dry and the sweat under her arms burns like acid, but she tries to appear composed, in control of this situation. Maybe this woman is just some kind of charlatan, not a dangerous criminal.

To her surprise, the woman bends down to pick up her purse and takes out her wallet. She removes one card, and then another, and hands them to Helena. One is her government-issued ID, and the other is a white keycard with the logo of CuttingEdge Medien GmbH.

"Your name is Helena Bachlein. You're thirty-three years old, and you were born somewhere outside of Bonn. I can't think of what the town's called right now. I met your parents when they visited last year. You can ask them." Doro pauses for a moment, maybe catching her breath, maybe waiting for a reaction. Helena considers calling her parents, right now, to ask them, but maybe that's all part of the trick. The woman wouldn't have mentioned her parents if it didn't play into her hand. Besides, she still doesn't have their number.

When Helena doesn't respond, Doro continues. "You had a tabby cat named Bienchen and a dachshund named Franzi when you were growing up. You studied marketing at Humboldt University and graphic design at BTK. You don't like whipped cream on your hot chocolate and you can't stand when people cut in line. You're a very private person and don't like when people talk about their personal lives in front of everyone at work."

Helena can't breathe, can't even take all this in because of the blood pounding in her temples. How can she know these things? Who could've told her? But even as her mind frantically searches for explanations, a part of her already knows that this woman is who she says she is. But if that's true . . .

"You're not able to have children," Doro adds in a soft voice, looking down at her folded hands.

Helena realizes for the first time that she still has Doro's ID and keycard clenched in one hand, the other hand still poised over the phone in her pocket. She cancels the call, takes the cards in her left hand, and wipes the damp palm of her right hand on the rolled-up leg of her pants. She hands the cards back to Doro. For a minute, several minutes, neither of them speaks. They avoid eye contact with each other and sip their cold tea. Helena feels like she's going to cry, not because she's sad but because she's so exhausted, so weak, and she doesn't have the energy to figure this out.

"You hadn't been on a date in years," Doro continues after they've both set their empty cups on the table. "That's why my husband and I set you up with Tobias."

There's something caught in Helena's throat she can't quite clear out. When she finally manages to speak, she asks, "When?" She knows the answer to this question won't explain anything, but she has to start somewhere.

"You had a date the weekend of your accident." Doro is looking at her hands again, but Helena doesn't have the sense that she's lying. Rather, she seems embarrassed.

"Could you make us another cup of tea?" she asks. She needs to get Doro away from her, even if only for a few seconds, if only by sending her to the kitchenette at the other end of the room. She needs to be alone with this new information, alone among all the things she doesn't understand.

"Of course." Doro smiles as she takes the two cups from the table. They could still speak to each other from the sofa to the kitchen, but they don't have to. And that's a relief for both of them.

Helena closes her eyes and tries to put the pieces together. So Doro really knows her. Doro is her friend. But Doro doesn't know Joachim. She had a date with someone else a couple of weeks ago. But why? Why would she let Doro set her up with someone when she's married? Did she keep Joachim a secret on purpose? Was she cheating on him? Maybe there were others. She can't see herself doing something like that, but who knows what her motives were. Whoever she was a few weeks ago is just another person she can no longer remember.

She hears the low whine of the kettle getting ready to

whistle. So they'll drink another cup of tea, ask a few more questions neither of them can really answer. And that will be all for now. Because Doro can't stay too long. If she stays too long, Joachim will get home, and he'll have another version of the truth ready for her, another version of who Helena is. And things will make even less sense if she has to try to put those two truths, those two selves, together tonight. She doesn't have it in her.

Doro sets two cups of tea on the table and sits down again. She asks a few questions about Helena's injuries and when she'll be able to get her casts off. But they're like bad actors, saying the right lines while their thoughts are somewhere else.

Doro blows on her tea and takes a cautious sip. She looks up at Helena. "So you don't remember Tobias? Not at all?"

"Not at all." Apologetically, she adds, "The name sounds familiar, though." Of course it does. Like any other common name. "What's he like?" It isn't the right question, but it's one Doro can answer.

Doro considers. "He's blond and he's got a bit of a beard most of the time, smiles a lot. A really nice guy," she adds after a pause.

There's a touch of accusation in her tone, as if Helena had chosen to forget him. And yet he couldn't have meant so much to her, if they only had a date or two.

"How long had—have I known him?" she asks.

"Just since the Saturday you had your accident. He told my husband's friend, Hannes—that's his cousin—that the two of you really hit it off and were planning to get together again, but then you never answered any of his messages and his calls went straight to voicemail. Of course we told him you'd been in an accident as soon as I heard at the office."

There's something she wants to say but isn't, and Helena doesn't feel like prying it out of her. So they really hit it off that Saturday. But maybe he just saw it that way; maybe she had a terrible time. Maybe, accident or no accident, she wasn't planning to contact him again. That's not the point, though. The point is having met him at all.

"But you said I don't usually go on dates?"

"Not as far as I know, but . . ." Doro takes a sip of tea and sets down her cup, then picks it up again. "To be honest, Hel, I'm feeling pretty confused myself. We've been friends since the week you started, and the whole time I knew you as a woman who'd resigned herself to being single forever. Now I come over after what I thought was your first date in years, and you're talking about some husband I've never heard of. I mean, when did you move into this apartment?"

Helena drains half her cup of tea as she counts the years, straining not to forget the blank ones between then and now. It's a strange question, because she must already have been living here when she met Doro. "Just before I married Joachim, so about six years ago now."

"So you've had two apartments this whole time?"

"What?"

"Hel, you've had me over a million times. My husband, too, and a couple of our coworkers, some of your other friends. And it was never in this apartment. I've never seen this apartment before. You always lived in a one-room apartment in Wedding."

"Wedding," Helena repeats. That district borders this one, but Joachim thinks it's a bad part of town and never wants to go. Can it be that she lived a whole part of her life there, had a home and guests to visit her in it? She's long past disbelieving Doro; she just wants to understand the why and how of it. "But this is my home," she says.

When Doro doesn't answer, she gets to her feet and picks up her crutches. "I'll show you," she says.

Silently, Doro follows her as she hobbles through the apartment, opening her drawers, the shoe closet and the bathroom cabinet to show Doro the things that are hers. Doro follows closely behind her and examines each piece of evidence carefully, inspecting garments and looking in all the corners of each room.

When Helena finishes the tour and sinks onto an arm of the sofa, Doro asks, "What book are you reading now?"

Exhausted, Helena points at the detective novel lying on the coffee table beside their empty cups.

"That's not really your genre, is it?"

It isn't, but what does that prove? That her friend knows her taste in books better than her husband? "Joachim brought me it in the hospital."

"But where are all your other books?"

"What?"

Doro doesn't repeat the question. Helena looks around the living room, then gets up and goes to the bedroom again, scanning the perimeter as if shelves crammed with books had only just vanished.

"There was a flood . . ." she recalls aloud, relieved to have an explanation at hand.

"Was there?" It isn't just a standard response. Doro is genuinely asking whether there was a flood. And Helena doesn't know what to say.

"I think you'd better go," she says finally, surprising herself as much as her visitor.

"But Hel—"

"I'm very tired and confused, and I've had about all I can take for the day."

Doro opens her mouth to say something, then takes a deep breath instead. She picks up her purse from in front of the sofa and walks to the door. Before leaving, she turns around to face Helena. "Will you be all right?"

"Of course," Helena lies.

"I could come back tomorrow, after you've spoken to your . . . husband."

"Please do." Helena reaches around Doro to open the door. When the other woman has stepped out into the hall, she closes it and leans all her weight against it. She's sweating but feels chilled. How long until Joachim comes home? She doesn't know if she can face him. Was she lying to him all this time, or was he lying to her? Neither would really explain this. Does he know about Tobias? Maybe he wouldn't be so nice to her if he did.

She makes her way back to the sofa and lies down on her side in front of the blank television, the coffee table with two empty cups. In a way, this is her fault. She could've left well enough alone, didn't have to have all those ugly suspicions about her marriage. But she had to go down into the cellar and see what rats she could find. She couldn't have expected this, though. She only wanted to find out what she and Joachim were fighting about, and now she knows less than ever. At least, until Doro came through the door, she knew who she was.

She stays still a while, not thinking, just lying in the strange circumstances as if they were bathwater going cold. When she looks at the time, she realizes that Joachim could come home at any minute. With great effort, she lifts herself from the sofa, takes Doro's cup to the kitchen, and throws away the teabag. She washes the cup, dries it and puts it back in the cabinet, then lies down again opposite her own empty cup.

JOACHIM

Helena is on the sofa with a book when he comes in. With a book, not reading. She has it open across her lap as he puts down the groceries and comes over to kiss her, like she only just set it down. But he feels certain that the book is a prop, that she's been waiting for him all this time, watching for his arrival. Her eyes don't have the distant look of someone glancing up from a book, but rather something too alert. A predator waiting to pounce.

"Hello, darling," she says.

Maybe he's imagining it. Maybe she's just excited to see him. He glances around the apartment, thinking how small it must be for someone who has to stay here all day and—almost—every day. The few books he bought her, maybe some daytime TV, the empty cup on the table with a teabag hanging over the side. But he did give her a phone. She could've called . . . She could only really have called him.

"How are you?" He sits down beside her. She puts her book on the table and he takes her hand. It lies limply against his palm, neither rejecting nor reciprocating his touch. She might as well be sleeping.

"Oh, *I'm* fine."

He can't tell what she means by the peculiar emphasis she puts on *I'm*—that she's fine, but he isn't? Or that they aren't? Or maybe she's reminding him of her condition, as if he could forget.

"I got you an appointment for next week," he says, trying to keep the uncertainty out of his voice. He thought she'd be happy about that. He looked forward to coming home to tell her, to her happiness. "Dr. Meier is highly respected in the field. I did some research. He can see you next Friday. I'll take you." He swallows and adds, "Of course."

"Friday?" she asks, for all the world like a woman with a jam-packed social calendar who might not be able to make this date. Or is she complaining because the appointment isn't sooner?

"That was the earliest I could get." Another lie—he could've brought her in today—but then each little one is just part of the big, overall lie, isn't it? So, in a way, he hasn't been that dishonest. Once he's told her, once he's taken back his one big lie, it'll all be clear between them.

That's why he took the appointment for next Friday, instead of one this week. He told himself he needed to make arrangements. But what arrangements? He could've just called his office the morning of. Everyone understands what an emergency is. They've been nothing but understanding since he first mentioned the accident. What will they be after, if any of this gets out? If they ask about his wife a few months from now, what will he say?

He's so caught up in this new thought that he doesn't immediately notice Helena's silence. She has so many silences, his wife; the silence of retreating so far into her own mind that she's out of earshot, the silence of watching and listening so intently she forgets to say anything. But this is one of her menacing silences, a silence she uses to speak. She doesn't just happen to be silent; rather, she's actively not speaking. But the appointment isn't that far off. She can't be angry about that. He needed the time. He needed the fixed deadline of the appointment, a date by which he has to come clean, but he couldn't face it right away.

His instinct is to ask what the matter is, but he's afraid of what she'll say. Maybe if he just pretends not to notice, everything will be fine.

"I'll get dinner started. Do you want anything to drink? I

brought some red wine. You know, Dr. Hofstaedter said you should have a glass now that you're off the painkillers. Good for the blood." He's aware that he's rambling, giving away his nervousness, and comes to an abrupt halt on his way to the kitchen.

"Sure," she says. "I'll have a glass."

When he brings it to her, he's again startled by the expression on her face. It isn't hostile, but rather what he expected her to look like when he came in—distant, barely present enough to take in his words. But she's not reading now. *Where are you?* he wants to ask, but instead busies himself in the kitchenette, pretending she's too far away for them to speak. He scrubs the potatoes and puts them in a pot of boiling water, spoons some curd cheese with herbs into a bowl and chops up vegetables for a salad. He has the eerie feeling of being watched the whole time, as if she were staring, unblinking, unmoving, at his back. But when he glances over, she's reading her book. Or at least she has it open.

She doesn't say a word until they're both seated at the table and he's serving.

"Thank you for cooking."

Even these innocent words sound strangely empty, her tone like that of a foreigner who knows a few polite phrases, but never gets the delivery quite right. Again he wants to ask what the matter is; again he stops himself.

Finally, it's Helena who breaks the silence. "Where are my books, darling?"

The question startles him. It takes him a moment to recall the answer to questions like this. "But I told you," he says a few seconds too late, "so many things were ruined by the flooding."

"So they're all gone?"

"Some of them might be in the cellar. We were reorganizing things right before your accident."

For her, it makes no difference whether they're in the cellar or another part of town.

"I'll have a look tomorrow after work. I'm too tired to carry them up tonight." He can stop by her apartment and pick up a box or two. She must be bored with the stupid bestsellers he bought. Maybe that's all this is.

"Thanks." Another pause. "Joachim?"

"Yes?"

"Do I keep a diary?"

He chews longer than necessary, biding his time. She did, at least at the time of their separation. He saw it once when she'd run down to sign for a package, leaving it on the nightstand. He couldn't help picking it up. She'd just started a new page, and all she'd written was: *that I hate him and only want*—she must've been writing when the delivery man rang. She was gone a few minutes, but he had no interest in reading more. That was a few days before she moved out.

"I'm not sure." He takes a sip of wine. "If you do, you haven't told me about it."

"I've kept a lot of diaries in my life. I thought it might help if I had a recent one to look at."

"I'll have a look in the cellar tomorrow." He never considered the possibility of a diary. If she reads her own record of their separation before he can explain, he'll have no chance at all. What if she knows she kept a diary and is testing him to see if he's lying? He'll have to bring one over, but keep her from reading it. Distract her somehow. Or hide it during the day. Just a little more time. Things are going well between them now. He just needs a little more time like this, and she'll be ready to hear the truth. Ready to hear and accept his side of the story, like she never was before.

"Was it because I was leaving?"

"What?"

She takes a bite, chews, swallows and sets down her fork without taking her eyes off of him. "You said we were reorganizing things. Was it because I was moving out?"

So it's not about the diary. Or the books. One less trip to make, anyway. Again, he overchews his food, takes a long swallow of wine. What can he say? Is there an answer that will keep her from asking more questions? Which answer is less of a lie, when her books aren't even in his cellar to begin with?

"Yes," he finally says, because that's the less favorable answer,

and therefore the one she's more likely to believe. He's ready
for a barrage of questions now, for a minefield of half-truths
he'll have to navigate, for anything but the question she actually asks.

"Did I ever . . . I mean, as far as you know, did I ever cheat
on you?" She's blushing and her voice is apologetic before
he's answered. Is that what's been on her mind all evening?
Where did she get an idea like that?

"No, never." As long as she doesn't ask whether he ever
cheated on her. They've still never agreed on the answer to
that question. But she doesn't ask.

"And you never suspected me of anything like that? Never
had your doubts, or didn't think I was where I said I was?
Anything like that?"

"Never," he says again, refilling their glasses. He carries
their empty plates to the kitchen sink. Helena, cheating on
him? Helena, the pillar of righteous anger who told him he'd
poisoned their marriage? Impossible. "Not once did I ever
have reason to suspect anything like that. Why?"

She waits until he's back at the table to respond. "I thought
that might be the reason I was moving out."

"No, that wasn't it." Which of course begs the question of
why she *was* moving out. Or rather why she did. He has to
keep things straight or he'll end up even more confused than
she is. When she doesn't ask the question he expected, he gives
her an answer of his own accord. "It was more complicated
than that. We were always fighting, and at a certain point we
just wore ourselves out. We couldn't live like that."

"What were we fighting about?"

He can tell her heart isn't in the question. Does she not
care, or is she thinking of something she isn't saying? Maybe
they can agree to leave the past behind them, and live based
on what comes next. Would he want that? If it weren't for the
past, Helena would just be a good-looking stranger. The past
is the special bond between them.

"Nothing, really," he says. "Just little things, one after the
other, but it added up." Is that the truth? You could say they
separated because of that letter from Ester, but that wouldn't

be true, either. That was the last straw, but the camel's back had been at the breaking point for a long time. If it hadn't been that, it would've been something else. Or maybe they would've kept bickering and sniping at each other forever. What is it that makes things so much easier now?

"I remember us fighting," she says vaguely, like someone listening to a more interesting conversation at the next table.

Will things stay easy? Or will they inevitably fall back into their old patterns? He remembers that feeling of helplessness, as if he were being made to speak against his will, seeing himself moved along the path to a fight, unable to turn back. Or was he only unwilling?

He takes the empty wine bottle to the recycling crate, and then returns for their glasses. Sometime before she left, she told him he wasn't made for marriage, that he'd never really committed to her. "This is the exit you've been searching for all along," she said. And he was silent, suffocating with hurt and rage and terror, until long after she and her things were out of his apartment.

"We should get ready for bed," he says.

Helena is fixedly watching the point across from her where he used to be sitting, and he has to repeat himself.

"Yes," she says. "I think we're both tired."

He falls asleep on his side of the bed with one hand resting on her stomach, raised and lowered by her breath. He's afraid to move closer tonight, but he needs to feel that she's still there.

HELENA

Helena wakes once, before Joachim, from a vivid dream she forgets immediately, but feels sure contained one of her lost memories. She wakes again when he gets up for work, and then a last time after he's left. In his absence, she feels a strange, heavy guilt that it takes her a moment to place.

Then she recalls Doro's visit, and the fact that she'll return today. What will she say when Doro asks what Joachim said? That she didn't ask him? In a way, she did. She found out that either she wasn't cheating on him, or he didn't know she was. It must be the latter, since Doro set up that date. She still can't think what would've prompted her to do something so against her nature. She must've been absolutely miserable, or else Joachim must've done something so horrible she felt driven to it. Or was that simply the person she'd become over the years, a change in her character she can no longer remember?

He said they'd separated over nothing. But how could that be? Of course, they fought a lot, and they'd been fighting for a long time. Some before they were married, and more after. But there must at least have been one last fight, one specific point in time when the decision was made. Why doesn't he want to tell her about it? Is he protecting himself, or her?

While she brushes her teeth, she tries to imagine what her right leg looks like under the cast. Not much longer until she can walk without crutches. It's strange that such an obvious physical injury could heal faster than whatever's going on in her brain. She's gotten so used to thinking of it all as one big package that it's hard to believe it won't all be over at once.

She rinses her mouth and washes her face. When it is over, whatever secrets Joachim is keeping from her, or whatever she kept from him, won't matter anymore. At least, they won't be secrets from her.

It's late and Doro could be here soon, so she sits down on the bed to dress, the clothes catching in awkward bunches on her casts. Afterward, she goes back into the bathroom to wrench a comb through her tangled hair—she must've moved a lot in her sleep—and tries to trick her foggy mind into remembering either her last dream this morning, or the person she was just before she stepped in front of a truck.

So she had an affair. Or many. She had a double life. A second home Joachim knew nothing about. She can't picture that now because she's just thinking of the facts. What she needs is to remember how she felt at the time. Hurt, maybe. Or angry? She and Joachim were fighting. Maybe she felt like he didn't love her anymore, that it was just a matter of time until he left her. She could've been looking for someone to comfort her. Or did she want to hurt him? But then she wouldn't have kept the whole thing secret.

The doorbell interrupts her thoughts, and she puts her half-combed hair into a sloppy bun before buzzing Doro in. Because of course it's Doro. Who else could it be?

"Are you all right?" Doro asks as soon as Helena opens the door. Her eyes move around the room, searching for other occupants.

"Same as yesterday. Come in."

Doro pours two cups from the pot of coffee Joachim left, and they sit next to each other on the sofa again. Helena watches Doro and waits for a cue. She notices a dimple in the woman's chin, a strange feature in the rather thin lower part of her face. Out of place somehow, until the theme is echoed by her round cheeks. Helena feels that she knows this dimple, but of course she might've noticed it yesterday. What's a dimple in some woman's chin, anyway? That's not going to answer her questions.

Doro puts milk and sugar into her own coffee, a bit of milk and no sugar into Helena's. Helena watches carefully, waiting for her to make a mistake, but the coffee is the exact shade of brown she makes for herself every day. She finds herself wondering whether Joachim knows her that well. But he's usually at work, not there to prepare the individual cup. It's strange to think of Joachim with Doro here, just as it was strange to think of Doro last night. They exist in two different realities. She might as well start demanding an explanation from Joachim for something someone said to her in a dream. But this is really happening.

"I was worried about you," Doro says. "After I left, I wasn't sure I'd done the right thing, leaving you here by yourself."

"But I was fine and I wasn't by myself. Joachim came home a little while later."

Doro blows on her coffee, puts down her cup and slicks back an invisible wisp of hair from the top of her ponytail. "That's actually what I was worried about. I didn't know what might happen once you confronted him."

"Oh." Helena lifts her cup with both hands to drink. She knows Doro's words aren't meant as an accusation, but still. She should've confronted him. Or been honest, whatever you want to call it. She should've said, *Something funny's going on here. Why do I have two apartments and why has my friend never heard of you?* Why didn't she? No one could blame her now, whatever she did before. No one could hold things against her that she can't remember doing.

Doro waits another moment, then asks, "Well, what did he say? When you confronted him?"

"Not much really." Helena knows what the next question will be before she hears it.

"You *did* confront him, didn't you? You did ask for an explanation?"

"Not exactly. I asked whether he'd ever thought I was seeing other men. He said he never had. I didn't mention this other apartment you were talking about." The way Doro looks at her with her lips slightly parted makes her feel the need to justify herself. "What could I confront him about? I don't even know what's going on. Maybe *I'm* the villain, here. Did you think of that? This could be a case of me going behind his back and him not knowing a thing about it."

"I thought of that, but I don't think that's it. You had a full social life and you were always having guests over, sometimes until late at night. You have a bed in your apartment; I assume you slept in it. You've never mentioned this neighborhood to me. And this business about a flood is a little too convenient. Ask your neighbors upstairs whether a pipe burst."

Helena feels the blood draining out of her, leaving her cold and immobile. Everything Doro is saying makes sense. Hasn't she had thoughts like these at the back of her mind? Not about the other apartment, of course, but the flood, the way it seems only to have affected *her* things . . . and now this story about her things being in the cellar. Are they both lies, or was the flood story meant to cover for moving her things because she was moving out? But why moving out? She already had another apartment. And if that's not the revelation that led to their separation, then what is?

"Are you all right?" Doro asks again.

"Just a little dizzy. I haven't eaten yet."

She lets Doro make her toast and bring it to the table, lets herself be treated like more of an invalid than she really is. When she's finished eating, Doro says, "I have an idea."

Another shudder passes over Helena. She knows she isn't going to like it. But she does her best to smile. Doro is helping her. You can tell a good medicine by its bad taste.

"Let's go to the registry office," Doro continues. "Your address must be on file there. We can find out how long you've had that other apartment."

She's calling a cab before Helena can refuse.

• • •

It's easier than Helena expected to get down the stairs, now that Doro's here to carry her crutches and take her by one arm.

She doesn't quite see the point of this outing. Knowing how long she's had this apartment won't tell her anything. She wants to know *why* she rented it, not when. And they won't have that kind of information on file. Maybe Doro just wants to prove that she's been telling the truth. Not that Helena doesn't believe her. Not that she's quite able to.

The sight of the registry office, located in a sprawling complex of familiar brick buildings, reassures Helena. She's been here a thousand times for some errand or other—replacing a lost driver's license, doing the paperwork for her marriage, registering at Joachim's address. It's not the kind of place where strange revelations are made.

Doro helps Helena up the steps and leaves her in one of the chairs along the corridor while she draws a number. They're lucky; the wait isn't very long. Most people are at work by now.

"Tell me about yourself," Helena says when Doro sits down next to her.

"What?"

"I don't remember anything about you. Here you are, doing all these things for me, and I feel like you're a stranger."

"But Hel, that'll pass—"

"Still."

Doro puts her chin on one hand and considers. "Well, I'm from Schwerin originally. I studied some in Berlin, then later in London, then I worked in Hamburg, Frankfurt, and Berlin. I started at CuttingEdge Medien about a year and a half before you. I do mostly motion graphics and some 2D design with you. I have a husband, Georg, whom you've met, and we have three children and two rabbits. You wouldn't have met the rabbits, I guess, because they're always in the kids' rooms." She pauses and looks at Helena to see whether she's given the right answer, or at least said enough.

"Okay," Helena says. Is it enough? She still doesn't remember any of it. Will that change when she sees the specialist, or will she never get back those years? She and Doro will have to become friends all over again. Maybe they won't really be friends, but only feel obligated to pretend, because of the past. When, all the time, she won't feel any closer to Doro than to any other random stranger. But that's not fair. Doro's being so nice to her. They'll be real friends again, sooner or later. She tries to get a hold of the things Doro said, to picture her husband, children, and rabbits, to recall being seated at a crowded family dinner table. But she catches herself imagining it and trying to call that a memory.

She remembers other friends, Susi and Thomas, Magdalena, Sara, Sepp . . . These and many others are clear in her memory. When did she last see them? Are they still friends? Why hasn't she heard from them? You'd think they'd come by and see how she was doing. But maybe they don't know about the accident. Maybe they've fallen out of touch. That can happen with old friends. Just because they were close a few years ago doesn't mean they are now.

And then Doro is pulling her to her feet and pointing at the screen where her number is flashing, helping her down the hall to desk number 23.

The bureaucrat has a sour look on his face as the door opens, which softens when he sees Helena's crutches. He starts to get up, then settles into his chair again, rubbing his thick gray mustache as Doro helps Helena into one of the two seats across from his desk. How different this is, Helena thinks, from sitting in these two seats with Joachim, giddily telling that woman we wanted to get married.

"We'd like a copy of her registry record," Doro says.

"ID?"

Helena fumbles in her wallet and hands the man her ID. It occurs to her that she still doesn't have the keys to the apartment, that she won't be able to get back in later. What will she tell Joachim? But what nonsense. He probably already knows more than she does.

"Bachlein, Bachlein…" The man searches for the file on his clunky computer.

Helena looks over at Doro, who gives her a reassuring smile. What is there to worry about here? Since there's no outcome that will answer her questions, there's neither anything to worry about, nor to hope for.

"Here we are," the man says as the oversized printer next to his desk clatters into motion. He hands Helena a piece of paper and wishes them a good day. Then, remembering something, he asks to see her ID again.

Helena hands it to him without looking up from the piece of paper. There it is, her registered address for the past two-and-a-half years. She can't believe it. But she has to. It's printed in clear black ink, leaving nothing open to interpretation. What could've possessed her to register there? And how could she have kept it from Joachim?

"Excuse me," she says, just as the man starts to say something to her. They both stop and then start talking at once again. Finally, he waits for her to continue. "Is this the only address I'm registered at?"

"It is. If you want I can also give you a list of your former addresses, but then, you already know those, don't you?" Helena stares at him without responding. "While you're here, I'm just going to put a new address sticker on your ID. It's still got your old address for some reason."

Helena watches, unable to move or speak, as he pastes a sticker with an unfamiliar address over her ID. When she doesn't reach to take it from him, he sets it on the desk, and Doro tucks it into Helena's wallet.

"Thank you," she says for Helena, and takes her friend by one arm, not because Helena can't walk on her own, but because she doesn't seem to know it's time to leave.

• • •

Outside the registry office, Helena leans against the railing of the staircase and tries to regain her balance. She looks down at the paper, up at the green and gray branches cutting across the hazy blue sky, and down at the paper again.

She knew that she had this apartment, that she'd had it for a while. So what's the big deal? She already believed Doro or she wouldn't have come here in the first place. Still, it's somehow more than she expected. How could she have had the life this paper says she did for over two years, and have no idea about it? The strangest thing is that she's *only* registered at this address. What would make her cancel her registration at her and Joachim's apartment? Does he know? He hasn't said a word about this apartment. And it's not like the registry office would call him up and say: *By the way, your wife just told us she doesn't live with you anymore.* But Doro said it would've been impossible for him not to know.

"Are you okay, Hel?"

What a question. "Sure," she says. "I'm just a little bit confused."

"Me, too." Doro steps out of the way of a group of foreign students paging through photocopied documents, then offers Helena her arm to help her down the stairs.

"And now?" Helena asks when they've reached the bottom.

"I think we should take a look at your apartment."

JOACHIM

Joachim takes a long lunch break. At first, he thought of going by Helena's to get some books so he could go straight home after work. But he decides against it. He'd have to bring the books to the office with him, and people would ask questions. He wants them to keep seeing him as the faithful husband looking after his injured wife, handling a difficult episode in their otherwise peaceful, normal married life. If everyone around him thinks that, maybe he can, too.

Instead, he walks along the canal, enjoying the mellow warmth of the sun through the thin film of clouds. He feels the same strange blend of anticipation and regret he felt as his last year of school came to an end, and later his last year of college. But what is there to regret? If he's careful, if he doesn't make any mistakes, he has everything to look forward to. Helena's already feeling better, and her condition will only improve. He'll tell her the truth any day now, and then that will be behind them. She'll remember everything sooner or later, the good times as well as the bad. But what she'll remember best is what's most recent, the way he looked after her when she was hurt, the way they managed to put all their fights behind them and be together like they always should've been.

His heart races and he walks faster to keep up with it. The clouds are melting away from the sun, and when breaks in the vegetation reveal the water, the light on it dazzles him. A future with Helena. That's what he has, or will have when everything's sorted out. Somehow, he hasn't thought much further than getting her settled in his apartment and making it look like she never left. But that's just what's going on now, something that will soon come to an end. It's their future he should be thinking about. Going away for long weekends, giving each other a massage after a stressful day at work, having good friends over for dinner and wine. It all seems so ordinary, and yet so impossible. They should move to another apartment. Maybe that's the problem. His place is already so full of memories it's hard to fit the future in. They'll at least have to redecorate. Something like that, something new to signal that they're really starting over.

His mind is so full of plans that he steps onto the bridge without waiting for a break in traffic. A car honks and slams on its brakes as Joachim jumps back off the road.

"Asshole!" the motorcyclist behind the car yells, either at the driver, Joachim, or the whole world.

Joachim waits for them to pass and then continues across the road. You'd think he'd be more careful after what happened to Helena. What if he'd been run over and it had ended just like that? Helena would never know quite what had happened. She'd figure out the past few years sooner or later, but no one could tell her, not even her own memory, all that he'd done and had planned for them. She'd only know that he lied to her, without ever understanding why.

His chest clenches with a sudden, powerful sadness that stings all the way up to the corners of his watering eyes. He has to remind himself that it didn't happen, that he's fine and they still have everything ahead of them. Maybe it's only the change in light on this stretch of the canal—the trees taller, the shadows deeper, and the path closer to the water. It's just the car that startled him. He veers to the right to dodge a jogger shouting into his Bluetooth headset, then continues slowly, watching the dusty path at his feet. He'll ask Helena where she wants to move to, what part of town she wants to try out. They could adopt a dog. Maybe even a kid, once things are more stable. They aren't that old yet. They could take turns working from home.

That would help patch things up, too. Not just with Helena, but with all their friends and relatives. Tom and Susi had him over once or twice after the breakup, trying to play the neutral parties, but for most of Helena's friends, he might as well have been dead.

Even when things were good, Helena's parents had taken a while to warm up to him, but he won them over in the end and he can do it again. He hasn't told his own parents about what's going on between him and Helena, but they always liked her. They'd be thrilled. He's still never heard the end of how he messed up the best chance he ever got. But his parents never were as supportive as hers. Anyway, once their old friends see that Helena's forgiven him, they'll forgive and forget, too. After all, what was he really guilty of? And if he was at fault, that's in the past and he's doing enough to make up for it now. Or they'll make new friends, he and Helena. Other sophisticated couples they'll go to readings and galleries with. For all the women he's been involved with since Helena, he realizes, he hasn't made very many new friends. Friendly acquaintances, sure. New and old colleagues he can grab a beer with, watch a soccer game. No one closer than that.

But sometimes you take a wrong turn. Then you always want to keep going and try to make the path you've chosen be the right way, try to follow it as far as you can. When what you really should've done all along is double back to the point where you went wrong, and fix your mistake.

That's what he's doing. He's done his time without Helena, tried out how that is, and he knows now that he's better off with her. He even likes himself better just knowing she's in his life. He'll tell her that. He'll tell her all the good things about her, all the things he loves. He won't keep it to himself, won't try to be the winner in the relationship and the fights and petty little resentments by keeping his feelings to himself. He'll expose himself, make himself weak and vulnerable, give himself up to her. If she sticks around.

He stops abruptly as if something had struck him, then stumbles to the nearest bench. That, that thought is the one he's been hiding from all this time. Thinking so hard about the distant future to keep from thinking about that one little question of the immediate future: whether she'll want to stay. He leans back against the decrepit wood of the bench and allows himself to think the worst: that she could hear all he has to say, all he has planned for them and is ready to sacrifice for her, and still say, *Sorry, you had your chance.* That she could simply walk out of his life again, the way she did three years ago. What hope would be left after that?

Sure, he survived it once and he could survive it again. But he doesn't want to just survive. He wants the bright future he's been cobbling together in his thoughts for the two of them; he wants to look forward to all those things, and a thousand others he hasn't had time to think of yet. He's not really religious, but surely there was some reason she came into his life again, some reason she stepped so blithely in front of a speeding truck. And some reason she never—officially, at least—severed the tie between them after she left.

He looks at his watch and gets up to hurry back to his office. He'll already get home late if he stops by her apartment again, or he can skip lunch tomorrow to make up the time. He tries to think of practical things, to plan how he'll start the conversation about their past, but the dull drone of dread within him rises to a point where he can hardly hear his thoughts. As he watches his leather shoes kicking up dust, he feels a painful certainty that all his hopes and plans were nothing more than the fairytales he repeated to himself as a child when he couldn't sleep. What will things look like when he and Helena finally wake up?

HELENA

"Well, here it is."

Helena nearly loses her balance when Doro stops in front of an old apartment building with crumbling molding on the façade and *DEATH TO CAPIT*— spray-painted on the front door, as if the left-leaning vandal had been interrupted in the middle of his work. She doesn't remember the graffiti, but that could be new; there are a thousand other half-visible sayings, threats, odes, and tags scrawled on the door beneath it. It could be any door, anywhere. She tries to make an association with the building, the crumbling stone and the windows curtained in a dozen brilliant colors. Which one is hers? She doesn't know. Instead, she feels like someone going to an apartment viewing, trying to picture the life she could have in an unknown house, once the lease is signed.

"Do you know if any of your neighbors has a spare key?" Doro asks, then cartoonishly strikes her forehead. "Oh, sorry."

For a moment, they can't hold back their laughter, but when the moment passes, the door to Helena's building is still locked.

"Let's have a look at the names," Doro suggests. "I might recognize one."

"Or I might," Helena says. This time neither of them laughs. She watches Doro staring at the list of names, one finger hovering over the buzzers, waiting to press the right one. Her face has the same strained concentration Helena's felt so often lately, trying to will herself to remember something it feels like she's never known.

"It's no use," Doro says finally. "We'll have to buzz until someone lets us in, and then I'll go door-to-door and ask."

Helena nods. What else can they do? She doesn't mind about the difficulty. In a way, it makes things simpler. There's no need to ask herself any questions now, only the task at hand: How will they get in? And Doro's going to handle that, so there's really nothing to worry about.

No one answers the first three buzzers. It's early enough for them all to be at work, but with any luck, there'll be an old lady or stay-at-home parent around, some students in a shared apartment.

When Doro presses the fourth buzzer, an irritable man's voice asks what they want.

Doro nudges Helena, who begins, "This is your neighbor, Ms. Bachlein, and I've forgotten my keys. I wanted to ask whether—"

"Ms. who?"

"Bachlein."

"Never heard of it."

The sound of him slamming down the receiver shakes both women so that it takes them a moment to continue.

So my neighbor's never heard of me, Helena thinks. Did I really live here? Maybe it's all just a misunderstanding. Then she remembers the man who lives across the hall from her and Joachim. He seemed like he'd never seen her before, either. Maybe she never really lived anywhere.

Doro continues to make her way through the buzzers. Toward the bottom of the list, a sleepy young voice answers. Helena has to explain twice, but then Müller / Göbek buzzes them in, after adding helpfully, "I don't know how you'll get into your apartment, though. Shit, right?"

The narrow foyer is cluttered with rusty bikes and third-hand strollers. The damp, earthy smell seems familiar to Helena, and this time, she doesn't second-guess herself, but sits down at the foot of the stairs to close her eyes and breathe it in.

"I'll go see if anyone's got your spare key," Doro says.

Helena nods. She feels she's on the brink of something. There's an idea, a sense of something in her like a word on the tip of her tongue, but one false move could scare it away forever. It's best not to pursue it.

She opens her eyes and rummages in her purse for a pen. She doesn't have any paper, but she limps over to the mailboxes and takes some moving company's flyer out of the junk mail bin.

She makes it with one crutch, and at first, the more obvious thrill of managing on her own overshadows a second surprise: how natural it was to walk over here. Like she knew exactly where she was going, like she'd done it a thousand times. Because she has. She looks up and sees her overflowing mailbox, the label with her name written on it. And that *is* her handwriting.

The building still doesn't look familiar; there's still only the slightest sense that she's been here before. But that's enough.

She presses the flyer against the wall and writes:

Dear Neighbors, A couple of you have my spare keys and I really need them because I've been in the hospital and lost mine. If you still have them, please call me at—

She has to look through her little prepaid phone to find her own number. She adds it and props the note above the mailboxes where everyone will see it.

Will it do any good? I always keep to myself, Helena thinks. Am I really the kind of person who lives in a city and knows my neighbors? She feels that, whatever else has changed in the past few years, that won't have.

But she lived in this apartment for two or three years. It's easy to forget how long that is, how much can happen in that amount of time. After all, the neighbors could've befriended her.

She can hear distant footsteps in the stairwell, but she can't tell whether they're going up or coming down. Poor Doro. There are a lot of neighbors to ask.

If she and Doro are so close, why doesn't Doro have her

spare keys? Again she feels a flicker of doubt. Then again, Doro never claimed to be her best friend. There could be any number of other, closer ones, all of them wondering right now where Helena is and why she doesn't get in touch. Doro's just the only number she had. And in Doro's place, she'd probably also feel obligated to get to the bottom of this. Someone has to, and she certainly wasn't going to on her own.

She looks again at her mailbox, the pile of ads spilling out of the open slot. There might be something worthwhile in there, too. A clue, so to speak. How long has she been away? There could be all kinds of important things she's been missing.

It's not just the keys to her apartment she needs, though. The key to her mailbox is gone along with the rest of them. She takes a step back toward the stairs, then stops and approaches the mailboxes again. This isn't a top-secret room at the Federal Intelligence Service. First she reaches her left hand into the slit and pulls out everything she can get without opening the mailbox. She drops the pile on the floor behind her. She can feel that there's more in there, but she can't get at it.

She runs her finger over the lock. It really doesn't look very complicated. She sticks her pen into the slot and jiggles it. No luck, but if she had something a little flatter . . .

Suddenly nervous, she looks over her shoulder. What if someone sees her? Let them. She's got an ID and a certificate of registration to prove this is her mailbox. Besides, who would break in with two casts and a pair of crutches?

She tries a hairclip, a folded-up piece of paper, the corner of her bank card and the zipper on her wallet. If only she had a screwdriver with a small bit! She's sweating and tearing through her belongings with tears of frustration in her eyes, unable to stop. Once she's tried everything she can find, she starts trying the same things over again, frantic, clumsy, scraping her fingertips and tearing her cuticles.

She breaks the clip off her pen and tries that; it's thin enough, but too short for her to get a good grip on. She opens up the pen and tries the spring and finally the ink reservoir. Her nose is running and tears are already streaming down her face when she realizes that the lock has moved. One more turn and the reservoir breaks, but the mailbox opens.

She gives a startled sob and pulls it open all the way, wiping blindly at her damp cheeks and nose with hands covered in thick blue ink. She hears footsteps behind her and readies all her explanations; she has the paperwork to back up her story, but she doesn't want to look crazy.

"There you are!" Doro calls from the bottom of the staircase. "Unfortunately, I couldn't find anyone who—Hel, what happened to you? Your whole face is blue!"

Sheepish, Helena takes her hand off the mailbox and lets the mail spill out. "I was crying and my pen broke. I just wanted to check the mail."

Doro's expression is frozen between concern and amusement, the dimple in one cheek belying the line of worry across her forehead. "Oh," she says, pulling a tissue out of her purse and handing it to Helena, "Good idea."

Helena dabs at her face until the tissue has a blue tinge. "What now?"

Doro sighs. She looks tired. But someone has to know what to do, and Helena certainly doesn't. "Let's sort out your mail and then call a locksmith," she says. "Luckily you have your ID with this address so they'll be able to open the door." Doro picks up a pile of envelopes from the floor and begins to weed the junk out from the actual mail. Helena returns to the mailbox for the last few things crushed into the bottom by weeks of mail being dropped onto them. She sees an envelope from her bank, her insurance company's newsletter, a greeting card with no envelope and . . .

"Doro," she says, but her voice dries up in her throat and she has to say it again. "Doro, I don't think we need to call the locksmith."

"What?"

In answer, Helena reads the greeting card aloud:

Dear Hel, I'm going to be in Manchester for a few weeks, so I thought I'd give your spare keys back. No use having them locked up in my apartment if you need them. Hope your weekend goes well!—here she'd drawn a winky face, maybe in reference to Helena's date. Did everyone know about that?—*Let's catch up when I get back. Love, Julie.*

"Oh, that English girl who was at your birthday party?" Doro asks.

"I think so." For a brief instant, she thinks there's a freckled face and an accent to go with that name, and then the image blurs. She remembers what she remembered, but she's no longer sure of it. The experience leaves her breathless. She's getting closer to something.

They take a few minutes to finish sorting out the mail, to read the postcard Julie sent a week after her first note, glance at Helena's bank statements and throw away all the outdated offers from the grocery store. They do these things not because they need to be done now, but because they need the time. To think, or, in Helena's case, to try not to.

Then Doro takes a shopping bag out of her purse, puts in all the important mail and offers Helena her arm. They leave her crutches beside the mailboxes.

On the third floor, Helena gets another thrill of fear or excitement when she sees her name above the doorbell. Maybe if they rang instead of unlocking the door, another Helena Bachlein, just like her but totally different, would open it and welcome them into her uncannily familiar life.

Doro opens the door but waits for Helena to go in first.

The recognition comes before the strangeness. After all the suspense, all the effort to get here and the fear of what they'll find, Helena enters a perfectly familiar room. There are her bookshelves, her bed against the wall, the two-person sofa with a folded newspaper on the coffee table in front of it and, in the corner, the little wooden desk where she sometimes works from home. The door to the bathroom, the kitchenette and the little nook overlooking the courtyard, with a folding table, two chairs, and that funny old picture of Port Louis.

The first thing she's really aware of is that she's been here over and over again in all the dreams she's forgotten in the past few weeks. She feels the terror of half-sleep, when the colors start to fade and the walls grow transparent, and you can't quite touch anything. But the chair she collapses into, the table she rests her elbows on, are solid, opaque, and very, very real. She's never been more awake, never more ready to believe she's dreaming, or less able to.

Doro is asking something but Helena can't hear it through her sobs. She's afraid of this place, of its ineluctable reality, all the uncertainties this one certainty creates. Have all her dreams, all her nightmares and the strange thoughts that crossed her mind between sleep and wakefulness been real? Has she dreamt the past few weeks?

No, they were real. Doro was there in that other apartment with her; all of that was real, too. No matter how little sense it makes, both of these places, both of these lives are real.

Her vision is a blur but she senses Doro leaving the room and coming back into it. She feels a hand on her shoulder and is surprised that it doesn't pass right through her. But the touch holds and things start to move toward their new positions without quite clicking into place. Then something wet is pressed to her forehead. The cold shock of it stops her sobbing, and she sits still as Doro wipes her face with a wet washcloth.

This is her chair, her table, her home, her friend; this is her life and this sobbing is her sobbing, the sobbing of ending a marriage that's already been over for years, of parting from a life she gave up so long ago, of all these pains, fresh and imminent, aching within her like dread of things to come, burning like deep and recent wounds. She longs to sleep dreamlessly, to forget all that she remembers now, forget even having forgotten. She remembers leaving Joachim, remembers it until that pain is her only memory, until she forgets where she is.

"It's going to be okay, Hel," Doro says, pulling out the chair opposite her. "I'm going to help you figure this thing out."

For just a moment, Helena wants to ask: *Haven't you done enough?*

JOACHIM

Joachim slogs through the day, struggling to come up with catchy puns for a supermarket chain's winter campaign. What's the matter with him? He used to enjoy his work. Sure, some of the customers can be a pain in the ass, and the rush deadlines are exhausting, but when it came down to the fundamental work, it was something he really liked doing. Until recently, he had no trouble working twelve hours at a stretch when he had to. Now, the last couple hours of each day are unbearable. All he can think about is clocking out and going home.

Home to Helena, he reminds himself. But is he really that eager to see her? When she's on his mind all day, it isn't exactly her he's thinking of. Rather, he's worrying about their past, and wondering what their future will look like. They aren't quite happy thoughts.

He *is* happy that she's there. It's nice to come home to someone you love, someone you know is happy to see you. But that's another guilty thought—is she happy to see him, or to see anyone at all? He can't make himself feel good about what he's doing to her anymore. It's gone on too long. And if he can't tell by looking at her, his own symptoms should make it obvious: he's sleeping poorly, distracted from his work, his mind constantly moving in the same obsessive circles. He's begun to have absurd terrors, like some neighbor coming over and telling her she didn't used to live with him, or her parents calling the police because she hasn't been in touch.

Even the happiness he feels in her presence has something of this terror in it.

Then again, maybe he's looking at it all the wrong way. It's not Helena but this bizarre situation that's wearing him out. The little trips to her apartment or office before and after work, the constant vigilance to make sure he doesn't let something slip. It's enough to do anybody in.

Dragging himself to the kitchen as if his body were a dead weight he has to carry, he tries to tell himself that things will be better soon. Wasn't Helena good for him the first time around? Got him to quit smoking, eat healthy, finally finish decorating his apartment, find a full-time job. But even as he tells himself these things, he knows that the weary anxiety he feels now is familiar, a fact he learned by heart during those months of fighting that wore them both to the bone.

He closes the door behind him, relieved to find the room empty. He puts a cup under the espresso machine and presses the button without bothering to switch on the lights. It got so bad at a certain point that he'd go on arguing with her in his sleep, holding grudges for weeks about fights they'd never really had. Sometimes, the very gnashing of his teeth would wake him.

She, on the other hand, slept more than ever toward the end. On weekends, she went to bed before midnight and slept until after noon, and during the week, she often came home from work and went to bed without eating. The last few times they could still bring themselves to try and make love, she either cried afterward or had to stop halfway.

"I can't help it," she'd say. "I just feel so sick."

It was never clear to him how much of her upset was real and how much she was putting on to punish him. Maybe she didn't know herself, and went so far out of her way to hurt him that she ended up damaging herself beyond repair.

But as he leaves the kitchen, his thoughts brighten with the lights of the hallway, and he reminds himself that nothing is beyond repair.

HELENA

Helena has nothing to say to Doro the whole way back to Joachim's apartment, nothing to say after a neighbor's buzzed them in and Doro's helped her up the stairs. Against her better judgment, she holds Doro accountable for what she suffered today, what it feels like she's never going to stop suffering. She's not sure if she'll ever have anything to say to her again.

"Will you be all right?" Doro asks. "Should I stay until Joachim comes back?"

"No, thanks. It'll be all right."

Doro looks relieved. Maybe she has nothing more to say to Helena, either.

As the sound of Doro's footsteps fades away, Helena tries to get a grip on things. It isn't that she remembers everything, but the memories are close to her now, within reach. At the same time, it's like trying to catch hold of a pack of stray dogs. She's only got two hands, and as soon as she reaches for another one, the two she's holding by the scruffs of their necks break free again.

If only she could write it all down, map it out in some kind of elaborate diagram and put all the pieces in their proper places. But there's no paper in her purse, not so much as a receipt to take notes on. Just her certificate of registration, and that won't be worth much if she starts to draw on it.

But the certificate is an important piece in the puzzle. A key fact that she both knows and remembers: She's lived in that apartment for a long time. She couldn't have named an exact date, like this document does, but she really had a sense of it when they were there, all the nights sleeping and mornings waking in that room, all her routines and habits.

She remembers very little about moving in, but if she focuses on this precise point, she can recall a heavy weariness coming over her all at once, her body suddenly incapable of carrying even the small cardboard box she had in her hands. She just couldn't take another step up the stairs.

And then Magdalena was behind her, taking her by the shoulders, saying something stupid, like *Earth to Helena*, to make her laugh. She did laugh, to please Magdalena, but every movement damaged her, her body nothing more than a thin paper bag full of broken glass.

Magdalena! she thinks with a sudden urgency, almost expecting her old friend to come up the stairs behind her now. *Where's Magdalena?* Sitting down on her—or Joachim's—doorstep, she tries to remember the last time she saw Magdalena. But she only comes up with a series of blurred images: Magdalena pushing her aside when she tries to help with the dishes, Magdalena pulling a ski cap over her long blonde hair as they come out of the movie theater—nothing significant. The very banality of these recollections suggests that they're still friends.

She can remember Doro now, and all kinds of anonymous faces moving through her life, faces she might be able to call by name if they were here now. Doro isn't her best friend but the one she sees the most of, and the most reliable. The sort of person she'd call if she needed help painting the walls or moving.

But she hadn't called Doro when she moved into her apartment; she must not have known her yet. When did she quit her old job? It can't have been long after her separation. It was probably *because* of her separation. She and Joachim met at that office, back when he used to freelance there. It must've been hard to keep going there, seeing their mutual acquaintances and remembering the first innocent flirtations in the kitchen or at her desk. Knowing she'd left him for good.

And there's the crux of everything: leaving Joachim. She remembers not only the blistering hatred and nauseous weeping of their final weeks together, but also her numb, cold resolution when she went to stay at Magdalena's without saying goodbye. She feels that she could remember more, could dredge up all that time, but she doesn't have the strength.

The thing to focus on is the main fact: She and Joachim split up years ago. As far as she knows, they haven't seen each other since. Which would explain why she barely has anything in the apartment, why the clothes he says are hers feel so unfamiliar. And why he's gone to so much trouble to keep her out of touch with anyone who might tell her the truth.

Now that she knows the extent of his dishonesty, she's surprised how easily she was taken in: that absurd story about the flood, the phone and Internet connection being out for weeks, the long delay in making a doctor's appointment, his going to her office five times a week to pick up and drop off her assignments.

But how could she have known? She woke from her accident fragile and blank, and all the things he said seemed to make sense. They even sounded true. He must've practiced. It can't be easy to lie with that much conviction.

She closes her eyes and rests her head against the door. Why is the truth so exhausting, when the lie was so simple? She feels as if she'll never sleep again, never be able to turn off her whirring, cranking, buzzing mind.

The thought of sleep makes her wonder what time it is, and she gets out her phone to check. It's not quite five, and her mind automatically starts to estimate how long until Joachim gets back, but she stops herself. Instead, she should figure out what to say to him.

She extends her left leg and one of the crutches falls from its position against the wall with a cold, solid thud. She waits for the door opposite her to open, for footsteps to come rushing toward her from above and below. She has a feeling strangely akin to guilt, as if she were at fault for knowing what she does. She ate the fruit of forbidden knowledge, and now she'll be cast out of this ambiguous paradise.

Which is what Joachim's been trying to prevent all this time. Has he been banking on her never getting her memory back? How long was he going to keep lying? He must be out of his mind.

The problem is that she can't quite believe he is. He created these illusions for her, not himself—otherwise he wouldn't have been able to pull it off. He must've taken her keys so he could get things out of her apartment.

Is it all some kind of cruel joke? An elaborate revenge on her for walking out and not being in touch for so long? But he's been so nice to her this whole time: What would the punchline be? Ha ha, Helena, I got you to believe that we're still in love?

So maybe this isn't a trick, at least not a cruel one. Maybe he's living this intricate lie because he likes it better than the truth. He must've seen her amnesia as a kind of tacit agreement, a willingness to accept his version of things.

No matter what this turns out to be—madness, revenge, wishful thinking run wild—she has to confront him about it the minute he gets back. If she doesn't, she'll make herself complicit in his lies, an accessory to forging this cozy little world. The only question is how.

JOACHIM

Joachim leaves work early in an effort to convince himself that he really wants to go home. In a way, he does. But even without daring to think about it, he knows that what he wants most is to go home to an empty apartment, to close the door behind him and collapse in some dark corner. Not to have to keep a smile on his face or ask the right questions; just, for a few minutes, not to be seen.

A train is pulling in when he gets to the U-Bahn station and he could make it, but instead walks slowly down the stairs, letting everyone else rush past. He pictures one of them bumping into him, knocking him down, his head bursting against the stairs like a water balloon. He's so vividly aware of his thin red blood running down the litter-ridden steps that he's surprised to arrive on the platform intact.

He remembers this sense of dread from various living situations, apartments shared with roommates or girlfriends that soon developed into the grounds of an elaborate cold war. There's no hostility between him and Helena now, but the feeling is the same: the desperate hope that he'll get home and find the door bolted, the lights out, so he can slip into his room before anyone else gets in.

But there's no chance of Helena being out. Not today or any day. That's what's stressing him out. When's the last time he was alone? He hasn't had the place to himself in over a month. The next train pulls into the station, and he waits for the passengers to flow out, then wedges himself in among the sullen construction workers and teenagers eating döner kebabs full of raw onions. A woman with an oversized baby carriage makes a snide remark to no one in particular when he doesn't get out of her way fast enough. At the last minute, a group of tourists jumps into the car, and he no longer has anything to hold onto. He struggles to stay on his feet between stops, borne up only by the density of passengers surrounding him. As if it weren't enough that they have to stand so close together, everyone within eyeshot is staring aggressively, blaming him for taking up space, judging him based on his clothing, hair, age, face, and inability to meet their eyes.

He can tell Helena he needs a few minutes alone. He'll say it's been a long day or that he's not feeling well. She might not believe him but she won't say anything. So much of marriage is like that. After a certain point, you don't even need to have the arguments anymore; each of you knows what the other is thinking but not saying, and what you would say if she said what she was thinking, and what she would say to that, and so on forever. After a certain point, you're too tired. You don't believe the polite social lies your spouse tells you, don't believe or like them, but you don't want to fight, so you pretend you do. And she doesn't want to fight, either, so she pretends to believe in your pretense.

Is that the worst thing in the world? The train lurches to a halt in a dark tunnel between two stations, and the baby carriage rams Joachim in the gut. He did want someone to come home to. He was happy about that, at first. Maybe it isn't Helena or him either; maybe it's just too much, her being there all the time.

And then the guilt comes like clockwork: She can't help it. He's the one who set things up to make her totally dependent on him. It's not my fault she's injured, he reminds himself. I didn't tell her to jump in front of a truck. On a certain level, though, he feels that it *is* his fault, and he begins to reproach himself for not taking her to an orthopedist or even a general practitioner since she's been out of the hospital. He wanted this pet so badly and now he isn't taking care of it.

Once, when he was very young, he won a goldfish as a prize at the town fair. His parents wanted to trade it in for a stuffed animal, but he was adamant, absolutely determined to have the bright, glistening creature that watched him with such dark and curious eyes from its plastic bag of water. For once, his parents gave in but made him promise he'd take good care of it. Of course he promised, and of course he did for the first few days, but then he forgot, or couldn't be bothered. Whatever the reason, he didn't feed his goldfish for a couple days, and his mother slapped him in the face when she saw it floating on top of the water.

My parents were too hard on me, he reflects as the train wearily drags itself down the tunnel. I was too young to look after anything on my own. They should've helped me. They've always expected too much from me, and at the same time they expect me not to live up to their expectations. His mother didn't slap him when she heard that he and Helena had separated, but she was just as convinced that it was completely his fault, his failure as a person, as she'd been all those years before, flushing the foul water and limp orange body down the toilet.

Helena's more forgiving, he tells himself. I wouldn't have married a woman like my mother. But forgiving his failings didn't mean she hadn't expected them all along, always known he was going to fuck things up. Wasn't it that way with Ester? Helena didn't let him explain. First she asked a few vague questions about what he'd been doing during the break in their relationship, then she interrupted his equally vague answers.

"I knew you'd lie about it. You're so full of shit." And she thrust that stupid letter in his face, stood there watching him read it. Never, never a moment alone.

"Let me explain," he said.

"I don't want you to. I never want to talk about this again."

He was so surprised in that moment, so relieved. He'd been sure she was going to leave him, that there was nothing he could say to stop her. It was like God had reached a hand in through the ceiling, caught her before she could reach the door, and turned her around.

For the first few weeks, he was like a man who'd died and

been brought back to life. He wanted everything to be perfect, better than perfect; he wanted her never to have a reason to look at him that way again. He agreed with everything she said, took her on expensive, well-thought-out dates and bought her small, tasteful presents. He didn't want to overdo it because it might seem like he was trying to buy her back if he brought home diamonds or something. Mostly, he picked up books by her favorite authors—he could still remember them back then—or nice things for their home. Pots of nasturtiums and amaryllises for the windowsills that were already crowded with plants. He pretended to believe the excuses she made to avoid sleeping with him and talked a lot about their plans for the future, to remind her that they had one.

At Alexanderplatz, the train empties out and he moves into a corner where he can lean against the Plexiglas wall separating him from the seats. It was exhausting then and it's exhausting now, but it was different then because of that elephant in the room, the fight she refused to have with him because she knew it would kill them, the fight that was there behind all the petty little arguments they started to have again once his initial relief subsided, and he was too tired to keep up his constant vigilance over her happiness. Up until the day he came home to find her gone, he was sure they could be happy again if they could just survive an honest conversation. But maybe there's no such thing.

He remembers the way she used to look at him in the last few months of their marriage, that wide-eyed, blank expression. At the time, he took it for anger, but now he believes it was simply shock; that, just like him, she could never quite believe how badly things had gone. She's not like his parents, after all. She may have asked too much of him, but she didn't marry him expecting the worst. And that was the most exhausting part, in the end: her endless disappointment.

• • •

He takes the stairs two at a time to get the grand entrance over with, but stumbles over something just as he reaches his floor. He bends down and picks up one of Helena's crutches. The other is propped against the wall, and in the dim corner by the door, eyes closed, is Helena.

Dead! he thinks, and in his horror there's also acceptance, as if this fact made perfect sense. Then she opens her eyes and looks up at him before he has time to compose his expression.

"Is everything all right? What are you doing here?"

"Good question," she says, and his stomach his halfway up his throat before she gives a hollow laugh and adds, "I guess I got myself locked out again. I wanted to see if I could get around on my own yet, and I forgot I still don't have the keys."

"I'm so sorry. I was meaning to make another copy. I didn't realize . . ." Didn't realize what? That she wouldn't want to be caged in his apartment indefinitely? He switches on the overhead lighting, although there's still enough light coming through the window for him to find his keys. With the lights on, he can see that her face is terribly pale, with a sickly bluish tinge. His mouth is dry and sticky and he wishes there were anyone else here, a neighbor, a stranger, to help him figure out what to do.

She puts out her left hand and he looks at it blankly before helping her to her feet.

"We need to make an appointment with an orthopedist," she says. "I want to know when my casts can come off. I wish you'd get the Internet fixed so I could find the number myself."

"You're right, of course. I'll call both of them tomorrow." He's so relieved to hear her say something ordinary that tears well up in his eyes. He turns to unlock the door to keep her from seeing. What was he so afraid of? It's true that she looks sick, that he was startled to find her outside of the apartment. But why is his heart still pounding so painfully? If she wants to go out, he'll make another set of keys. If she needs to see a doctor . . .

He recalls that she *is* seeing a doctor soon, one of the specialists in head trauma and amnesia Dr. Hofstaedter recommended to him. So here it is, so long in coming and yet so sudden he forgot to expect it, the time to tell her the truth.

She leaves one crutch by the door and uses the other to

limp to the bathroom. He listens to the water running in the sink, searching the sound for some thought that's just slipped his mind. Then he goes into the bedroom and closes the door, leaving the lights out. That's right; he wanted to be alone.

Well here he is, alone. Now what? Is he going to tell her when she comes out of the bathroom? And then what? Maybe he should take her out to dinner. She probably hasn't eaten all day. She's lost at least five kilograms since coming out of the hospital and she was never fat. He thinks of the goldfish. He feels sure now that he didn't even feel guilty for killing the little creature, only terrified of the punishment he would face, and more than that, of his own failure. And he's failing now: Helena looks miserable and unwell, and what he's about to tell her won't help.

HELENA

In the bathroom Helena washes her face over and over again until the soapsuds stop coming off blue, then puts on moisturizer, makeup, and perfume, combs out her hair. Does it matter what she looks like now? Once she's confronted him, they'll have bigger problems. Or he will. No matter how she wracks her brains, she can't come up with an explanation that would make his behavior acceptable, unless he actually has lost his mind. Which still doesn't seem likely.

She planned to confront him right away, was settled in and waiting for him when he came up the stairs, but something stopped her. Maybe it was how tired he looked, how helpless. He'd had a long day and it didn't seem fair to say it right away. Besides, she didn't want to make a scene where all the neighbors could hear. Of course, she could've started as soon as they got into the apartment, instead of coming in here. Maybe she just wants him to remember her pretty.

She thinks of his deception and her credulity, of the first time she saw him coming through the door of her hospital room, and that dinner on the lake. Of making love like it was the first time. No wonder it felt that way, since they hadn't touched each other in years. She's angrier at herself than him. Why didn't she notice? Sure, she couldn't remember leaving him, but there were so many signs, now that she starts to look for them. More than just her possessions, her very presence was missing from the apartment. She let herself be fooled by the familiar location and overlooked how strange it felt to be there. Somehow, she should've known.

She looks into the mirror a last time, trying to make her expression neutral. She wants to catch him off-guard, not give him time to prepare any lies or excuses. For once, she wants to hear the truth.

When she comes into the living room, he's gone, but he comes out of the bedroom before she has time to wonder where he is.

"Let's go out to dinner," he says.

"Sounds good." Because, after all, it doesn't matter where they talk. And because there's a guilty little voice in her head saying, you've gone along with it this long; what difference can an hour or two make?

JOACHIM

Joachim wants to call a cab but Helena insists she can make it without. She looks healthier now, even with a certain glow to her face, and he hates to think how she'll look a couple hours from now.

"You look nice," he says, then winces, waiting for the blow. He should've said it when he came in. But she didn't look nice before.

As if reading his thoughts, she says, "I got some ink on my face from a leaky pen. That's why I looked so odd when you got home."

"Oh." It's good to have an explanation; he should be grateful for such a simple, harmless explanation. But, somehow, it's not enough. It wasn't just her complexion that was strange when he came up the stairs, but the look in her eyes. And what was she doing slumped over in the stairwell like that? Fine, she was locked out. That didn't mean she had to sit there in the dark the whole time. Why didn't she call him? He would've come home faster if he'd known. How was he supposed to know she'd try to go down the staircase on a pair of crutches with no keys to the apartment? But it's not like she's blaming him. At least for now.

"I only need the one if you take my arm," she says, propping her second crutch against the wall beside the door. He notices she has a sweater on, although it's warm in the apartment. It is a bit cool outside, but he didn't think to remind her. She must've seen the weather on TV.

In the stairwell, he gives her his arm, but she barely puts any weight on it. Why is it that his heart sinks with each step she takes on her own? Surely they'll both be happier when she's more independent. He tries to think of all the things that will be better: meeting up outside of the apartment, making love without worrying about hurting her, having time to himself when she's out, her happiness at not being cooped up anymore. But there's a dishonesty to his thoughts, like when he was a child and used to pray that God would make him pious and good, when all he really wanted was for God to protect him from the long dark claws he dreamt of reaching in through his window at night, or coming out from under his bed. He always slipped that part in at the end, like an afterthought. He prayed as if he could hide his true thoughts from God, and now he thinks as hard as he can of wanting Helena to be well again, hoping against hope that he can convince himself.

Why wouldn't I want her to be well? he asks himself as he holds the door so she can hobble out onto the sidewalk. The sky has the pale glow that proceeds dusk, and the air is filled with that silence particular to evenings in late summer, when no cars ever pass by, and all the insects hold their breath. The only honest thought he has is: *I'm going to miss her.*

HELENA

The Italian restaurant is only a few blocks away, but Helena is sweating all over by the time they arrive. She no longer feels nervous; things will take their course without much effort on her part. All she has to do is remain calm and try to withstand them, like a boulder in the midst of a turbulent sea. This won't destroy her.

Joachim pulls out a chair for her at a table by the window, and a waiter rushes over to give them menus and prop her crutch against the wall. The other patrons glance over with expressions of pity for her, or admiration for his considerateness, then lose interest again.

"How was work?" she asks, though nothing could be further from her mind.

"Fine," he answers, as if nothing were further from his. What's he thinking about? Probably the best way to keep deceiving her. He always was a clumsy liar. She remembers catching him out before, the way his mouth opened and closed without words, like the gills of a landed fish. The walls are down now and she could remember what she caught him at if she tried, but she doesn't want to make the effort. Sometimes, fragments of memory move through her mind like traces of a dream: smudged fingerprints on the seal of an envelope and frantic, childish handwriting, nausea that struck her like a blow to the stomach, and his openmouthed helplessness. "How about you?" he asks. "It must be a pain to work from the apartment."

"It is," she says. "But luckily that'll be over soon."

The waiter comes back and she orders a bottle of red wine. Joachim hasn't even opened his menu.

"You don't look very well yourself," she says after the waiter leaves. "When I'm better, we should go on vacation." The words came out without her thinking, just habit. For a moment, she forgot that there is no future tense for the two of them. The fact that confronting him will mean ending this relationship has never been so clear to her. But he's already nodding and she can't take it back now.

"Where do you want to go?" he asks, and then that conversation starts, all the places in the world they want to see, but there's something hollow about it, and not just on her end. She has the feeling that neither of them is really present in this conversation. They're both just putting up a front, and now the two fronts are having a pleasant chat about travel plans, while their real thoughts lurk in the separate depths of their distant inner lives. She just has to say the word and another conversation will start, just as automatically, gaining a different kind of momentum.

"Helena," he says abruptly, reaching across the table to take her hand. But then the wine is there, and the waiter to take their orders, and it's hard to be in the same place again after. It's hard to be anywhere at all. She can't keep the situation in her mind for more than a few minutes at a time. She knows there's something on their minds, something unpleasant they have to talk about, but it feels like any old fight that needs to be made up.

"What did you want to say?" she asks.

"Just how much I love you."

Her throat is dry and she almost knocks over the bottle with her cast in her haste to take a sip of wine. He's still holding her other hand on the table, and she feels ashamed. Which of them is being more dishonest right now? Maybe he really does love her. His brown eyes have that sheen on them that could dissolve into tears at any moment, and there's a splash of pink on his cheekbones, though he hasn't touched his wine. But you can fake anything.

"I love you, too," she says, and though the response is automatic, saying it aloud isn't. She left too much space between his words and hers, time enough to wonder whether she's lying. She still can't get her head around it: almost three years. Did they talk to each other at all in that time, even about tax returns or picking up her things? She can't remember hearing from him, and now that things are starting to make sense again, not remembering means something. Not remembering means it probably never happened. She remembers buying herself a new SIM card around the corner from Magdalena's apartment, and maybe that was enough. If you really want to reach someone who lives in the same city as you and has dozens of acquaintances in common, you don't need a phone number. That one little obstacle was enough to keep him away. He never made much effort, not after they settled into their routines and he started to take her for granted. But he's sure as hell making an effort now.

The waiter returns with a plate of bruschetta and Joachim has to release her hand. She pulls it away as if from a hot stove. And then comes the small talk: The bruschetta is good. The wine, too. Are you supposed to pronounce the *s-c-h* in bruschetta like *sh* or like *sk*? They keep that up until the waiter brings their entrees and after he's cleared away their plates. There's plenty to talk about: the upcoming visit to the doctor, visits to other doctors after that, the progress of her recovery.

Beneath the warmth of the food, the wine, the candlelight, and Joachim's admiration, there's a cold, hard core to her when she sees the dishes being cleared away. The evening is ending now and she hasn't said a word. She flags down the waiter and orders an espresso before Joachim can ask for the check.

"I'll have the same," Joachim says. But it hasn't bought them much time, really. Just a few more swallows of this night, a few more spaces to slip words into. And still she doesn't know what to say.

The waiter sets down the two little cups on their two little saucers. Joachim taps his against hers and winks at her. She feels something shift within her, her guts a steep slope down which a hard, condensed ball of dread is about to tumble.

"Joachim," she says, but he says her name in the same moment, and then neither of them wants to be the first to speak. They sip their espresso and then she says, "There's something I need to ask you about."

"Anything." All the color goes out of his face. Somewhere inside of him, something's been switched off. She sees that he's afraid and wants to make an accusation out of that, but she's just as afraid as he is. Maybe more. She only remembers bits and pieces of their last separation, but that's enough to let her know how blinding the pain was, how heavy the lasting ache of disappointment. At the same time, she remembers being alone for those years that went by so quickly and yet lasted forever, much longer than she was ever married. She doesn't want to be alone forever, but she doesn't want to keep pretending just to put it off for a few more days or years. Fleetingly, she thinks of Tobias, whose face she can't remember, but whose name she can't forget. To think she started to believe she was the unfaithful one . . . But Joachim is still waiting for her question.

It doesn't come out the way she expects. "Joachim," she says again. "Have you ever regretted marrying me?"

He finishes his espresso and clears his throat. "I never thought of it that way before," he says. "At a certain time, I must've. But I don't now. I'd do it all over again, even if I already knew all the problems we'd have."

"Problems?" She can feel the tears gathering in her eyes. How absurd to still be taken in by these little speeches, the lies she's so hungry for she swallows them whole. She doesn't want to cry because it will only get them off topic.

Sure enough, he reaches across the table to brush away the drops gathering on her eyelashes like rain on naked branches. He wipes them off her cheek with the side of one finger, and she only wants him to hold her, to protect her from having to face all the lies he's told, or rather all the awkward truths she can't get to line up with his words. It's not fair that she has to be the one to speak.

"I'm just tired." She tries to keep the tears out of her voice but he's already signaling for the check, paying it and helping her to her feet.

"Let's just go home, make some tea and get to bed," he says, all the while stroking her hair from the roots to the spot between her shoulder blades where it stops, trying to soothe this frightened animal enough to get it back into its cage. And she lets herself be soothed and guided back into the apartment, because there's a chill in the air outside, because it's exhausting to be on her feet, because everything outside of this apartment is cold, weary, and hopeless; and because, whatever the reason, right now, this is her home.

She still has all the time in the world to tell him, or let him tell her. Maybe after the appointment next week, so he can believe it's a medical miracle, and beat himself up for having taken her to a doctor in the first place. Maybe before, maybe in the middle of the night, when she wakes from another of those strangely familiar dreams, or maybe after, long after, when the words have gotten easier to say.

JOACHIM

All week, Joachim dreams so many different scenarios that could've taken place that, when he wakes before his alarm on Friday, he isn't sure which the real one is. Did he tell her or didn't he? He looks over at Helena sleeping peacefully beside him and recalls the last few days piece by piece. What did she ask him last week? Whether he was sorry he married her. Where did that come from? Something must be the matter. She hasn't asked him anything like that since, didn't do anything to disrupt another weekend of him wheeling her along aimlessly between thunderstorms, another week of him going out and her staying home. But that doesn't mean it's not on her mind.

Maybe she senses something even if she can't remember it. It's not like they took a time machine back to before their separation. Those years still happened, and they're still there, somewhere inside of her. Will the doctor manage to draw them out today?

From all that he's read, there aren't many concrete treatments for what she has—or rather what she's missing. So maybe the doctor will just ask her some questions. What if he asks Joachim questions, too? That would make sense. To check whether her answers are right. If only he'd told her last week, or even last night. But then they'd be in no shape to see the doctor today.

The alarm goes off and he grabs for his phone to turn it off.

"Morning, darling," Helena says. He notices that she only

takes one crutch with her to the bathroom. The jerky motion of her limp bothers him. Or is it just the fact of her movement? He stretches and goes to the kitchen to make coffee. Just another morning, he reminds his racing heart.

In the cab, Helena chats with the driver, making trivial conversation about the weather and traffic the whole way to the doctor's office. He can't tell whether she's in good spirits or covering for his grim silence. Then again, why shouldn't she be in good spirits? She's been having a serious problem for weeks, and now it might get solved.

He waits two meters behind her as she hands her insurance card to the receptionist and says she has an appointment with Dr. Meier. He's surprised that she remembered the name, which he only mentioned once after making the appointment. But why shouldn't she? Dr. Hofstaedter explained that to him while Helena was still in the hospital, that there was a kind of amnesia where you had problems storing new memories, but that was different from what Helena had. That would be far worse. What if she couldn't remember a fight they'd had they day before? They'd have to have the same fight all over again, every day forever. Or maybe every hour, the same album playing on loop. But there's nothing unfamiliar about this nightmare scenario. Weren't they that way before, day after day, without any medical conditions? Always caught in the same moment of resentment and distrust.

Helena touches his arm and he starts. He didn't realize she was done checking in. He helps her into the waiting room, onto one of the white plastic chairs. He feels like she doesn't really need his help and is just humoring him. But it must be easier for her to walk with him next to her. He shouldn't always second-guess her.

The only other person in the waiting room is a stout, hearty-looking woman in her late forties or early fifties, whom they greet after sitting down.

Joachim looks at his phone. "We're a bit early."

"Better too early than too late," Helena says.

"Yes, of course. It's no good having to rush, especially in your condition."

A nurse comes to call the other woman, and the conversation fizzles out. Were they keeping it up for her benefit? Helena leans over the white plastic table next to her chair to sort through the selection of well-worn magazines. Ancient issues of *Spiegel* from before the last Bundestag election. Tabloids from last weekend. A special interest magazine for pharmacists and a greasy copy of *Gala* with outdated gossip about Europe's royals. She looks at the cover of each one and puts it down. Then starts through the stack again. She's halfway through when the nurse calls her.

Joachim stands up and then sits down again. Is he supposed to go with her? The nurse gestures for him to stay in his seat.

"We're just going to give her the MRI now to see how the brain trauma has developed. We'll call you in after."

Helena doesn't look at him, but leans on one of the nurse's arms. He can hear the beginning of their hushed conversation about her injuries. They'll probably ask her again in private, to make sure he didn't do it. Will they find out about the subtler injuries he's inflicted on her? No scan is going to detect the lies she's heard lately. And when they call him in after? Well, maybe he won't go. He could just walk out of here right now. He could say there was an emergency and he'll send a cab for Helena, pay the driver to help her up the stairs. He already has a foretaste of the wild exhilaration he'd feel if he walked out of this building, raced down the street through the warm, still air, and ran all the way home. Or in the opposite direction, as fast as he could.

But the fantasy is only so appealing because he knows it's impossible, because he could never bring himself to do it. The thing with Ester was probably the only really irresponsible thing he's done in his entire adult life. Unless you count what he's doing with Helena. But *irresponsible* isn't quite the word for that.

An elderly couple comes creaking into the waiting room, the man with a walker, the woman shuffling behind him. Both greet Joachim with heavy Berlin accents, then take no further notice of him. The woman holds the man's arm with a thin, veiny hand while she sits down, and then offers him her brittle arms to help him into the seat. When they're both sitting, he rests his hand on the knobby knee protruding through her loose pants, and she puts her hand on his. Joachim sees them smile at each other and then looks away again, because it was a private smile, just for the two of them. Their silence isn't like his and Helena's silence. He and Helena aren't able to talk, whereas this couple doesn't need to. They must be past all the uncertainties now, past all the fights where there are no winners, where nothing is ever decided.

And yet why should they have had it any easier than he and Helena? They must've overcome even greater problems—growing up in the war, trying to make a living in the hungry years after, spending a few decades getting used to a country that no longer exists. Maybe he and Helena don't have what it takes to grow old together. There's a dangerous lump in his throat, so he picks up one of the magazines at random, forces himself through an article about why the FDP is likely to lose its seats in the Bundestag. He's overthinking things. Helena isn't agonizing this way. Of course, she has the advantage of not being able to remember half the things he's worrying about.

HELENA

Helena leans a little more heavily on Sister Anne's arm than she needs to. After all, she's the injured party here. Even if she's the only one in danger of forgetting it.

All the way down the corridor, Sister Anne makes pointedly pointless conversation. How are Helena's injuries healing? What does Helena do? Is that her husband in the waiting room? So nice of him to come. Unpleasant to wait at the doctor's office by yourself.

In the examination room, she closes the door and starts setting up the scanner. Helena sits down uninvited on the cot in front of it; after all, her leg is in a cast.

"Did your husband do this to you?" Sister Anne asks from her crouched position next to the crowded power strip into which she's trying to wedge one last plug.

"No," Helena answers quickly. "I was hit by a truck crossing the street." For an instant, she has the feeling that she's lying. Didn't he do something to her? Didn't he do all he could to keep her from getting her memory back? It's strange that she isn't angrier at him. Just thinking about what's happened to her brain turns her stomach. And if it were up to him, the damage would be permanent. Maybe it will be anyway. She still can't remember why she crossed against the light at a busy intersection, or anything about the man she spent the afternoon with just before. Still, those are trivial details compared to what Joachim was trying to hide from her. Just incidents, not fundamental circumstances of her life.

But what should he have done? Not come to get her in the first place. That would've been the normal thing to do. He could've called her parents and let them handle it. Or Magdalena or Susi. And then? And then nothing. He would've stayed out of her life like he had all along. Or rather, like she made him.

And if he'd come and told her the truth right away? She still might not have remembered for a while, but she would've been able to learn the facts like new information. She probably still would've let him take her home. It wasn't Joachim who lied to her first; it was her feelings when she saw him.

What does that mean? Were her emotions, like her memories, set back to some earlier point in time? Or maybe something within her never stopped waiting for him to reappear, was relieved instead of surprised when it finally happened.

"I hope I haven't offended you, Ms. Bachlein. You know we have to ask that kind of thing."

Helena looks up, startled. "Oh, no, not at all. I was just thinking of something."

"Well, don't think too much when you're in there." Sister Anne indicates the scanner. "No, that's a joke—you can just relax." She gives Helena a set of earplugs to block out the noise and shows her a button she can press if she has a problem. "So there's really nothing to worry about at all," she says.

Helena lies back and tries to believe her, tries to separate the dull pings of the machine from the sound of her heart, close her eyes and keep from dreaming. But in the darkness of the machine, her heart beats back and forth between guilt and dread, sure that everything she's been doing her best to hide is exposed now. And she'll protest that she wasn't *always* faking it, but no one will believe her. She knows this scenario is absurd, but she can't stop picturing it to herself in a thousand different variations. Sometimes Joachim is watching, and sometimes she's all alone. It's as if Sister Anne had wheeled her into a private movie theater where she can watch all her worst anxieties in action.

With a great effort, she forces other faces into her mind. Doro, Magdalena, Susi, Thomas, her parents . . . All of them positive, supporting her, on her side. They know what she's been through. But then another face starts to appear in the crowded darkness: a young, but sickly woman's face, with matted hair and clumps of mascara around her eyes. The horror-movie moment where that woman reached out a clammy hand to grab Helena's arm strikes her with such visceral vividness that a tremor runs through her body. That woman, that woman, who was she? Where were they? Helena strains to build up the scene around them, not sure how much she's remembering and how much she's inventing. A doorway. They were standing in a doorway, Helena on the outside, that woman on the inside. Helena had come to see her and the woman didn't expect her. But why? It must've been that woman's—what was her name?—it must've been her apartment. Helena can't remember what she said or what the woman said when she opened the door, only the sickly horror of that cold, damp touch on her arm, and the terrible effort of trying to hold herself together, not disintegrate or run for her life.

Then the dull noises stop and she feels a warm touch on one of her arms. It must be over now. She still has her eyes closed when Sister Anne rolls her cot away from the scanner, but she can feel the light around her, protecting her, cleansing her of what she just saw. She opens them and tries, just for now, just until she's alone again, not to remember. She watches Sister Anne saying something for a few moments before taking out her earplugs.

"Are you feeling all right, Ms. Bachlein? You're quite pale and I noticed you shivering a bit during your scan."

"Yes," Helena answers without thinking. "I just remembered something."

"Something you'd forgotten? How wonderful! You'll be able to tell Dr. Meier all about it in a few minutes. I'll just get your scan printed out and then take you into the consultation room." She steps out, leaving Helena sitting on the cot. She knew there'd been something about another woman but it was too much to remember all at once. You have to take it in small doses. She knew it was something like that, but she thought: one step at a time. Until this moment, she didn't realize she'd seen the woman, been touched by her cold hand. She can hear some kind of machinery groaning through the wall, and then Sister Anne comes back in with a manila folder under one arm. As the nurse helps her to her feet, she remembers in sickening detail the moment just after, that woman's damp, cold hand drawing the warmth out of her pulsing wrist, when they both burst into tears: Helena's silently streaming down the burning skin of her face, and the other woman's sickly weeping, the strands of snot coming out of her nostrils that she didn't wipe away, her heaving gasps for air. She shudders and feels the tremor pass through her body into the solid, healthy warmth of Sister Anne at her side.

"Shall I get you a blanket, Ms. Bachlein? You seem to be a little chilled."

"That would be nice, thank you," Helena manages to say. She doesn't understand anything. She can't believe she'd go to the home of some woman Joachim was seeing, confront her like that. It isn't like her. And why was the woman already such a mess, even before Helena arrived? She lets Sister Anne deposit her in one of three vinyl-covered chairs opposite a sparse pressed-wood desk, where the nurse deposits the manila folder next to a metal penholder. She opens a drawer in the desk and takes out a form on a clipboard, which she hands to Helena.

"Please start filling this out," she says.

Helena nods and begins answering the questions: when and where she was born, her parents' names, whether she has siblings. The form is several pages long, and that reassures her, having so much paper to put between herself and whatever's about to happen.

"Would you like me to get your husband right away, or would you prefer to speak to the doctor alone first? Many of our patients find it helpful to have someone there to help them put together the memories they're missing and—"

Helena surprises both of them by cutting her off. "Why don't I see the doctor first so we can discuss the medical aspects? I don't want to worry my husband unnecessarily, and we can call him in after."

"Of course." Sister Anne steps out again.

Every second alone is a victory and a torture. Dr. Meier will be here at any moment, and then what? With all these hours and days and even these last minutes to prepare, she still hasn't decided what she wants to tell him. The truth? She can't do that to Joachim. Wouldn't he be in some kind of trouble? There must be a law against deceiving a sick person this way. Certainly they wouldn't leave her in his care. She could tell the doctor part of the truth. She could say that she'd started to remember things, things from much earlier, but not yet everything. He may be a specialist, but he can't see into her head. If they start to talk about what she remembers, she can come up with some harmless memories, ones that won't change anything, and tell the doctor about those. And when they call Joachim in? Then it won't just be about what she says. He'll have to explain things, too. That's what they want him for, isn't it? To tell her about the things she can't remember. As if he could tell her about all those years he wasn't there. It's a relief to know that the responsibility is Joachim's, that it's his decision how much to say. But it's also terrifying to have so little control. Can she cover her ears as he speaks, shout at the top of her voice that she isn't ready to know?

The door opens and a handsome Middle Eastern man in a lab coat comes in. Helena's surprised at how young he is. As if only an old man could know anything about memory.

"Dr. Meier." He comes over to give Helena his hand so she won't have to stand up.

"Ms. Bachlein."

He sits down behind the desk and takes out the images from the manila folder. Helena makes her way through the names of all the schools she attended and a list of her relatives, what she majored in and her first job. Sister Anne returns with a notepad and pen, then sits down one seat away from Helena.

"You can finish that later and fax it in," Sister Anne says, indicating the form.

Helena nods, and then the silence seems long to her, so she explains about the accident again. Sister Anne already knows and the doctor must, too; it must all be there in her folder. But once she's started she can't just stop in the middle of things, so she speaks as fast as she can, stumbling over her words, until she's reached new ground.

"When my husband came into my hospital room I knew exactly who he was, who I was, all kinds of things. I felt confused about what had happened and why I was in the hospital—I couldn't remember any of that. But in terms of our lives, I wasn't aware of anything missing. It all felt . . . normal." It's strange to talk about that first meeting, strange even to remember it. She feels as if all the memories she's regained were much more recent, and her accident had been years before. It's even stranger to think of Joachim seeing her before she regained consciousness, seeing her lying there, and having to decide what to say when she woke up. Maybe he'd already decided. Did he plan it from the moment he got the phone call, or was it a spontaneous whim? But he couldn't have planned it that far in advance. Even the doctors didn't know she had amnesia.

"When did you first become aware that you couldn't remember certain things?" the doctor asks.

She thinks back. It's hard to identify with that vague woman in the hospital gown and all the bandages. Was that really her, or did she only see it in a movie? But if it wasn't her, she'd remember what the face with the bandages looked like, instead of the view through them. "I was confused about the date," she recalls. "I wasn't sure what the date was, not even the year, and when I saw it, it seemed strange to me." She pauses to give Sister Anne time to finish taking notes.

"And what else?" the doctor asks. His elbows are resting on the desk and he leans forward, looking genuinely eager to find out about her case. It makes her feel like someone with an interesting story to tell rather than a patient. He must love his work. His enthusiasm makes her want to speak freely, and it's hard to remember what she's supposed to say and what she isn't.

She hesitates for a moment. But this is a thing she's allowed to say; even Joachim said it. "My husband told me we'd decided to separate. I couldn't remember that and I think that's when we both noticed how much I'd forgotten."

"So you had decided to separate from your husband, but he still came to check on you when he heard about the accident."

"Of course," she says, although there really is nothing natural about it, even less than the doctor thinks.

"Are you separated now?"

She feels herself blushing, although it's the next logical question and answering it shouldn't be difficult.

"No," she says after a few seconds. She doesn't use the time to think about her answer, but rather to force herself not to think. If she really started asking herself that question, they'd be here all day.

"In other words, in light of the accident…?"

"We sort of put that on hold."

"Whose decision was it to separate?"

"I suppose it must've been both of ours."

"You suppose?"

"Doctor, I am being treated for amnesia." As soon as she's spoken, she regrets what she said, and regrets her tone even more than her words. If only she'd managed to say it lightly, make a joke of it. But the reminder came out defensive. Not that he's accused her of anything, not yet.

He gives her a tight smile. "That's why I ask, of course. It's important to define the boundaries of your ability to remember so we can work on these trouble areas. I take it you don't remember why you separated, either?"

"Not exactly. That is, not the specific moment I decided to, but we'd been having problems for a long time. So I can imagine . . ." Did the doctor notice her slip-up? The fact that she just called it her decision? If he did, he isn't giving anything away.

"Well, that's one reason we like to have a family member or close friend at the appointment to clarify these things. What else have you had trouble remembering?"

"Pretty much everything about the past few years. I'd

changed jobs but I didn't remember the new company I was working for, or friends I'd made there."

"Have you been on sick leave since the accident?"

"No. I've been working from home. It's the same type of work I've always done, so it wasn't that hard to pick it up again." Like her marriage. The same way it had always been, so it was easy to pick it up again. But it isn't the same, is it? It feels different this time. When you come down to it, though, not much has changed. They may be fighting less, but they're no more able to speak to each other than they've ever been. The realization knocks the wind out of her and she has to struggle to get air into her lungs again, keep answering the doctor's questions about where she's from and when she moved to Berlin fast enough to sound natural, slow enough to give Sister Anne time to write it all down, mark the boundaries of her memory like the map of some theoretical country neither she nor the doctor will ever know.

By the time Sister Anne goes to get Joachim, Helena's exhausted from the strain of remembering, replying, always measuring her words to say just enough. She tells the doctor in the past tense what she couldn't remember, but never says that she remembers it now. Always, *I noticed that I couldn't remember . . .* and never *but now I can.* When Sister Anne returns with Joachim, she almost expects to be sent out of the room so they can interrogate him in private, not give him and his so-called wife the opportunity to compare notes. But Sister Anne simply shows him to the seat next to Helena and asks whether anyone would like a cup of water.

Joachim

When Sister Anne returns with two paper cups of tepid water, Joachim takes both from her, gives one to Helena, and then slowly drains his without looking up. He isn't thirsty but it's a way of slowing things down, one millisecond at a time. Maybe he can keep draining little cups of water until their time here is up, until it's the next patient's turn and the doctor has to ask them to leave. Once he's emptied his cup, he doesn't know what to do with it. Helena's only taken a couple sips from hers, and has it balanced on one knee. She's facing toward the doctor, but he can feel her watching him out of the corner of one eye as Sister Anne takes her seat again and turns to a fresh page in her notebook. He crushes the empty cup in the palm of one hand and holds it there, hoping no one will notice. He glances over at the nurse, and then fixes his eyes on the doctor like Helena is.

This guy looks like he just finished medical school. Maybe that's a good thing. Maybe he hasn't seen enough to get what's really going on here. What is really going on here? Even Joachim's having trouble keeping track. Is he here to help the doctor treat Helena's amnesia or to prevent her from remembering?

"Let's start with the basics," Dr. Meier is saying. "Why don't you tell me about your relationship with Ms. Bachlein?"

Joachim can feel sweat gathering between his palm and the crumpled paper cup. What if Dr. Hofstaedter warned

Dr. Meier to check up on him? He shouldn't have asked her for advice. She was suspicious of him the whole time. But it's a perfectly normal question so there must be a perfectly normal answer.

"We've been married for six years now," he begins, and wonders where to go from there. What level of detail is the doctor asking for? Does he want to know what their relation-ship was like, or just have some kind of time line? "We'd been dating for a couple years before that," he continues. "We met at the advertising agency where Helena used to work. I was freelancing at the time and sometimes had projects there."

The doctor asks Helena whether she remembers all that and everyone turns to watch her nod once, twice, three times; yes, that's all true. Joachim turns to see Sister Anne noting it down.

"Did you live in the same apartment that whole time?" the doctor asks once the nurse's pen comes to a rest.

Joachim hesitates. It almost seems like a trap. Whether he and Helena were still married all this time is open to a very loose interpretation, but an address is an address. He didn't move, though. "Yes," he says. "The same one we live in now." He looks over at Helena for a reaction, some conspiratorial wink or twitch of her face, but her expression is impassive as she nods a couple more times. So nobody's in on this with him; he's all on his own.

"And you remember that apartment?" the doctor asks Helena.

She clears her throat. "I do, but not everything looks the way I remember it. When I came home from the hospital, I noticed some changes."

For just an instant, the doctor's thick, elegant eyebrows dart up, then settle again. "What did you notice, exactly?"

"A painting I remembered was missing and not all of my things were there."

"What kind of things were missing?"

Helena is searching the doctor's face for some kind of cue, and Joachim wishes she'd look at him instead, so he could tell her to say . . . well, something. But she doesn't take her eyes off the doctor's face, and Joachim wouldn't have known what the right answer was, anyway.

"My clothing," she says. "My books, shoes, that kind of thing. I had things in the apartment, but not all the things I remembered."

The doctor looks in Joachim's direction and he wishes he had just one sip left in his crumpled paper cup, anything to dribble onto the sudden, excruciating dryness of his palate. "Mr. Schmidt, where are your wife's things?"

"Pardon?" Joachim croaks, although he understood the question perfectly. He clears his throat.

"The things your wife remembers that aren't in the apartment—where are they?"

"Oh, you know." Even Joachim resents his own superior tone. "It's not like she remembers everything like it was right before her accident. Some of the things she's been asking about I haven't seen her put on in years. She probably gave them to charity ages ago and then forgot about it."

He finds himself unable to keep looking into the young doctor's dark, unflinching eyes, and bends to put his cup on the floor. Sister Anne grabs it and tucks it into a pocket of her white uniform.

"And the other things?" the doctor asks.

"Some things are in the cellar." With relief, Joachim recalls that Helena already heard this lie, so it doesn't count as a new one. "We'd packed them up because we planned to separate for a while."

"A while?" the doctor repeats.

Joachim nods as the muscles in his throat go through the motions of swallowing without any saliva to smooth the way. "Yes, we hadn't really come up with a specific amount of time." Except forever. Helena's disappearance still stings like a recent wound if he presses on it, but he's kept it out of his head this long, and he can keep it out for another half hour. So what if she never wanted to see him again? That was another Helena in another marriage in another life.

"Your wife doesn't remember why you decided to separate," the doctor tells Joachim. "That definitely falls within the time frame affected by her amnesia, which seems to go back around three to four years, including the point at which she started her current job."

Helena leans behind Joachim's back to whisper something to Sister Anne and the nurse stands up.

"I'm just going to help Ms. Bachlein to the bathroom," she says. "We'll only be a minute."

Joachim watches them go like a train he just missed. But when the door closes behind them, a new ease settles over him. Does it really matter what he says now? The doctor can't tell whether he's lying, and if telling Helena the truth will help her remember, then it doesn't matter whether he does it during this session or in the privacy of their apartment. Why does there have to be a witness to his confession? He won't let himself be fooled by that stern medical gaze or the fine lines that appear and disappear from the doctor's young forehead. Dr. Meier doesn't know anything more than Helena's recent medical record and whatever Joachim tells him.

"There was no one reason we decided to separate," Joachim says, and realizes for the first time how true this is. It always went without saying that Ester was the reason they split up, but now he sees that that was just an occasion for them to finally do it. After all, if he and Helena hadn't "taken a break," he'd never have met Ester. It could've been Ester or any other fight. She was just the sign they'd been waiting for.

"But there must have been some reason," the doctor persists. "Your wife wasn't sure what it was but she implied that it was her decision to leave. It seems to me that she wasn't sure that the separation was just a temporary arrangement."

"It's true that it was mostly her decision. Helena was—" He clears his throat again and wonders why the past tense seems so much more fitting. "Helena can be a very moody person. If she gets upset about something, she may sulk about it for days, or she may do something impulsive." That's it: Helena's a bit unstable, an unpredictable type who could walk out on him over nothing. That's enough of an explanation for now.

"And what did she get upset about in this case?"

"I don't—"

"Mr. Schmidt," the doctor interrupts. "I understand that this is a difficult topic for you to discuss with a stranger, or even with your wife. But you do understand that her mental health is at stake? Please do your best to think back to what this particular fight was about."

Their time must be almost up by now. Maybe he should just come clean, or start to. Once he opens his mouth to speak, all of this may disappear, like a bad dream you wake from in the last crucial instant, before you have time to die. "Helena thought I'd cheated on her," he says. "We'd been fighting a lot and already talked about a trial separation, but things got especially hostile over that issue and that's when we actually decided to go through with it."

"Had you?"

"What?"

"Had you cheated on her?"

"No." The single harsh syllable tastes like a lie, but it's what he thought at the time, and what he'd say if he and Helena were having the same argument now. He didn't cheat. Or if some greater authority should step in and tell him that it *had* been wrong to sleep with Ester, that he *had* cheated, then it would still be true that he hadn't meant to. And isn't that what it comes down to? Not the physical act of sex with another woman, but whether he betrayed Helena in his heart.

He has to ask the doctor to repeat his question.

"Why did she think that?"

Joachim answers in a single breath, not allowing himself time to think, because he's already told the truth now, and he might as well. "We'd taken some time off before, just for a short amount of time, and I was involved with another woman during that period. I stopped seeing her the second Helena told me she wanted us to get back together, but . . ." He looks to the doctor for help, but his expression is as blank as ever. He could just as easily be watching a dull soccer game as hearing about the most difficult period of Joachim's life. No nod for him to go ahead, no sympathetic smile of *I'm a man, too* brotherhood. And what was it all about, ultimately? That he hadn't told Helena about Ester or that he'd been involved with her at all? He can't remember now, and maybe he never really knew.

"Your wife didn't believe you?"

"I didn't tell her about the other woman right away," he says, but the confession brings him no relief. If only Helena were here now, they'd be over the hurdle and in the home stretch. If only he'd already spoken Ester's name aloud in front of her. But he's done enough. She slipped out just when he needed her, but as soon as she comes back, the doctor will catch her up on everything she's missed.

"She found out, though?" the doctor asks.

Sister Anne opens the door with a clatter as if to dispel any suspicions that she was eavesdropping. It doesn't matter whether she was, or Helena was. If they were, Joachim won't have to say everything twice. Sister Anne helps Helena back to her seat and resumes her position with the notebook on her lap.

"That won't be necessary," the doctor tells her. "Our time is just about up. Ms. Bachlein, your husband has indicated to me that your decision to separate was largely based on your unfounded suspicions that he was cheating. I want you to spend at least an hour discussing this difficult but potentially rewarding subject this evening. An emotional event like that leaves its marks on the structure of our brains. In general, spending about an hour a day going over the facts can be very helpful. Try to come up with a time line of major events first, and then fill in the more minor ones. You can finish filling out that form and bring it with you to your next appointment for a guided discussion. In the meantime, I'll review the results of your scan."

Joachim starts to say something, but when the doctor stops to listen, he finds he has nothing at all to say, not now and maybe never again.

"I don't want to give you false hopes," Dr. Meier says, turning to Helena now, "but many patients with retrograde amnesia do spontaneously recover most of their memories after a certain point. There's no medical proof that talking about the past will help that process, but it will certainly help you to get along in the meantime."

She nods but doesn't say anything.

False hopes, the doctor said. And that's what Joachim has had all this time. Thinking it was just a matter of saying a few words to Helena and she'd be healed. When the whole thing is just a ticking time bomb, no way of knowing whether she'll snap out of it on the way home or this time next year.

The doctor turns to Sister Anne. "Give Ms. Bachlein and Mr. Schmidt an appointment two weeks from now."

Sister Anne takes Helena's arm again to guide her out to the reception area, and Joachim follows slowly behind. A time line of the events, the big ones and the little ones filled in, the whole space of the last few years jammed with fine print until there are no more blank spaces, nowhere left to hide. And yet the doctor told Helena her suspicions were unfounded. Was he trying to help Joachim, or spark Helena's interest so she'd insist on a discussion?

He doesn't notice that the nurse has already given them a new appointment until he feels the weight of Helena's grip being transferred from Sister Anne's arm to his. Not that she's a burden, he thinks, walking her to the elevator. She's just the weight he needs to keep from floating away. Something to keep him grounded. The talking treatment will help him as much as her, maybe more.

HELENA

Neither of them speaks until they've left the building and crossed the street away from it. There's a thin gray cast over the sky that makes it seem later than it is.

"So that was the big expert on amnesia," Helena says, trying to keep the relief out of her voice. For a while there, she really thought she was going to get caught. But of course no expert could see into her thoughts, and it would be hard to prove she was faking such a tricky condition. "Talk for an hour a day. I could've thought of that."

"Still . . ." Joachim says, but doesn't continue.

She doesn't ask what he wanted to say. She doesn't really want to know.

"Should we catch a cab?" he asks after a while. "I would've called one but I didn't know what time we'd be out."

"That's okay."

They stand for another moment without moving. But it's okay; it really is. No matter where they go from here, for the moment, everything's okay.

"Are you able to walk a bit?" he asks.

"Sure," she says.

They start in the general direction of the apartment. It doesn't make sense because there's no way they can walk the whole way, and he was supposed to go to work after, but for some reason, it's the only thing they can do.

They're far out in the West in a residential area interrupted only by businesses that don't rely on foot traffic: an architect's office, a divorce lawyer, the doctor they just left. Most of the windows on the ground floor have flower boxes on the sills. Geranium, impatiens, geranium, geranium, pansy, and then an empty one. A convenience store next to a jack-of-all-trades cobbler whose sign features pictures of all the things he can repair: high heels, boots, belts, locks, keys, knives, razors.

"Just a minute." Joachim deposits Helena against the brick wall of the shop and steps inside.

His absence startles her, as if he'd vanished while they were walking side by side. She knows he didn't drop her roughly against the wall, but when she replays the scene to herself, it seems like he did. The whirr of machinery inside the shop cuts through the songs of invisible birds. And they're supposed to talk for an hour this evening. About that other girl, or how there wasn't one.

His reappearance startles her as much as his disappearance. She shifts her weight back onto her crutch and they walk another few steps without speaking.

"It was something I was meaning to do," he says when they reach the end of the block. "You know, since yours got lost in the accident." He hands her a set of keys.

"Thank you." She has the terrible feeling that this gesture means more than it seems to, that something incredibly important is happening now, but she can't grasp it. When they happen across a taxi letting someone out, Joachim waves to keep the driver from pulling away. He has the cab drop him at his office before taking Helena home.

JOACHIM

The hours of the afternoon fly by. Joachim can't remember the last time he worked with such concentration, the whole ad campaign coming together perfectly. It's for a hip new line of organic sodas, and he balances the aggressively neon color scheme of the packaging with brilliant photographs of natural wonders: the Great Barrier Reef for Peach Passion, the Grand Canyon for the cola flavor. He takes a break from that project to update the cutesy pick-up lines for a series of billboards advertising a new hotel reservation site, and even the trite wordplay seems to flow straight from his brain to the keyboard. He's so focused he nearly jumps out of his seat every time one of his colleagues speaks to him, but then everyone knows he's having a rough time.

As the sky begins to lighten in advance of sunset, he puts off going home half an hour at a time: he'll stay 'til six, 'til six-thirty, 'til seven. He knows Helena will be annoyed that he's still at the office after seven, and he's surprised she hasn't texted to ask when he'll be back. It's not his fault he has to stay this late, though. If he hadn't spent the morning taking her to the doctor's office, he would've left ages ago. Maybe she understands and that's why she hasn't said anything.

But as the time on his monitor approaches eight and the office empties out, he has to admit that nothing he's doing is urgent. The only thing due tomorrow was the billboards and he had them finished by five. He can't finalize the soda campaign until the graphics artist gets in tomorrow, so there's nothing much to keep him here. He tells himself he's taking advantage of a rare burst of inspiration, of energy he hasn't had in weeks. That it would be a waste not to get in the hours today rather than cramming them in later when his mind's all over the place again. Still, even after he's shut down his computer, he hesitates, drags his feet as he takes old coffee cups to the kitchen and stops by the bathroom to wash his face, which suddenly feels unnaturally warm. Maybe, just maybe, he doesn't really want to go home.

It isn't just that Helena will be angry at him for coming home so late, and it isn't even that he should've told her he was going to. In fact, it isn't that at all. In his current state, her anger would wash right over him without soaking in. As he clocks out and walks slowly to the U-Bahn, he admits to himself that he still doesn't know what to say to her about the affair, their separation, his appearance at the hospital . . . in short, about anything. And that'll be the first thing she wants when he comes in, the big therapeutic discussion about things she didn't even want to talk about at the time.

Telling the truth has lost its appeal now that he has to. He was going to make this big, noble sacrifice, admit to terrible mistakes she has no recollection of him making, and officially change his ways. Now he has a homework assignment from some specialist who just finished college, an endless hour to fill by helping Helena make accusations. When all he wants is a couple glasses of wine and to fall into bed. They'll probably have to talk about it over dinner. She'll time it to make sure she's getting the exact right amount, not getting shorted by five minutes of memories. And it's not just tonight, is it? They're starting off with the worst topic but this is going to be every evening for the foreseeable future: hour after hour of a conversation he doesn't want to have.

The train pulls in, leaving him stranded exactly between two doors. He pushes into the crowded entryway and stretches his arm painfully to catch hold of a yellow rail.

The worst part is that he'll have to lead the discussion. Helena barely knows what they're supposed to be talking about.

She won't even know what questions to ask. At least if this were a fight, if she were furious with him about something she could remember, she'd get the ball rolling. She'd accuse him and he'd defend himself or admit wrongdoing, draw in a couple mitigating factors. The talk would hardly fit in the single hour allotted to it as she explained just *why* she was so upset and how what he'd done was *particularly* hurtful. As it is, he'll have to chip away at the long silence one word at a time.

When he reaches the apartment, he stops and listens for the TV or the radio, or Helena still typing if her day's been as long as his. But he can't hear a thing. He remembers the day he came home to find her sitting on the sofa, so blank, watching for him, and a shudder runs from the arches of his feet to the roots of his hair. It shouldn't be like this. It shouldn't, but it is. He plasters a broad smile on his face and opens the door. All you can do is make the best of it.

The living room and the kitchen are silent and empty. The only light is above the kitchen table, where a covered dish of food is pinning down a sheet of paper.

"Going to the appointment made me so tired," she's written, and then an arrow toward the bowl: "It's a salad so you don't have to warm it up. Love you."

No mention of the discussion they were supposed to have. He turns over the note, reads it again, and pours himself a tall glass of red wine. Well that's all right, then. Is it possible that she forgot? He doesn't see how she could have. It was pretty much the only thing that came of the whole appointment. Maybe she just wasn't up for it. If she was really exhausted and didn't even know when he'd get in? He should've contacted her by seven at the latest. The note doesn't sound angry, though.

He drinks the glass of wine and pours another while he picks at the salad, only sitting down halfway through his meal. What if she wakes up when he comes in? Or if she's not asleep at all? There's no way of knowing when she wrote this note. She might just have gotten into bed the second he opened the door, and be waiting there for him, ready to start talking after all.

If she is, then so be it. He'll tell her he's too tired and they can do it tomorrow. If she really cared, she would've stayed up to have it in the first place. He needs his rest. There's nothing worse than an argument in bed for keeping you up all night.

He moves as slowly washing the dishes and getting ready for bed as he did leaving work, putting off the potential discussion one minute at a time, but when he opens the door to the bedroom, Helena's so sound asleep she doesn't even flinch. She's sleeping on her left side and breathing so gently he can hardly hear her. Poor thing, he thinks, and is startled by the dizzying tenderness that rushes through him. Drifting off beside her, he wonders why the feeling came as such a surprise.

HELENA

On Monday, Helena wakes to the low, brilliant sunlight of early fall. As usual, it takes a moment for her thoughts to settle into place. Joachim's gone now, the weekend passed without discussion, the start of another week. She picks up her phone. Still just the three numbers. She texts Doro and asks for the number of their office, then gets up and dresses.

By the time she's ready, Doro's answer is there, with a little "You okay?" tacked on to the end. Is she?

"Sure," she writes back. "Will explain later." Then she calls her office to say she won't be able to complete any assignments today. The woman on the other end asks how things have been.

"All right, but it's a slow process," Helena says, trying to put together the pieces of this woman's face. Her voice sounds familiar. A harsh, efficient voice, its gentleness ill-fitting now, like a tutu on a bodybuilder. She misses the woman's next remark but says she's probably going to get her casts off soon, and then she'll be able to come back to the office. The woman says she's glad to hear it. Helena murmurs something and hangs up.

She saves the number of her office and goes out into the living room, moving between one crutch and the wall. She can't tell whether she's getting stronger or just used to her injuries. The air is cool and her skin feels chilled as she follows the tangle of cords from the phone to the modem. The wires coming out of the back of the modem lead behind a bookshelf, and she's careful not to put any weight onto her right side as she bends to put her left hand behind it, feel for the outlet until she can tell that nothing's plugged in. She fishes out the power adapter from the modem with her crutch and passes it to her left hand. When she plugs it in, the green lights on the little black box come on and the cordless phone chirps a few times. Slowly, she gets up again.

What a stupid, obvious trick. He didn't even disable the modem or cut the cord or anything, just unplugged it. And this is the first time, even after realizing it was all a big hoax, that she thought to check. It bothers her that he made so little effort.

She takes the phone to the table with her and starts up the laptop. Google tells her the nearest ten orthopedists and the third one she calls can see her. It's strange to be able to call someone this easily, to reach for the world that was at such a far remove, and find herself touching it. She calls a cab and then searches through her old emails for her parent's phone number.

She saves it in her phone and dials.

"Long time no see," her mom says when she answers the phone.

Helena explains that she lost her old phone and couldn't find the number, that the Internet was cut off. She doesn't say where. Last time they talked, the call was so short she can't remember what she managed to say. Does her mother even know about the accident?

"I didn't want you to worry," she says, "but I wasn't doing so well for a while after I got hit by a car. I'm doing a lot better now," she adds in the same breath, because she still doesn't want anyone to worry.

"Why didn't you tell us? We would've come and picked you up. Dad and I could've looked after you. What was the matter with you? We would've driven up and gotten you."

Before her mother can go on telling Helena everything they would've done if they'd known, she interrupts with a catalogue of her physical injuries. After a pause she adds, "And I was having trouble remembering some things. I hit my head when I fell. But it's not that unusual and now I remember pretty much everything except right before the accident." Everything except the areas of the past she's too afraid to delve into, could only remember if she wanted to. But that's not the same as amnesia. The things she doesn't want to remember are still there in her head, a shelf of books she chooses to keep closed. She could open them at any time.

"But how have you been getting on?" her mother says. "You don't even have an elevator in your building! And you live all by yourself." She starts to tell Helena all over again how much better they would've taken care of her, and that makes it easier to say what she has to say now, easier than if she had to toss the words into a glaring silence where they'd stand exposed and alone.

"The hospital called Joachim. I didn't tell them to. I was unconscious and the police came up with him as my next of kin. He offered to take care of me until—"

"Joachim?" Her mother sounds more surprised to hear Joachim's name than she was about any of Helena's injuries.

"Yes."

"Joachim?" her mother asks again. "Your—"

"Yes," says Helena. "I guess he felt like it was the right thing to do."

"But Joachim—" her mother starts to say, then doesn't seem to know where to go from there. The name has an uncanny effect; each time Helena hears it, she feels a little more estranged from him, a little more shocked to have spent all this time in his care. It seems almost possible that she didn't really, that it was all merely a strange thought that crossed her mind in half-sleep, and later came to seem like the memory of something real.

"It's a long story. I'll tell you more about it later, but I've got a cab coming to take me to the doctor. How are you guys, anyway?"

Before she hangs up, she gives her mother her new number. She sits still for a long time after, exhausted by the prospect of the day ahead of her, of all the days to come. She felt this way last Friday night waiting for Joachim, totally exhausted by the talk they were going to have before she'd heard a word of it, until she came up with her brilliant escape plan. If only you could always pretend to fall asleep before the difficult moments came; if only you could always say, *It's a long story*, or *I'll explain later.* But even lying next to Joachim with her eyes closed that night, even helping him fill another weekend with irrelevant outings to parks, restaurants, and a movie, she knew she hadn't really escaped, that nothing could be put off forever.

In the cab, she tells the driver the address of the doctor's office and carefully straightens herself up, fixing the clothing that got mussed in her slow, clumsy struggle down the stairs, smoothing her hair and dabbing the sweat from her forehead with a tissue. She considers asking him to come back for her, but she doesn't know how long she'll be. Maybe the doctor will just tell her to go home and keep taking it easy.

At the doctor's office, she gives the receptionist her insurance card and hobbles into the adjacent waiting room. She still feels sweaty and somehow distorted, as if she were a blurry picture someone had pasted into this crisp, clean room with its empty wooden chairs against the wall, its untouched magazines laid out in a fan across the coffee table. There's no window in the waiting room, but the bright overhead lighting gives the impression of sunlight.

This isn't like the other appointment, she reminds herself. Bones are bones, either broken or not, and there are no secrets in mine. Anything the doctor asks will be about concrete facts: how long she's had the casts on, how her arm and leg feel.

The nurse comes for her before she's gotten up the courage to disturb the elegant arrangement of magazines. He offers her his arm and leads her down a short, silent corridor. This must be the off-season for broken bones: too early for ice, too late for the reckless accidents of summer.

In the examination room, the nurse sits behind a small desk with a laptop after depositing Helena in a creaky chair. He asks general questions about her health, and then about her injuries: how she got them, when, where she was treated. He has a bland, unlined face that could be twenty-five or forty, and hair cut so short she can't make out the color.

After he's filled out the necessary forms on the computer, he excuses himself and goes to get the doctor. Now that the effort of getting herself here is over, now that there's nothing to do but wait, Helena feels wearier than ever. She could slip off to sleep right here, head against the wall, the back of the chair creaking slightly under her weight. She closes her eyes. She must've slept even less than she thought these past few nights. Certainly, Joachim fell asleep before she did; she heard that subtle shift in his breathing, opened her eyes just wide enough to catch the tell-tale parting of his lips. Nothing keeps you awake like pretending to sleep.

She feels a deep, primal resentment against him, blaming him for her weariness, as if he'd snatched the sleep away from her, taken it for himself. And a more rational kind, wondering why he didn't bring her here himself, why it doesn't occur to him to take her to a doctor unless she asks. He shouldn't have picked her up from the hospital if he wasn't going to take care of things like that. It's not like he did her such a big favor; if he hadn't come, she would've gone to stay with her parents and seen half the doctors in town just to be on the safe side. They would've watched movies and sat on the porch feeding the birds, spent a few weeks catching up. It would've been restful and healthy to recover that way, without all this confusion about a relationship she got over years before.

She opens her eyes, feels the glaring whiteness of the room, the stillness of it, around her but not soaking in, not penetrating the dark chaos within her. Did she ever really get over it? Why was she alone for all those years? He surely wasn't. Of course he hasn't said so, but he must've had all kinds of women around in that time. Even in their break of just a few months, he managed to pick someone up. But that's not the point now, no need to think about that other woman, her clammy hand closing on Helena's wrist. The point isn't whether he was alone, but why she was.

Did she still love him? What she feels for him now is too difficult a question to ask herself when the doctor could come in at any moment. But did she still love him, all those years when she was alone? When she looks back, it seems she barely thought of him, but he must've always been there in the back of her mind, an unfinished thought and a problem she never solved. You never think about the white walls of your apartment, but they're there around you all the time. Maybe the problem was that she never really allowed herself to think about Joachim.

At first it was hard not to, but she forced herself. In the beginning, at Magdalena's, she was a wreck, but then she had the new apartment and the new job to distract her. She went to Ikea and to tumbledown antique shops in her neighborhood; she took long walks with her headphones on so she wouldn't have to think. In the evenings, she watched movies or read books so there was no room for anything else, and when she got up in the morning, all she thought about was doing well at her new job. It was all she allowed herself to think about.

She made new friends, saw less of the ones who'd seen her through her separation, and kept the groups strictly separated. She never mentioned that she had a husband. When he came up, she said simply "my ex," because that's all he was, an X, something she'd crossed out of her life. Mostly she avoided telling stories that he played a role in.

The door opens and she tries to compose her face, and then her thoughts, to answer the doctor's questions. But it's only the nurse again. He apologizes for the delay—how much time has passed?—and says that the doctor wants them to take new X-rays first. As he helps Helena one door further down the hall, she imagines that the doctor isn't here at all, that it's all some kind of trick, dragged out one minute at a time. After all, that's what her life outside of this practice turned out to be.

She feels something like dizziness that has nothing to do with her physical balance, and forces herself to concentrate on holding first her arm, then her leg, still between two navy blue partitions as the nurse takes the X-rays.

This time, the wait for the doctor isn't long. The nurse leaves with the X-rays and returns a few minutes later with a heavyset blonde woman, about Helena's age, who'd look more in place on a milking stool or behind the counter of some old-timey inn. Dr. Ahnen says that Helena's bones have healed and the casts probably could've come off a few days earlier.

"You'll have some swelling in your foot and ankle for quite some time, but that's normal. You're going to have to be careful, of course."

Half of Helena listens carefully to all the things she should and shouldn't do with her arm and leg, nods at the appropriate intervals, but the other half has already left the doctor's office even before her casts are off, is speeding away. Yet, in spite of her rushing thoughts, when she limps out of the office, one arm and one leg so pale, hairy, and loosely fleshy they no longer seem a part of her, she has no idea where to go.

She shuffles over to the next bench and sits down. She takes out her phone to check the time and sees that she has another message from Doro: "Heard you called in sick. What's going on?"

She calls Doro and tells her about the doctor with no idea what else she plans to say until it comes out of her mouth. "Hey," she says, "do you think you could put me in touch with Tobias?" She pauses. "Again?"

"Of course." For whatever reason, Doro sounds relieved.

• • •

Helena's heart pounds as she listens to Tobias's phone ringing, but slows once he picks up. She doesn't recognize his voice. It could be any male voice with the faint relics of a Bavarian accent, an expectant "hallo" and a last name she doesn't recognize. She should've had Doro call him. You don't always have to make things harder on yourself.

"I don't know if you remember me. My name is Helena." She starts to add, "I'm a friend of Doro's," but it isn't necessary.

"Helena!" Now his voice is warm with an enthusiasm she wishes she could share. "I'm so glad to hear from you! Doro told me about your accident, must've been right after I saw you last. How are you?"

It feels like being mistaken for someone else. "I'm okay," she says. "I just got my casts off."

She lets him go on for a couple minutes, listens to his relief that she's okay, his barely concealed excitement about this call. Funny that she could make someone this happy without knowing who he is.

She says, "I'd like to see you again."

"How about tonight?"

They arrange to meet in Joachim's neighborhood, but she hangs up disappointed. She was so sure he'd ask her to the same café, do everything like before, until it all somehow clicked back into place. End things the way they started. Somehow. Except that it would only be a blind date on her end.

She didn't tell him about her amnesia or Joachim or any of it, but maybe Doro already has, either directly or through the series of relationships connecting them. He didn't mention it, but then what would he have said? Maybe asked whether she remembered him.

Even with the cast off her leg, she doesn't have the energy to drag herself back up all those flights of stairs. Or to be in that apartment right now.

She makes her way back to it, but only opens the front door of the building long enough to shove her crutch in and let it fall against a wall. It doesn't really matter whether someone steals it now.

The door falls closed behind her and she keeps walking, although what she wants most is to sit down and not move for a good long time. It's frustrating to feel this weak, to have to force herself to take such small, slow steps in order to keep moving at all.

She wants to stop at the closest coffee shop, the one she pictured escaping to a few infinite weeks ago, but when she reaches it, it's empty and the sign has been removed. She heads toward the café where she's meeting Tobias in a couple of hours. It's just as well. Why drag herself around again, when she can collapse right where she needs to be? Just collapse and wait.

A few yuppie parents, dragging their toddlers to and from the playground, give her funny looks. Is she that disheveled or is it her slow, deliberate shuffle, like something out of a zombie movie? She should've held onto her crutch. Then everybody would think, *Oh, that poor injured woman*, and not *What's wrong with* her?

It doesn't matter. The stares pass her by, and after all, these aren't her neighbors, this isn't her neighborhood, and in a way this isn't her life, isn't even her. Just somebody passing through somebody else's life. Even if that somebody is the person she was a few years before.

In the café, she exaggerates her limp so other patrons make way for her instead of staring, and collapses on a brocade chaise longue that's seen better days. The place is already pretty full— emaciated hipsters drifting in and out of the smoking room, tourists hunched over laptops on antique schoolhouse tables, stay-at-home parents treating themselves to coffee and cake, absentmindedly rolling strollers back and forth with one hand. The throbbing in her ankle is like heat and a low drone all around her, occasionally rising to drown out the other noise. She rolls up one leg of her jeans and examines the contrast between the dark swelling and the pale skin around it.

It's a lot of time to kill without a book, but she has a couple of things to do before Tobias gets there.

First, she flags down the heavily pierced rockabilly waitress, who tells her to order at the bar until Helena points out her injured ankle. Then she has to wait for her latte to arrive, position it carefully on the unstable 1950s kidney table, and rummage through her purse for her phone.

And then she has to call Joachim.

He misses her call and calls back, so that's a little more time past.

"Are you okay?" he says, instead of *hello*.

"Yeah, everything's okay. I just wanted to let you know I got an appointment with an orthopedist, but she could only see me this evening so I probably won't be back when you get in."

"When's the appointment? Should I come take you?"

"No, no, you'd never make it in time." She cups her hand over the phone to keep out the potpourri of voices, espresso machines, and chairs scraping across the decaying wooden floor. "I'm already in a taxi. I just wanted to let you know."

"Do you want me to pick you up afterward?"

His attentiveness fills her with a mixture of guilt and fury: How can she lie to someone who cares so much, and why did he only start caring so long after the fact? "I don't know how long I'll be. I'll let you know. Bye!"

He's already started to say "I love you" when she hangs up.

She extends her left arm to its utmost length to pull a newspaper off the rack behind her by its wooden handle, and again she feels a strange thrill of recognition. But she knows she's been in this café many times, with and without Joachim. Was it something in the paper? Something she saw out of the corner of her eye? Nothing jumps out at her as she scans the headlines, and the feeling doesn't return.

It was so easy to lie to Joachim, so easy to believe in what she was saying. It might as well have been true. Was that the way—is that still the way—he feels lying to her? The necessity excusing everything, making a lie plausible, even to the one telling it. She feels closer to him in this complicity, and then abruptly, unbearably distant: They're always deceiving each other, never on the same end of the lie. There is no understanding between them.

• • •

She's bored and hungry an hour before Tobias arrives, and then clammy and shaky as the time gets closer, the newsprint sticking to the palms of her hands. She knows from his eagerness to meet her that she made a good impression the first time, but she doesn't know how. In a way, Tobias is a time traveler—he already knows what the future looks like after they meet, and she still has no idea.

Worse still, she doesn't know what she felt the first time around. There was no time to confide in anyone, no time to give anyone a quick review of the date, before her accident. But whatever she felt must've been strong enough to take her mind off the traffic lights.

She still expects to recognize him until someone taps her on the shoulder and she looks up into the pleading smile of a tall man with unkempt blond hair and the beginnings of a beard.

"Helena, it's me," he says. Her confusion must be apparent.

"Oh." She shifts toward the headrest of the chaise longue to make room for him. He puts out one hand as he sits to keep from coming into contact with her extended right leg.

"Must've been a pretty bad accident," he says. "How'd it happen exactly?"

So there's that to talk about, at first, repeating the facts they told her at the hospital. And then he excuses himself and goes to the bar for two glasses of red wine, and by the time he comes back, she's pulled herself together enough to ask whether he heard about her memory loss.

He didn't. So then there's that to talk about. He smiles whenever he looks at her, which is almost constantly, except to wince when she tells him the details of each injury. The attention is flattering and she likes the patient, peaceful way he sits and takes the information in, likes his hearty laugh when the conversation permits.

"So I can make all the same jokes I did on our first date," he says, "and you'll still laugh?"

"Did you make a lot of jokes?" It's strange to talk about a common past with someone this new to her. She does feel a certain ease in his presence, but she can't be sure whether that's familiarity, or only a natural sympathy between them. In a way, it doesn't matter. They know each other now.

"I have no idea," he says. "I was so nervous that I couldn't think what I was saying."

"Why's that?" she asks, because she knows she's supposed to. It's kind of a line but she doesn't mind it, coming from him.

"I guess I didn't expect you to be so beautiful."

She feels herself blushing, though she saw that coming a mile away. He's blushing, too, red in the face like a lumberjack who just felled a day's worth of trees. To fill the sudden silence, he tells her where they first met—that bar, that night with Joachim, that pang of not-quite-remembering—and that they both got there too early.

"It was a million degrees out, and we were both hiding inside like we didn't want to meet each other at all."

"Maybe we didn't."

Another shared laugh, and then she wonders how long this can go on before she has to tell him about Joachim. It's a question she puts off answering, one she lets Tobias' deep, soothing voice drown out. He tells her anecdotes about growing up in Freising, just up the river from Munich, his work as an architect, and his bad dating experiences since his divorce.

She realizes or decides that she likes him. It isn't the usual process of falling for someone—it's too self-conscious. Rather, she realizes that she must've liked him the first time they met, that he's the sort of person she'd choose to continue seeing. The clarity of this knowledge seems almost cynical, but it can't have felt that way originally. She would've been excited rather than relieved. She would've looked forward to hearing from him and seeing him again, been eager for the future. Now, without even thinking about where she and Tobias will go from here, she already feels that this is the end of something.

I married too young, she thinks. Or, if not that, I married too—something. Too completely, too recklessly. I married so that there wasn't enough of me left after.

She tells Tobias more about herself, observing her own growing awareness that this is a man she could be with, and be happy with. It doesn't matter whether she *will* be. The possibility is there, and that says it all: She could be the woman who loves Joachim, and she could be the woman who loves Tobias. She is both women, right now, without loving either of them. Is that all love is, recognizing the possibility between yourself and someone else?

There's a lull in the conversation, and he takes their glasses back to the bar. It's funny to think that she can see him now, see him any number of times, and go back to Joachim unchanged, the same person she was when she went out. For the first time, she understands how people cheat, not in clumsy, accidental affairs like Joachim's, but routinely, coldly—the way she once believed he'd betrayed her. It isn't something she wanted to know, especially not about herself.

When Tobias comes back with two more glasses of wine, she says, "I haven't even told you the strangest part of the story."

JOACHIM

Joachim wakes with a start when he hears a door close. The room is dark and it takes him a minute to realize he's on the sofa, not in bed, and then another to remember why. Helena. The doctor. He was supposed to be up waiting for her call, ready to pick her up. He must've drifted off. It was such a long day. He feels for his phone but it's lost somewhere in the sofa cushions. He has a crick in his neck.

"Helena, is that you?" Outside, the sky is completely dark. What time is it? How long did her appointment take?

"Shhh, Joachim, go back to sleep." He hears her uneven steps sliding across the floor. Is he imagining it or did she slur her words? No, she's just tired. She had to get to the doctor's office and get back all by herself. Still, something doesn't make sense here. Why would she tell him to go back to sleep when he's on the sofa, not even covered with a blanket, so obviously waiting for her?

"Turn the light on," he says, sitting up, somehow not quite able to stand. "I have to get in bed, anyway."

Another moment of darkness—is she hesitating or feeling for the switch?—and then the lights come on. Her face is flushed, her hair tousled, half out of its ponytail. One leg of her pants is rolled up to expose pale skin where her cast used to be, and the thin silhouette of her arm under her sweater shows that that one's gone, too.

"Your casts," he says, sinking back into the sofa cushions.

"Yeah, I got them off. They did some X-rays and my bones were healed."

He feels himself overflowing with a warm gratitude he could never express to Helena or anyone, a prayer answered before he dared to make it. She really was at the doctor's office. It must not be as late as it looks. It's starting to get dark earlier.

"How do you feel?"

"Good," she says, without moving from her position by the door. "My ankle's still pretty sore, but at least I can walk around."

"I'm sorry I didn't come pick you up. I must've fallen asleep waiting. What time is it?"

"I don't know," she says, almost before the question is out of his mouth, as if she'd been waiting for it. "I was so hungry after the doctor's that I stopped to get something to eat." She must know how her voice sounds, because she adds, "I had a couple glasses of wine to take the edge off my ankle, but I guess I'm not really used to drinking more than a glass anymore, because it went straight to my head."

There was something else strange, something he meant to ask her about before he fell asleep. Then he remembers: that crutch lying in the entryway of the house, abandoned. He would've worried if he hadn't just heard from her that she was in a taxi. "Was that your crutch downstairs?"

"Oh," she says, shuffling into the kitchen. "Yeah. I didn't want to take it in the cab with me, so I left it there."

Another answer that makes sense, so that's okay. Or it should be. He hears the faucet running as she pours herself a glass of water, but he can only see her as a silhouette because she left the overhead light off in the kitchen. Shaking off his stupor, he gets up to get ready for bed.

When he comes out of the bedroom in his pajamas, she's locked herself in the bathroom. He finds his phone on the floor beneath the sofa and sets his alarm for the next morning. He's surprised to see that it's after midnight. How late was the doctor's office open, and how long was Helena at a restaurant by herself? The strangest part is that he has no missed calls.

Not only did she not ask him to pick her up from the doctor's office, but she didn't even ask him to meet her for dinner. And it wasn't a quick dinner, was it? Not just something she grabbed on her way back. She sat down in a restaurant, ate, and had a few glasses of wine. By herself?

He settles into bed and closes his eyes against the swarming, bewildering darkness around him. Maybe she met a friend for dinner. Why doesn't she say so? Maybe she just isn't saying much because he was so tired; maybe she'll tell him about it tomorrow. Maybe.

He hears the bathroom door open, the bedroom door open and close, feels her weight sinking in next to him with the cautiousness of someone trying not to wake a sleeper. There's nothing he can accuse her of. He doesn't even know what to be afraid of now, but he is, very definitely, afraid.

"Helena," he whispers, trying and failing to keep the urgency out of his voice.

"Mm-hmm?" She's tipsy, tired, comfortable in bed. He shouldn't bother her but he can't help it. He has to say something, anything. He has to somehow get ahold of her in this strange, shifting darkness. Otherwise she might not be there when he wakes up.

"Let's go away together," he says.

"What?" She's already drifting away from him, going away all by herself.

"This weekend. Friday, after work. Let's go away for the weekend." The idea forms piece by piece in his mind until it seems already real, inevitable. "We can stay at some country inn in Brandenburg or Meck-Pomm, catch the last sunny days. Just the two of us. We can finally have some time to talk."

"This weekend?" she asks, and her voice is suddenly harder, no longer muffled by wine or drowsiness. "Are you sure?"

Her wariness startles him. She always wanted to go away for the weekend; one of her constant complaints was that they never took any trips together. And it's not like he's talking about hiking, just a couple days of sitting out by some lake, watching the clouds pass. And talking, having to talk, because there'll be nothing else to do.

"Of course I'm sure. I'll rent a car and pick you up after work on Friday. We can come back Sunday."

"Okay," she says. "If you want."

Through the darkness, he feels her awake beside him for a long time after.

HELENA

Helena considers putting off her return to the office until the next week, but on Friday she decides to go in for half a day. She can't put it off forever. She doesn't discuss it with Joachim, who leaves while she's still in the shower. It must not have occurred to him that she'd want to go in this week, or maybe ever again.

Before she leaves the apartment, she throws a couple of changes of clothing, her toothbrush, and cosmetics into his backpack, recalling how incapable she was of carrying it down the stairs just a few weeks before. A lot can change in a few weeks. Sometimes, it seems to her that more has changed in these past couple of months than in the three years before.

Has anything really changed, though? All of this around her, this old life draped over her, is just a temporary illusion, a trick of the light that will pass as the sun moves across the sky. She's the same person she was before the accident, and the life she has outside of this apartment is there waiting for her to pick it up again. Even Tobias was more or less waiting for her call.

Can it all be over just like that? Was this time with Joachim just a random episode with no consequences? One that will, afterward, seem like a bizarre, anachronistic dream? Or is it the start of a new time in her life? They have the weekend to find out.

The weekend. How unlike him to suggest it out of the blue. He never wanted to go out of town. When they were married, it was hard even to drag him on a day trip to one of the lakes outside Berlin. Is there some special purpose to this trip, or is he trying to show her that he's changed? But she's changed, too, and not necessarily in ways that makes them more right for each other.

The thought of the weekend reminds her that she needs to call Tobias and say she won't be able to see him, but she puts it off, tells herself he might not be up yet. She's tempted to take a taxi to work, but she's made too much of a habit of that already, and she can't afford it. Besides, just like going back to her office, the U-Bahn ride there is part of getting back to normal life.

She texts Tobias from the train to say she won't be back until Sunday evening. She says she'll call him later, although she isn't sure she wants to. His reaction to her story about Joachim was, understandably, less than enthusiastic. She didn't expect him to be happy about it, but she expected . . . Whatever it was, he didn't give it to her. She still wants to see him again, but she can't ask him to wait forever for her to figure this out. Not that it's her fault. Crossing in front of that truck might've been, but not the rest of it. But maybe she was too hasty in leaving Joachim the first time around, and that's what's making things so difficult now.

She clocks in a little late for the flextime system, but nobody cares about that now. Uli, on her way back to the HR office as Helena comes in, is the first to greet her, the face to go with that voice on the phone. She claps Helena on the shoulder and then removes her hand, not quite sure how delicate Helena is. "Well, are you back in shape?"

This question repeats itself in one form after another as Helena makes her way to her desk, a blur of faces and inquiries and concern. She feels dizzy by the time she sits down next to Doro, but the overexertion is mental rather than physical. She didn't even try to call up all these incidental faces or names during her convalescence, and now the familiarity of them rushes at her in a confused jumble, more information than she can process at once. Luckily, she doesn't have to call anyone by name, just nod and smile and thank them for caring, tell everybody she's going to be okay.

"Should I tell everybody to piss off?" Doro asks with a wink as Helena carefully takes her seat.

"Only if you can say it nicely."

"I hate to be the hundredth person to ask, but are you okay? I'm not just talking about your bones."

"More or less," Helena says. "Let me see if I can remember my password for the worklist, and then I'll tell you about it in the kitchen."

The little employee kitchen, with a window overlooking the small courtyard, gives Helena a sense of long-forgotten familiarity, something like what she always feels driving past her old school on the way to visit her parents. Doro takes a mug out of the cluttered cabinet and puts it under the espresso machine for Helena, as if she might no longer know how. Helena closes the door.

"Did you call Tobias?" Doro asks.

"I saw him Monday night."

"And?" The growl of the espresso machine comes to a halt and Doro hands Helena her mug, puts in one for herself.

Helena pours some UHT milk into her cup from the Tetrapak on the counter. "I didn't remember him." She leans against the wall to take some of the weight off her leg. Golden light is coming through the little window, but in an hour or two, they'll have to put the lights on. It's that time of year when things are more brilliant, more intense, but briefer. "I liked him," she adds, "but."

Doro seems to already know what the problem is, to have known all along. Helena is too slow for this fleeting, golden season. "Are you still staying at Joachim's?"

Helena nods.

"Did you talk to him about . . . everything?"

Helena shakes her head. "He wants us to go away for the weekend. I guess we'll talk about things then."

"Do you think you'll . . .?"

Doro doesn't finish her question but, whatever it is, Helena doesn't know the answer. Instead, she tells Doro what it was like to see Tobias again, as if for the first time.

"Apparently he really likes you," Doro says.

Helena nods again. He offered to let her stay at his place if she still needed help getting around, or to help her move back into her old apartment. He couldn't understand how she could continue to stay at Joachim's. But it was all too abrupt. She couldn't leave just like that, in the middle of the night. She wants to leave gradually like light fading from a window pane, its departure unnoticed until dark.

"Where are you guys spending the weekend, then?"

Helena shrugs. "Somewhere nearby. It didn't seem like he had anything planned."

"Well, I can't say I envy your position." There's something in Doro's voice that Helena dislikes, the implication that she doesn't envy Helena's position, but if she were in it, she'd handle it a hell of a lot better. Doro doesn't know, nobody knows, what this is like. It isn't a normal situation. Time has always moved forward steadily without stopping or asking anyone's opinion. It isn't fair that Helena has to sift through it now, decide what to keep and what to throw away. Doro's never had to choose between two different versions of herself.

"I guess I'll let you know how it goes," she says.

• • •

Helena tells Uli she has a doctor's appointment and has to leave early. If there's some advantage to getting run over, it's that no one asks you for a doctor's note.

She takes the bus from her office to her apartment, and the familiarity of the route is jarring: every graffiti, every train station, every used car lot, grocery store, and pothole along the way is still stored in her memory.

She doesn't remember where she hid that letter all those years ago, doesn't even remember hiding it, but she knows herself, knows she wouldn't have been able to look at it, wouldn't have been able to throw it away.

She finds it in a moving box at the bottom of her armoire,

mixed in with college papers, old Christmas cards, and faded ticket stubs from movie theaters and airports. Still in its envelope.

The return address is unfamiliar, but she remembers the station where she got off last time, and when she gets there, she squints at the minute streets winding through the station map until she finds it.

It's a ways from the station and her right leg is trembling by the time she reaches it. The door to the building is propped open and a moving truck is parked out front. Helena makes her way in and through the courtyard to the rear building, where she stops to rest before starting up the stairs.

It would've been easier if the front door had been locked. It would've been easier to ring, wait a few seconds and limp away relieved that no one was home. It still would've counted.

Even now she doesn't know what she wants here. What can she possibly say to Ester? She barely remembers what she said the first time: They screamed at each other a bit, and then cried for a long time after. In the same room, but not really together. At some point, Ester opened a bottle of whiskey in the kitchen, and they both had a couple of glasses, still not really together, just miserable in the same place. Ester's kitchen had a ripe, garbagy smell, and there were fruit flies hovering in it. Her roommate, a mousy girl with glasses, came home not long after Helena called Magdalena to come get her, and Helena was relieved that Ester wouldn't be alone. She didn't want to be responsible for her.

By the time Magdalena arrived, Helena was drunk and didn't know why she'd come. Ester was sitting in a creaking kitchen chair with her head in her hands, saying something like, "God help us."

As far as Helena can remember, they didn't talk much about anything; there was just that first moment when Ester opened the door, knew who she was and grabbed her by the wrist. The last thing she remembers of the visit is looking over her shoulder as she left—did she say goodbye?—and being startled by how young the other woman was, just a girl really.

When she reaches the right landing, she stops to catch her breath. Is this really happening? How can it be that Ester still lives at this address? Helena's presence in this building feels abrupt, as if she'd skipped over the entire process of getting here, simply stood up from her desk and found herself outside this door.

She rings once, briefly, hoping again that no one's home. But a rosy-cheeked woman with henna-red curls answers almost immediately. She's put on a little weight, dyed her hair, and it takes Helena a moment to recognize this calm, puzzled face as the same person who opened this door years before. Ester doesn't recognize her.

"My name is Helena Bachlein," she says. "I was here a few years ago about . . ." She doesn't know what word to put into this blank, how to sum it all up. "About Joachim Schmidt," she says finally.

Ester's face goes completely white and then turns a deep pink, all her blood let out at once and then dumped back in.

"Please come in," she says.

Helena can't be sure how accurate her memory of the apartment is, but if it was anything like the chaos of dirt and dim lighting she recalls, a lot has changed. The hallway is crowded but tidy, with two shoe racks and a row of coat hooks painted to look like the legs of a caterpillar. Ester shows Helena into the kitchen, which is also a delicate balance of clutter and tidiness. The stack of dishes drying by the sink glistens in the sunlight coming through the window, but seems seconds away from collapse.

Half the wooden table Helena sits down at is covered in piles of papers, magazines, and groceries; the other half is so freshly polished she pulls her hand away from the damp surface.

"Can I get you something to drink? A cup of tea?" Ester asks.

"Sure. Thank you." For a moment, Helena wonders whether she's made some kind of mistake, wandered into the wrong apartment. Was the name on the door really Ester's? But no stranger would've let her in this quickly.

"I notice that you're limping," Ester finally says as the

kettle's coming to a boil. "Did you hurt yourself?" She sets two cups of fennel tea on the table.

"Yes," says Helena. "I was hit by a truck crossing the street. In fact, that's why I'm here."

"Oh?" Ester looks so surprised that she must already have come up with another explanation for Helena's arrival. Helena can't imagine what it could be. She's still not sure what she's doing here herself.

"You know," she begins, without knowing what else to say. The cry of a baby from the next room interrupts the silence before it can spread too far.

"Excuse me." Ester leaves and returns with a minute infant in blue pajamas. It goes on wailing but still seems to Helena to be in another room, not quite there. Or maybe she's the one who isn't quite here.

"I'm sorry," Ester says, draping a blanket over her chest and arranging the baby under it, "but if I don't feed him, he'll be screaming the whole time."

So she has a baby, Helena registers belatedly. For half an instant, she's sure that this is Joachim's baby, the one she said she got rid of, but she dismisses the ridiculous idea before she even finishes thinking it. This baby is only a few weeks old; the other one would've been walking and talking by now.

Anyway, that would've been too easy. Just ring Ester's doorbell and find everything undone, the affair ended amicably, the child on her lap, no hard feelings.

Life isn't like that. The future, even the present, is brimming with possibilities, hundreds, thousands of decisions to make every hour. But there is only one possible past, and no one can change it. Is that what Joachim's trying to do? Go back and overwrite what really happened, insert a new history? Even if she hadn't gotten her memory back, it never would've worked. She would've sensed that something wasn't right. Even right after her accident she sensed something. And sooner or later, someone would've told her. It's not like the whole world lost its memory.

"You were saying you were hit by a truck?" Ester prompts her.

"Yes, I lost my memory and a lot of things got very mixed up for me. I remember almost everything now, but I'm still trying to make sense of things."

"I can't imagine," Ester says. "All that seems like a lifetime ago to me. But I'm glad you're here, actually." She sounds more weary than glad. She probably has a lot to get done today, things to take care of in her normal life. "There was something I meant to say to you once, but I never got around to it."

Helena sips her bland fennel tea and nods.

"It wasn't as bad as I made out. I mean, for me, it was that bad—I was a mess. But it wasn't all Joachim's fault. I'd dropped out of college a couple weeks before, after a really bad breakup, and I was sort of at loose ends. 'Sort of' is an understatement. I was a mess," she says again. "Anyway, he seemed so stable and dependable. I didn't tell him how young I was. I mean it's not like I lied about my age but I didn't mention it. I laid off the drugs and got a job as a waitress. In my head it was like all this stability was coming from him, you know? I didn't believe I had it in me to get myself together."

Helena nods again. These are not things she needs to know, not anymore, but they may still be things Ester needs to say.

"He told me the first time we met that he was married but it sounded like . . . I don't know. I guess the only thing I really blame him for is making it sound like *he* wasn't sure. When what it came down to was, he wasn't sure whether you'd want him back, but he was gonna come running the minute you did.

"He'd already stopped seeing me by the time I realized I was pregnant. When I came to tell him, he didn't want anything to do with me. I don't know if you've ever felt like you were just a placeholder for somebody better? It's a shitty feeling. Really shitty. And I didn't really have anybody I could go to at that point."

"You must've been . . ." Helena starts to say but trails off.

"And then he offered me money," Ester says, switching arms underneath the baby and adjusting her blouse before she removes the blanket. "I would've given anything to have somebody help me, tell me what to do, you know? And here he was, saying he'd pay for the baby, for the abortion, whatever.

I knew what he was really saying was he'd pay to never see me again."

Helena nods and wonders whether she should tell Ester about Joachim trying to set back time.

"Anyway, I'm sorry for what I did," Ester says. She drapes the now drowsy baby over one shoulder and burps it. "I mean, he should've told you himself, but it wasn't right what I did. I guess I wanted to hurt him, and maybe I wanted to hurt you for being the one he wanted instead of me. What do I know. Maybe I hoped you'd take off and he'd come back to me, make it a real relationship with a future. I was just a dumb kid. I don't even know if I would've wanted that."

"You're seeing someone now?" Helena asks.

"Or did I just get myself knocked up again?" Ester's laugh sounds uncomfortable, as if she finds her own joke tasteless. "No, I'm married now. In fact, it's lucky you came when you did. We're moving to a bigger place now that we got the kid."

"How nice." Helena can't bring herself to ask any of the normal questions like where they're moving to or how old the baby is. There's a long silence as they finish their tea.

"Did you stay together?" Ester asks.

"No," Helena says. Because they didn't. Even if they do now, it won't change the fact that they didn't then. Nothing ever will.

"I'm sorry," Ester says. She sounds sincere but not too upset about it, maybe because the girl who sent that letter to Helena is such a stranger to the woman she is now.

"If it hadn't been that, it would've been something else," Helena says.

"Did you remarry?"

"Not yet." The laugh they share is almost sisterly, but doesn't last. If there's something Helena meant to say to this stranger, she can't remember what it was.

"I guess I'd better be going."

She accepts Ester's offer to call her a cab. Neither of them refers to the fact that they'll never see each other again; it would somehow be impolite.

JOACHIM

Waiting to pick up a rental car, Joachim finds himself sweating, breathless, constantly checking the time as the customer at the head of the line gives an interminable explanation of which car he wants and what for. Joachim reminds himself over and over again that there's no hurry, that he and Helena didn't settle on a specific time, but he can't convince himself to relax.

When he finally reaches the counter, he tells the harried teenager with sweat stains under the arms of his pale blue uniform that he wants a car to drive to Brandenburg for the weekend; he doesn't care about the rate and he doesn't want any deals. "Whatever's quickest."

The young man's eyes dart once over Joachim's face, maybe so he can describe it to a forensic artist later.

"I want to surprise my wife by picking her up from work," Joachim says, and the clerk nods, grateful for the explanation.

Fifteen minutes, a half-dozen signatures, and a swipe of his bank card later, Joachim is in a small Opel, speeding when traffic permits, and cursing when it doesn't. He has his phone in his pocket and his nerves strain for the slightest vibration, Helena calling to ask where he is.

Only when he's parked a few blocks from his apartment and gotten out does he realize how sure he's been, all along, that if he isn't fast enough, she'll be gone by the time he gets back.

He takes the stairs two at a time, but as he opens the door to the apartment, he feels a strange calm: either she'll be there, or she won't. For this one moment, everything is out of his hands.

She's on the sofa, her right leg propped up on the arm. She's wearing a sweater and dress pants and looks poised, somehow too poised for someone lying down to read a book. And there's too much color in her face. Her hairline is damp, either from sweat or from washing it off. He can distinctly smell her deodorant and the warm, sweet scent of her perfume, the heat of her body dissipating it throughout the room.

But he's covered in sweat himself. Maybe she's excited about their weekend away together, or dreading the therapeutic talks they can't keep putting off forever.

"How was work?" she asks, slipping a bookmark in to hold her place, and setting the book on the table. There's a backpack at her feet and he realizes he hasn't packed.

"Oh, nothing special." He's unable to recall a single moment of his day before now, as if his wife's condition were catching.

His wife. Well, the weekend will decide that. Funny how casually they come, the moments that decide your whole future. A couple hundred kilometers on the road, a hundred words or so, and that's it: all you have, and all you'll ever have.

He wants to cancel this trip now, abandon the rental car, unpack her things. "How about you?" he asks. "Did you get a lot done?"

"Not really. I went to the office for half a day, but of course I had to spend half of *that* time telling everybody what it's like to get hit by a truck."

He can't speak. All his organs are crawling up his throat, eager to abandon this sinking ship like so many rats. There's probably something he should say but they're choking him.

"Oh, I saw you hadn't packed," she adds. "So I threw a couple things into the backpack for you. You don't need your razor just for the weekend, do you?"

He shakes his head and, with great effort, manages to swallow his heart and lungs again. "Thanks. I'll just change my shirt and we can head out." His throat feels raw, like he accidentally inhaled underwater and came up spluttering.

He changes into a clean t-shirt and sweater, and tosses his damp shirt, stinking of anxiety, into the washing machine. In the bathroom, he splashes cold water on his face and drinks it out of his cupped hands. There's no need to panic. She went to the office but she can't have found anything out or she would've said something. Or not come back here in the first place. Maybe she just spent the whole day listening to people she didn't recognize tell her to get well soon and that they'd missed her. With any luck, she didn't even mention him, didn't say *my husband* and hear them all ask, *What husband?* She must've managed to slip away from all that concern in her own wary, retiring way, and simply work for a few hours.

It's the only real possibility, the only explanation for her peaceable silence. And she packed his things. Packed them into a bag with her things, mixed together, difficult to separate. She wants to go on this trip. If he tries hard enough, he can, too.

He dries his face, sprays on some aftershave and stretches his mouth into something like a smile. When he comes out, she's wearing a light jacket and a scarf, and is lacing up her sneakers.

"By the way," she says. "They finally switched the Internet back on, so I looked up the best way to the Autobahn from here."

"The Internet?" That sucker-punch feeling again, and he was already winded.

"Yeah, you know, that magical thing you can use to look up information on a little box?" She laughs. "You must've unplugged the modem while the service was cut off and never plugged it back in. I plugged it in and voila! We can take Bornholmer up through Wedding and we're practically at the exit."

"Thanks," he says, maybe a little later than appropriate. "I guess we can head out then. I can always use the GPS on my phone once we get going."

She laughs again, but this time it sounds harsh, almost violent, against the dull, dizzying shudder of his heartbeat.

"What do we need a GPS for? You can't find out how to get somewhere unless you know where you're going."

His forced laugh burns his throat but also clears it out, like a shot of something strong. "Sure," he says. "Good point."

He picks up the backpack and follows her out. Before he locks the door, he pokes his head in for a moment, feeling like he's looking at something for the last time.

HELENA

On the Autobahn, a sudden freedom fills the car. They roll down the windows and turn the radio up loud, the latest pop songs neither of them knows. Helena puts down her sunshade to dim the intense light of the sinking sun. They're heading south because that exit came first. It doesn't matter anyway. At this time of year, nowhere within an hour or two of Berlin will be particularly warm.

They joke about the unappealing names of the places they pass and the dull-sounding roadside attractions: a historical sawmill, a mining exhibit, a museum of woven handicrafts. But after a while, the joke gets a little old, and Helena begins to wonder where they *are* going to stop.

"And ideas yet?" she asks.

"What?"

She turns down the music and asks again, louder, because the windows are still open, the air screeching in to drown them out. She begins to feel cold and puts hers up.

"To be honest, I don't really know Brandenburg," he says. "It's so close but I guess I haven't seen much of it."

"I guess we never went away for the weekend," she says. It's the kind of thing you're not supposed to say in a fight: always this, never that. But it doesn't matter now. After all this effort to hold onto her, is he really going to dump her because she criticized his vacation plans? And then a sinking feeling of guilt: It isn't fair to keep leading him on, making him think it's all going according to plan, winning her over, when really . . . *But that's what he gets for lying to me in the first place,* she reminds herself. *Why should I be honest when he isn't?*

"We never used to," he corrects her.

After an hour or so, they stop at a gas station so she can use the bathroom. Dusk is eating away at the edges of the sky like age at the corners of an old photograph. She's ravenously hungry but he doesn't want to stop for dinner until they've arrived. Wherever that's going to be. The only reason it doesn't turn into a fight is because she can't be bothered. Instead, she demonstratively buys a pack of stale trail mix and eats it in the parked car while he does some belated research on his smartphone.

"Why don't you ask the guy in the shop if he knows somewhere?" she asks. "He probably lives around here."

"No, I think I've found something. The 3G's just so slow."

It *would* be like this. They never went out anywhere unless she planned it. Even if he wanted to take her out to dinner, even if it was a special occasion, he never gave any thought to where they should eat. And the few trips they did go on were spoiled for her because of his complete unwillingness to get involved in the planning. Well, except for that vacation in Mauritius, but that had been at the beginning, a misleading exception. He always left everything to the last minute and figured things would work themselves out, when really all that ever happened was that *she* worked everything out.

And now, for once, she let him have his way and be "spontaneous" about things. Which is why she's spending her Friday night choking down mealy peanuts in a dark parking lot in the middle of nowhere. You forget the old fights when you're not together anymore, and you wonder afterward what used to bother you so much. But the fights are still there, waiting to be resumed the moment you get involved again. Which is why you don't. Or shouldn't. She feels a heavy, indigestible certainty in the pit of her stomach that she made the wrong decision. What if she'd stayed in Berlin and seen Tobias again? But even seeing him would've been about Joachim.

"How about Rosenteich?"

Startled, she spills an assortment of raisins, nuts, and unidentifiable shriveled objects onto her lap. She gathers them together, opens the door and throws them on the ground.

"Maybe they'll still have some roses in season, right?" he says in a put-on, cajoling tone that embarrasses her.

"Where's that?"

"South of Cottbus."

"Cottbus?" Her only association with the place is as a grim region of empty concrete socialist buildings and emptier streets she once passed through after Reunification. But countryside's countryside, and they'll have to sleep somewhere tonight.

"Sure," she says. "Sounds great." It's not always possible to keep all the sarcasm out of your voice, or to be sorry about it.

JOACHIM

It takes them another forty-five minutes to find Rosenteich, but it feels three times as long. Helena's snippy and unpleasant, and it's impossible to talk about anything without her disdain for the whole enterprise showing through. She's always cranky when she's hungry, he recalls, and tries to make that an excuse for everything. But the specter of a weekend spent fawning and dodging her criticism in some East German ghost town rises up and haunts him for the rest of the drive.

When they finally arrive in Rosenteich, which supposedly borders several swimming lakes and a forest with extensive hiking trails, it's even smaller than he imagined: a main street with a gas station, a combined butcher and bakery, a discount grocer, an eerie-looking hotel—some of the letters in its neon sign brighter than the others—a bank with cracked glass where someone must've thrown rocks, and then private farm lots, increasing in size as the road deteriorates into a thin dirt path and he turns the car around. No streetlights, no sidewalks. But at least there's a hotel.

She hasn't spoken since they arrived, but then what should she say? It's too dark to make out much and what they can see is hardly worth the mention.

"Maybe we can get dinner here, too," he says, pulling into the nearly empty parking lot of the massive concrete hotel. A few lights closer to the entrance reveal that it's painted a sickly shade of yellow.

"I'm sure they have a restaurant," she says. "There's nothing else around."

"Is this okay?" he asks, opening the rear door to get the backpack.

"It's perfect. Right in the heart of things."

But at least they're laughing together now.

JOACHIM

The restaurant manages to seem at once makeshift and insti-
tutional: a few plastic tables and chairs in a large room, rem-
iniscent of a hospital cafeteria, with no menus and no other
customers. But then, it's a little late. None of the colors in the
room matches: the teal, neon yellow, and red geometric pattern
on the threadbare carpet, the dingy cream-colored tablecloths,
the heavy maroon drapes over the window through which
they could otherwise see the parking lot, and the optimistic
sky blue walls speckled with out-of-date ads for activities in
the region. They take a table close to the windows and are just
on the point of leaving when a sturdily built young blonde in
what must be traditional local dress stomps over to their table
and hands them two greasy laminated menus.

"Good evening!" She sounds like a child imitating some
particularly foolish phrase used by adults.

Helena orders a beer without looking at the menu, and
Joachim says he'll have one, too. In the girl's relatively long
absence, they look over the menu—adorned with grotesquely
pigmented photos that look like they were taken in the 1970s—
with its uninspired fare of schnitzel, pork knuckles, and baked
pasta.

"Well, we made it," he says, reaching across the table to
touch her hand. It's strange to think there would've been a
cast in the way not long before. That's how quickly things
happen—getting hit by a car, getting left by your wife, getting

a cast removed—any of those things can happen in just a day. It seems to him now that he didn't do enough with the time allotted to him, that he could've lived out the last weeks with Helena differently, better, in a way that would make him sure of himself now. Sure of them. Life is full of missed opportunities, but what a chance to have wasted.

"I wouldn't want this to be any different," she says with a mischievous dimple in one cheek, but he can tell that, in a way, she means it. It's not too late, not yet. After all, the great opportunity of all this was even seeing Helena, speaking to her, knowing where she was again. It's not over as long as she's here with him.

• • •

The only person at the reception desk is a balding man with a forehead like a boulder about to start an avalanche and a dingy mustache that's neither brown nor gray, but rather like something whose real color is hidden under an impenetrable layer of dirt. He tries to sound surprised that they don't have a reservation.

"Just walking in on a Friday night!"

"But surely you have a room available," Joachim says. "It's off-season and your parking lot is empty."

"Be that as it may . . ." the man says balefully, but doesn't continue.

Joachim feels an irrational fury he can barely contain, and he's relieved when Helena goes to sit on one of the dusty plush seats lining the otherwise bare walls of the entryway.

"Look," says Joachim, grinning in a way he fears might be more frightening than friendly, "We were hoping to stay here for the weekend. Your hotel was recommended to me by a friend, but if you don't have any rooms . . ."

With a visible effort, the old man returns Joachim's grimace of a smile. "We do have a room or two," he admits. "It's just that we don't generally allow check-ins after six."

Joachim looks over his shoulder. Helena is resting her head against the wall. He can't tell whether she's angry or just tired.

"I understand," he tells the man. "And I'd certainly be ready to pay extra for the inconvenience."

Although this is the moment the old man must've been waiting for, greasing the wheels of the transaction costs just twenty euros. Perhaps he's afraid Joachim will leave if he asks for more.

"What type of room would you like, Sir?"

"The nicest you've got."

That turns out to be a chilly but rather large room with a queen bed, a bathroom—which the mustached man emphasizes several times—an ancient TV set and a poorly done painting of the night sky on the ceiling, which has a small additional light in case guests want to leave the stars on overnight. The price, which was probably jacked up especially for Joachim, is less than that of a decent single room in Berlin, and far less than he would've been willing to pay to get Helena alone here, outside of everything they've already lived, and try to make something new.

"The front desk is now closed until morning," the man tells them, closing the door behind him. He can't hope for another such windfall tonight.

Helena takes off her shoes, switches off the main light and flops down on the bed, looking up at the ceiling. "It's actually quite charming."

Joachim feels the praise fill and warm him, as if he'd decorated the room himself.

"Did you bribe him?" she adds.

"A little."

And then they're laughing, and then they're flipping through the regional stations on the TV, laughing again and making love in a drowsy, end-of-a-long-day way, nothing like the romantic union he imagined for this improvised second honeymoon. Still, he thinks afterward, somewhere between consciousness and sleep, at least we were together, at least we are . . .

He wakes in the middle of the night and gets up to switch off the night sky, which he blames for disturbing his sleep. But afterward in the dark, he's filled with a deep and terrible loneliness, an indefinable anxiety that makes his heart race painfully. He wants more than anything to wake Helena, make her save him from this, keep him from being alone just for a few minutes.

But she'd only be angry, and he doesn't want to start a fight that would keep him up even longer, so he forces himself to lie still, pulsing between smothering heat and bone-chilling cold, watching like a continuous film reel in his mind all the things that could go wrong, and all those that already have.

HELENA

They wake late the next morning, and Helena has the vague, dissatisfied feeling of almost, but not quite remembering her dream. The drive, the arrival at the desolate hotel, and especially her meeting with Ester seem more like a dream than whatever flitted through her subconscious. When she turns to Joachim, she sees that his eyes are already open.

"Hey, you." She leans over to kiss him on the cheek, and the gesture has an echoing hollowness even as she feels the old ache of affection rise up in her. If only there were a way to start over. If only there were a way to be together now that had nothing to do with having been together before.

"Morning, darling."

But that was never what she wanted. Didn't she move and change her number to keep just that from happening? If he knew what was going through her head, he'd say what he always did, that she was overthinking things. That she could never just enjoy the moment without agonizing about the future.

She gets up to open the window. Only when a cool, fresh breeze comes in does she realize how oppressive the air in the room was, the stale smell of the room itself and the humid warmth of their bodies. Outside, everything is fresh and new. It must've rained overnight. Even the cracked pavement of the parking lot is glittering in the light of day.

That's what they need, too: something to wash away the

past and let the light of a new day shine on them. Maybe she'll say something like that when he finally starts to talk to her. Or she could just say, "Shhh, I know all that. We can forget about it now." And he'll explain why he decided to play this strange little game, and she'll tell him how long she's known. Or they won't mention it; one lie will cancel the other out.

He joins her in the shower, and until they leave their hotel room, they're strangely quiet, like young lovers trying out new things. She switches the ceiling light on and off as they step out, but it hardly shows up against the brilliant light of noon.

JOACHIM

The hotel restaurant isn't serving breakfast so they stop in the bakery for lattes, croissants, and bottles of water to take with them. The pervasive smell of meat from the other side of the shop overwhelms any scent of baked goods or coffee until they get outside. Joachim shows Helena the two dots on the screen of his phone indicating how close they are to the nearest lake, but he can tell she's not really paying attention.

"Do you feel up for the walk?" he asks.

"If we go slowly."

By the time they finish their breakfast, they're on the dirt end of the road, passing farmhouses that look far more ramshackle by daylight, large but largely patched together from scrap metal and wooden boards. A couple of them look abandoned. They turn off to the left down an even narrower dirt path interspersed with clumps of horse shit. He keeps finding himself a few steps ahead of her and having to stop. She moves with steady caution, like someone looking for footholds in the face of a cliff.

He feels that it would be wrong to speak to her now, to break that concentration. But the pressure of silence begins to suffocate him. He doesn't know what to say, only that he needs to say something. There aren't even many birds out, and the only consistent noise is the distant drone of the highway, something like the sea before you're close enough to make out the crash of each individual wave. The forest looms ahead of them a long time without seeming to get closer, and then, abruptly, they're in it, with half the light and double the silence. The threadbare canopy over their heads is a patchwork of dry conifers and half-changed leaves, sometimes red, yellow and green on the same tree.

Either the lake is farther away than it looked on the map, or he underestimated how slowly they would move. Their gradual progress down the dirt path seems eternal, the way they came now covered over by trees, identical to the way they're headed. At the same time, this could be the very safety he's needed, an eternal moment, a path that never ends in either direction, the beginning and end the same. His heart aches with the knowledge of it.

"Helena," he says.

She looks at him with a startled, wild-animal look, then covers it over with a smile.

"I love you," he says. "I love you so much."

And she watches with large, blank eyes and says nothing, maybe because she wants to know why he's telling her this now, or maybe because she doesn't love him anymore, doesn't have anything to say in return.

"When we were together before, we decided to take some time off," he says. His own voice sounds strange, as if he were speaking through some thick physical barrier. "I was involved with another woman during that time. We hadn't talked about whether that was okay, but I guess I thought it was. I wasn't sure you and I were ever going to be together again. I was . . ."

"I understand," she says.

"You do?" He's so sure this mercy must be some kind of trap that he's afraid to feel relieved. In all their years together, in all his apologies, excuses and explanations, there was never a moment like this, when she understood.

She nods and he hurries to continue, before she runs out of understanding or before he's tempted to leave something unsaid.

"She got pregnant and I wasn't really there for her. You and I were back together, so of course I'd stopped seeing her. Then she came and told me and I didn't know what to do. I didn't know how I could help her without somehow betraying you and there was so much pressure. It was all so immediate, I felt like I had no time to decide." Even now he feels his breath quickening, as if the decision had to be made all over again. "It seemed like she wanted to keep the baby so I told her I'd help support it but I was going to stay with you. I didn't tell you. I know I should've but I was too scared and it didn't seem fair. I knew you'd take off if you heard, and that wouldn't have been fair because I'd ended it with her, and I was never with her again once you said you wanted to come back. And then she went and had an abortion and wrote you a letter about all of it, and half of it wasn't true but you never believed me. You believed everything she said and then it was all downhill. There was no fixing things after that. You took another couple months to really leave, but it was over when you read that letter."

"Look," she says, and for a moment he continues to look at her, the expression of childish wonder on her face, but then she points ahead and he sees the lake opening up as the path winds downhill, the reflection of autumn sunlight almost blinding when he looks straight at it. "The lake," she adds extraneously.

They're at the bottom of the hill on the sandy shore before he can summon the courage to speak again, but Helena, peering through the rushes, interrupts him to point out a brave group of swimmers paddling at the opposite end.

"How can they!" she says. "I wouldn't even want to take off my clothes at this temperature, let alone get in that water!"

He feels a creeping sense of alarm, the way he did in the hospital when she greeted him so familiarly, like they'd seen each other just hours before. Is it possible that she didn't hear, didn't understand, has somehow forgotten what he said? Why doesn't she respond? He looks away from the group of swimmers and back at her, squinting and raising one hand to her eyebrows to block out the sunlight, grinning in a slightly breathless way, like someone rushing into a stiff wind.

"I should've brought sunglasses," she says. "I don't suppose I have any anymore."

"Helena," he says, and grabs one of her shoulders, holding in the urge to shake her until she's really listening.

"Yes, Joachim," she says, "I know."

"You know?"

"Yes, I know all about that girl sending me that ugly letter." And then, dismissing his amazement with a flippant wave of one hand, she says, "Can't we sit down soon? I'm not supposed to be on my feet for this long."

He nods, and even this slight movement wracks him with dizziness. Now he feels that he can barely keep up as she starts to shuffle around the lake, looking for somewhere to sit. "But how?" he finally manages to say.

"Who knows how these things work?" she says. "Maybe I dreamt it. Look, just there, there's a patch of grass that will still have sun on it for a couple hours."

The strange thing is that she doesn't seem to be covering for anything or trying to change the subject. It genuinely must not bother her. Does this mean she knows everything else, or just about the affair? How long has she known and not said anything? It can't have been long; she'd never have been able to hold something like that in without at least checking whether it was true. Unless it was so obviously true, such a clear, plausible memory, that there was no need for her to check. Unless she knew it for certain from the moment it crossed her mind. But if she knows, if she's still here with him, knowing and having known, doesn't that mean that she's accepted it?

He spreads out his jacket for her to sit on, but she perches on the very edge to make room for him. Still, she didn't say she loved him. She didn't say and he can never ask, could never ask something like that. Better never to know than to make a fool of himself. Besides, he'll find out soon enough. Her very gentleness alienates him. Is this woman really his wife, or simply a stranger? His Helena never had any sense of proportion, would never have been capable of weighing his mistake in light of their whole relationship, and deciding it wasn't worth ending things over. For his Helena, every discussion was the be-all and end-all, every fight an Armageddon they had only the slimmest chances of surviving. And his Helena always wanted to talk about everything, except the one time they most needed to talk. Who is this woman next to him, resting her hand on his knee and smiling at the glittering surface of this all but abandoned lake?

When he stares out at the water, everything around it seems to move and flicker, as if the water itself were still, and the sky, the mottled color of the trees, its rippled reflection. He wants to relax, close his eyes and enjoy this moment with Helena, her presence beside him warm as the autumn sun on his face, but he can't. Some creature inside of him is crouched with its hackles up, waiting for a sign of danger. He can't soothe it or coax it to sleep. If only she'd say something.

They should be able to be silent together. They've known each other long enough, intimately enough, for that. But instead of feeling that he doesn't need to say anything aloud, he feels that he can't. Does she feel the same way? Is she also desperate for him to break this silence, smash through it like the hard surface of the water cut by a swimmer's strokes? She isn't saying anything either, but he feels like it's his fault, either because he started a discussion he doesn't know how to finish, or because the discussion's already over and he has nothing more to say.

If this were a first date, it would be going badly. She'd think later, and maybe he would, that they had nothing in common, nothing to say to each other. And yet there's so much going on inside him now; he's brimming over with things he wants to communicate to her. It's only the words that are missing. How clumsy human interaction is, how we get in the way of ourselves, trying to speak with our mouths underwater, or make eye contact through a blindfold. Putting our hands to opposite sides of a wall, guessing where the other person stands, not even knowing if our fingers are aligned, if, the barrier having fallen, we would even be touching.

"Do you remember our first date?" he asks, just to say something. Once they start talking, no matter what about, they'll be light years closer to an honest discussion.

"Of course," she says too quickly, and he remembers what a sensitive subject remembering has become.

"I didn't mean—"

"I remember it perfectly. We got drenched."

He laughs. He'd just graduated and had only been in Berlin a few months when he asked the pretty intern at the office where he was freelancing for a date. He didn't know anywhere to take her. It was June and he figured something outdoors was a safe bet so he packed a picnic and asked Helena to meet him near Tiergarten, the only park he knew at that point.

It was cool and overcast when he left his house, drizzling by the time he met up with her; he was late and she was early.

He stopped and bought an overpriced umbrella in one of the tourist shops lining Unter den Linden and opened it over both of them. It had a picture of the red East German Ampelmann on one side, spreading out his arms to stop pedestrians from crossing, and on the other side the green Ampelmann, strolling confidently ahead in his fedora.

"You can't be serious," Helena said when he told her his plan. But she came along anyway, and by the time it started pouring, they were too deep in the park to seek shelter, and soaked to the skin so quickly it wouldn't have been worth it.

"Wow," she said. "This'll be a date to remember."

He would've been mortally embarrassed, but there was too much water pouring down his face to do anything but laugh and try not to swallow too much of it. When they finally found their way out of the park, they were at Potsdamer Platz, where they stopped in the Arkaden to buy two beach towels, and then stumbled into the Cinemaxx to see the next showing of a forgettable romantic comedy and discreetly eat the damp picnic lunch he'd packed. When they came out of the theater, the sky was a brilliant blue without a trace of white, and the sun was strong enough to start drying up the puddles on the sidewalk, though not their clothes.

After an experience like that, the only possibilities were for her never to speak to him again, or for them to become very close, very quickly. He worked from home for a few days in case she didn't want to see him, but when he got up the courage to call the following Thursday, she demanded,

"Where have you been?" and immediately accepted his offer of a second date, "indoors this time."

"Well, it's your own fault for not talking me out of it," he says now, watching the last of the swimmers exit the lake and disappear behind a large towel.

"I don't know what I was thinking."

"Helena," he says again, and she looks at him without saying anything, her mouth a thin flat line, a blank she won't fill in. He wants to ask: *How can it all have been for nothing, laughing with the water running down our faces and mud up to our knees, and all that came after? How could that ever just end?* But instead he says, "I guess it's a good thing you're starting to remember more."

"Yes," she says, "I guess it is."

There's something wrong here. Of course it's a good thing. Even if he has his reasons for not being unreservedly thrilled that she's getting better, at least she should be happier about it. But maybe it's because the things she's starting to remember are ones she'd rather not know. Or not that she doesn't want to know about them, just that she'd rather they hadn't happened.

Telling her about Ester wasn't the big epiphany he was hoping for. For one thing, of course, she already knew. For another, she didn't seem to care. And it's a lot harder to give excuses and explanations if nobody's accusing you of anything. What good are all the things he's been meaning to say now?

At the very least, he thought it would be more difficult, that she'd cry and maybe he would, too. At least then she would've seen how hard it was for him to open up about it. She might've thanked him for his honesty. But what good was honesty when she already knew? He didn't know that she knew. That has to count for something, that he was the one to bring it up. More than anything, what's missing is the relief he expected. He was going to feel better about everything; there was going to be a weight off his shoulders. But there's still a burden weighing him down.

"There's something else I've been meaning to say."

She doesn't look up. Only by following her gaze does he

notice that the light's gone off the water, that the surface is darker now, gentler on the eyes.

"We separated again after you found out about that other woman. For . . ." Somehow, it would be indecent to name a number. He'll admit it if she asks, but he needs to cling to this last shred of mystery now. "For quite a long time," he says.

"Okay," she says. Instead of asking the obvious questions, she lies back and rests her head on the ground, closes her eyes.

He waits a moment. "Do you want to talk about it?"

She takes so long to answer that he begins to wonder whether she's fallen asleep. Just as he's about to ask again, she says, "Joachim, I'm tired, I'm hungry, and it's getting cold. What I most want now is to go in somewhere and get something to eat."

"Are you too tired to walk back? I can run and get the car. We'll go get something to eat outside of Rosenteich. You know it's not far to the Spreewald from here. We could take one of those gondola rides like you always wanted." To his horror, he realizes even as he's speaking that it was not Helena, but Leila who always wanted to go to the Spreewald and take a boat ride down the meandering river.

If Helena notices, she doesn't say. Maybe she did always want to go there. There were so many places they never made it to. "Don't be ridiculous," she says without opening her eyes. "You'll take ages. I might as well come."

"No, no, I'll be faster on my own and I'll park at the edge of the woods. You can start back the way we came and I'll meet you halfway. You have your phone, right?" The last thing he needs is Helena lost in the woods, him having to call some kind of park rangers to search for her.

"Yeah," she says. "Of course."

"I'll be quick." Her forehead feels cool against his lips, and she doesn't move.

• • •

Just a few steps up the dirt path, Joachim feels miles away from Helena. He looks back after a minute or two, but because the path goes uphill, all he can see is a small patch of the lake through the trees, nothing of where he and Helena were sitting. A few more steps and even the dull glow of water has disappeared.

A cool, insidious breeze is blowing, one that sneaks into all the openings in his clothing, up his sleeves and down the collar of his jacket, spreading over his skin in a chilling embrace. She isn't dressed warm enough for the weather, and he hurries ahead, eager to finish this task, be on his way back to her instead of away from her.

He passes no one on the path, and his steps are obscenely loud in the eerie stillness interrupted only rarely by the grave, harsh call of a raven or hooded crow. It's still hours until sundown, but in a way, the sun has already left the sky, the brilliant warmth skimmed out of it, leaving only a wan, milky light, devoid of color.

And she didn't want to talk about any of the things he told her. He can't make sense of it, can't even really think about it. All his questions about her mood, her state of mind, are outweighed by a creeping primordial dread. He has to get out of this forest, has to look up at a sky free from the sharp dark spears of these pines, the mottled clawing branches of these ashes and alders. He was sure it would go quickly without Helena to slow him down, but with no change in the view ahead of him or behind him, he begins to wonder whether he's moving at all.

He runs up the path to be sure he's really getting somewhere, then stops to catch his breath. His own breathing sounds guttural, animal. And then he closes his mouth, breathes through his nose, and realizes that the growling sound isn't coming from him.

The sudden, foreboding noise seems inevitable now, the ultimate conclusion and vindication of his growing sense of dread. The most primitive part of his mind looks around for weapons while the possibilities flash through it—a wild boar? A wolf that wandered over the border? A vicious dog?

Even as the growl becomes a roar, he can't see any movement to the right or left, behind or ahead of him. When he finally looks up, the fear of an instant before is still too real, too present, for him to laugh it at. But as he watches the slow, graceful ascent of a hot air balloon over the tops of the trees, its billowing sides a rainbow of colors far beyond the canopy of autumn leaves, he finally starts to breathe again.

The progress of the balloon is impossibly slow, or maybe time has slowed down for him to watch it emerge from the trees like a radiant butterfly from its dull chrysalis. The roaring is a steady drone that fills the whole forest as, for him, the balloon fills the whole sky. It must be half a kilometer away to launch without getting caught on the trees, but its presence is so bright, so immediate, that he can see nothing else.

He watches for a long, long time as the balloon rises and shrinks almost imperceptibly from his whole field of vision to what could simply be a helium balloon whose string slipped out of a child's fingers.

Still, even when nothing remains but a speck in the sky he isn't quite sure he sees, still he waits. Will the miracle repeat itself? Is there some kind of hot air balloon station over there beyond the trees? It can't be that someone just keeps one in his backyard.

Some time after the balloon disappears, he walks on, unable to escape a sinking feeling that only at that exact spot could he see a balloon rise, that by taking even one step forward, he's missing something extraordinary and terribly important, something he'll never have the chance to see again.

The forest around him no longer feels empty; rather, it seems to continually shiver with anticipation, to be filled with rising and falling murmurs of excitement. But even as the long-awaited exit to the street emerges ahead of him, he's filled with a terrible loneliness. Helena should've been there, should've seen that with him. She won't understand, if he tells her later, how it felt to be torn out of the silence by that growing roar, to feel the depths of animal fear rise and suddenly give way to awe. She won't know how brilliant the colors were, how they took over the whole sky, drained the life from its pale blue. It will only become an anecdote, a minor incident on a long walk. The ache of it fills him, and he feels that his whole body is only a thin strip of fabric over it, stretched taut by the dry, hot blast of isolation burning and expanding within him.

At the edge of the street, he crosses his arms over his stomach and breathes deeply, trying to hold it in.

• • •

By the time he's pulled over by the edge of the forest and left the car, even the ache of his loneliness is only a memory, as incidental as the experience that caused it. But the sense of separation, of having moved that much further from Helena, remains.

He hasn't gotten far when he sees her ahead of him on the path. He calls her name and she raises a hand in greeting. She's still too far away for him to make out the look on her face. He breaks into a run.

"Well, somebody's got a lot of energy," she says when he reaches her. "It's all I can do to drag myself along."

"Do you need help?"

"What are you gonna do, put me in a wheelbarrow?" Her laugh is harsh, mocking his concern. Or maybe his helplessness, his inability to really do anything for her. He feels anger rise up in him, but her expression is so vague he can't even focus his resentment on her. She's not really thinking of him, at least not as a presence at her side, right now, on this path.

"You'll never guess what I saw," he says as the car comes into view. Because you can feel anger, you can resent somebody, anytime. He doesn't have to hold on to the feeling now.

But she does guess. "That hot air balloon? I saw it from the water. Must've been pretty close."

"It felt like it was right next to me. When I first heard the sound, I thought it was some kind of animal." He tells her and keeps telling her about it, recalling trivial details, expanding on his physical and mental sensations in those few instants, but the more he says, the less he feels he's really sharing the experience with her. It would've been better to say nothing at all, simply to know that they'd seen the same sight from different angles, and let her ability to guess what he was about to say pass for real intimacy.

"Do you want to stop back at the hotel?" he asks.

"I've got everything I need. How far is it to the Spreewald?"

The question startles him. In the short space between his misguided suggestion and this moment, he managed to forget that she agreed to it. So there's that to get them through the rest of the day, or for them to get through.

"What's the matter?" she asks as he starts the car and pulls back onto the pockmarked dirt lane.

It feels strange to hear her ask that. She was always the one receding into herself, waiting to be pried back out of the shell that clamped down after every slight, even the imagined ones. Or wanting to be left in it. And he was always the one to ask what the matter was, and never really get an answer—at best "nothing." What answer can he give her now? There are things you can't put into words, subtle things you never catch sight of, currents moving through the air or slight tremors in the ground beneath your feet. He understands her better than ever, but has never felt less understood by her. It feels like being inside her skin, behind her inscrutable dissatisfaction. But is she inside of him, or is he just lying there somewhere, empty and discarded?

"Nothing," he says. "I guess I'm just hungry."

• • •

Not long after getting on the Autobahn, they stop at a gas station for sandwiches and coffee from a dispenser. Helena said she couldn't wait. They eat in the parked car, silent, not hostile, but not quite together. Joachim finishes first and opens the GPS on his phone.

"Should we aim for Lübben or Lübbenau?"

"To be honest, I have no idea."

He's grateful to her for not mentioning that she never wanted to go to the Spreewald, not asking him where he got the idea. If he had to, he could always pretend that she simply forgot about it, but lying to her about such a trivial thing would set back all he struggled to do this morning.

That thought reminds him that they didn't really talk about any of it, not enough to give her a clear idea of the events, or him a clear idea of how much she really remembers.

It's never the right moment to bring up a subject neither of you wants to talk about, and he grins at her as she reaches to turn up the radio. They sing along with the trite chorus of a song they heard three times on the way from Berlin, mumbling through the parts they don't know, catching each other doing it, laughing again. He feels a complicity with her that's the closest they've been in days.

Helena

Helena wants them to park the car as soon as they get to Lübbenau, but Joachim insists on following the small streets to find a space closer to the water.

"You've strained your leg enough as it is," he says.

Some perverse impulse makes her say, "I'll be the judge of that," but she hurries to add, "Thanks for looking out for me, though," as if she could simply paint over her previous remark.

He parks the car outside of a chain supermarket up the road from the little marina. As they get closer to the water, almost every house they pass has a sign advertising rooms to let. She wants to make a joke about how they could've come here in the first place, but she knows he'll be offended instead of laughing. And maybe it wouldn't quite be a joke. As far as she knows, she's never in her life planned on visiting the Spreewald, let alone told him about it, but if he's so sure this was her dream getaway, he could've planned it from the get-go. It's hard to say things like that aloud, hard to convey the particular mix of fondness and frustration you feel.

Behind the marina, there are a few old railcars from the former Spreewald Express that used to run back when the region was glamorous enough to have its own tourist train. Or before everybody had a car.

"I wish we'd come in this," he says, knocking on the metal side. A tour guide in a historical conductor uniform glares at him over his cigarette.

"Yeah," she says. "That would've been the way to do it." It's as close as she can get to saying what she means. It's okay to tell him he didn't do this trip right if doing it right would've required time travel. And maybe, after all, it would have. Not back to the glory days of the Spreewald Express, but early enough in their own relationship for it to have made a difference. A romantic getaway rather than an apology for never taking her on one.

The marina is lined with wooden booths selling a variety of products neither of them has any interest in buying: a thousand kinds of pickles, cucumber schnapps and liqueurs, bottles of linseed oil in all shapes and sizes, pickle key chains and stuffed toys. Postcards of sights they haven't been to see.

Joachim stops for a long time at each booth, maybe trying to drag this out, make it seem like more of an event. There aren't very many customers and he shouldn't get the sales-people's hopes up. But maybe he wants to get her a present. Surprise her with it later. It would play into the whole setup he seems to have in mind. Not that there's anything here that would be remotely appealing as a gift from your husband, but it's the thought that counts. She goes back to look at the postcards, and then to use the public toilets at the other end of the paved square behind the marina. On her way back, she passes slowly by the row of larger souvenir stores and the ice cream shop, where a family in brightly colored windbreakers is clutching ice cream cones and squinting optimistically at the patchwork of clouds overhead. If he wanted to surprise her, he's had the time.

And that's true in more ways than one. Birthdays, anniversaries, Valentine's Day . . . At most, he did the bare minimum: a last-minute bouquet of flowers, a gift grabbed without time for consideration on the way home from work, dinner out somewhere. She knew women whose boyfriends and husbands wouldn't celebrate those occasions on principle, and she was grateful to him for his sense of duty. But it was never quite what she wanted. Expensive jewelry that wasn't really her style, when she'd rather have had something cheap but personal. The flowers that would've meant more if they'd come when she was having a rough week at work, or just because, for no reason at all, to surprise her. And all the outings she had to plan herself, leaving no room for surprise.

She sees him at the far end of the little market and waves, but stays where she is, facing the river. Two men deposit the last two elderly tourists on a crowded dark brown gondola, one of them unties the ropes mooring it in place, and the gondolier plunges his long pole into the water.

The people on the gondola wave to the people in the marina as the boat moves away, and the people in the marina wave back. Helena joins them halfheartedly, feeling like the interceptor of a greeting meant for someone else. A few mossy paddleboats splash out after the gondola, and then there's a lull. Nobody in the marina really seems to be doing anything; they're not shopping at the stalls or in the stores, not eating or drinking or waiting for the next boat, but simply standing or sitting around on the broad steps going down to the water. It's not even warm or bright enough for them to be sunning themselves. And yet everyone seems to be having a good time. Maybe it's just that she's the only one standing here all by herself.

"Hey!" Joachim claps her on the shoulder. "Why don't we see about tickets?"

There's a line at the little ticket booth that doesn't seem to be moving, and the young couple—are they teenagers or already a little older?—ahead of Helena and Joachim is arguing fiercely, the girl in an over-annunciated don't-care-who-hears-me tone, and the boy in a pleading, embarrassed whisper. Helena gathers that the girl wants to take the longest, most expensive boat tour since they came all this way, but the boy wants them to just rent paddleboats, since he paid for a room at the pension and doesn't have much money left.

"Please, darling, you're embarrassing me," the boy says, and the authoritative way he says "darling," makes Helena decide that they're a little older, maybe twenty or twenty-one, away for their first vacation without parents or friends.

"*You're* embarrassed?!" the girl hisses. "How do you think *I* feel?"

The line inches forward. Now there's just one group of well-tanned retirees ahead of the young couple.

"*I'll* pay for it," the girl insists, but the boy doesn't want that, either. Apparently the vacation is a gift for her that he can't quite afford.

Helena wants to interrupt them, to tell them it's not that important, that they should just do one or the other and forget about it; there will always be enough fights to have. She's so intent on the outcome of the argument that she forgets Joachim is standing next to her until he steps forward, claps the boy on the shoulder and hands him a fifty.

"This is for shutting the hell up," he says.

The two young people look at each other, openmouthed, and then at Helena for an explanation. She looks away and pretends not to be involved. They can't seem to decide whether to be grateful or offended, but finally the boy says, "Thank you, Sir," and closes his hand over the bill.

Helena follows Joachim out of the line and back to the row of shops.

"I'm sorry," he says.

"What for?"

"Embarrassing you like that."

"I wasn't embarrassed," she lies. She wants to be the right person for him right now, the person who would appreciate and understand the full meaning of his gesture, and not see it as a show-offish impulse.

"Should we get an ice cream?" he asks. "I don't think they'd feel comfortable with us on the same boat."

"Sure." It's cool and the tip of her nose already feels damp, but if he wants an ice cream, who's she to rain on his parade? She'd feel better if she actually wanted it. Not just the cone but the whole package. There's something going on in his head right now that's miles away from where she is, and the funny thing is, he seems to think it's about her. About them. So why does she feel like she's watching somebody else's romantic moments from outside? No, she'd be more comfortable if that little were expected of her. It's more like playing the romantic lead without knowing any of the lines. And he doesn't even seem to be acting.

Her feet feel chilled in her shoes once they're out of the sunlight, waiting in front of the refrigerated counter of the ice cream shop. The older woman behind it is impatient, as if there were a line out the door behind them. Or any line at all. She must be afraid that, if they think about it too long, they'll change their minds.

Joachim orders a scoop of vanilla and joins the saleswoman in watching Helena.

"I'll just have a coffee," she starts to say, but she can already see a twitch of disappointment at the corner of Joachim's mouth. Guess he's already got a pretty clear idea of how this scene should look, the two of them with their ice cream cones. If only it felt less scripted. "A scoop of coffee ice cream," she corrects herself.

"Mocha?" the saleswoman asks.

"Yes." Like it matters what she orders now. She gets what's going on here. How often has she been in his place, been the one to plan out every detail of a perfect day and be disappointed when he didn't go along with it? Without ever having said a word about it. Not that you could say anything without ruining it. You needed your partner to know without being told.

He pays and they walk back to the waterfront. So this is what he wants, the two of them licking ice cream cones in the late afternoon sunlight, his arm around her waist. There's nothing wrong with that. But the very insistence with which she tells herself that means there must be.

She's relieved when they board the next gondola, Joachim helping her into the back row long before the rest of the boat fills up. This is what she needs now: nothing to do, nothing expected of her, just sitting down and letting herself be carried away.

Most of the passengers making their way onto the boat are couples, mostly older, then one family with three small children at the front, a group of twenty-somethings in the middle. Almost everyone has the same accent and is probably from a fifty-kilometer radius of this boat. It's the end of the season and the end of the day. The end of a lot of things.

A man makes his way down the narrow side of the boat offering drinks and candy. Joachim buys two beers and hands her one. She's starting to feel time again, not just the fact of the past years, but time as a physical quantity piled up between here and there. She can tell because she's starting to notice when he pays for her, to know how much time passed without anyone treating her to anything, without any of those little gestures that signal "this is a date" or "we're a couple."

She wonders whether Tobias paid when they first met. She can't remember, and of course, she couldn't ask. But he did pay for their drinks at the bar.

The thought of Tobias is an uncomfortable one she's managed more or less to avoid until now. She holds her breath a moment, until the gondolier pushes the boat away from the dock, happy in the brief illusion that she can move away from this unwanted thought as easily.

Just past the marina, the shore on either side of them loses all resemblance to a town, alternating between forest undergrowth and pastures. The scampering speckles of sunlight on the silent, green-black water have the excruciating beauty of something you don't have time to take in fully, like the sudden, full-throated rise of a flock of startled birds.

The gondolier tells them about local cottage industries, the route they're traveling, and the Sorbian culture that was prevalent here before the Third Reich. Like any good tour guide, he peppers his informational program with bad jokes and teasing remarks to members of his audience. When he notices Joachim holding Helena's hand, he begins to refer to them as "The Honeymooners" and makes it a trope of his speech that the two are too smitten to listen to his remarks. Occasionally, one of the old women sasses him back and everyone laughs along when he addresses her as "young lady." They stop at a few makeshift stands along the river selling spiced pickles, horseradish, and obscure liqueurs and sweets from the GDR.

Helena's smile is painful, and she feels her hand sweating into Joachim's despite the cool air. She isn't one of these

uncomplicated people with their jokes and their straightfor-
ward relationships. Joachim might be, but she isn't. She's the
only one on board faking it.

But maybe she is just overthinking it. Maybe she can turn
all that off, just rest her head on his shoulder and watch the
million shades of green, gold, red, and black moving by, the
sky wanly shifting toward sunset, and not think about all the
things she can't say to him, or hasn't.

It works for a few seconds, and then for a few minutes.
And then not at all. It's nice to be here with him, to drift so
smoothly and quietly down this water, waving when they pass
another boat, listening to his pulse through his collarbone,
flattered by his attention and pleasantly surprised not to be
alone. And she's attracted to him—not wildly, but enough. If
she met him at a party now, if they had no history whatsoever
and he gave her his number, she'd call.

But the fact is, they do have a history, and even if she manages to forget that and enjoy this moment for what it is—a
meaningless disjointed episode, outside of time—he can't. It
means too much to him.

The sun is all but below the horizon when they dock again,
and the little market stalls have closed down. Joachim stops
her and kisses her at the edge of the water, but no one teases
them now, no one claps or makes a joke. This is real, or it's
supposed to be.

Something is lost with the onset of darkness, and even
he seems to feel it. This was the last and only full day of their
vacation, and now it's dark; now it's practically night, just
the void between today and tomorrow. He wants to get the
car before dinner, but she insists that they look around on
foot. She feels her right leg trembling with each step, a mass
of shapeless flesh.

They stop at the first likely place, a half-lit, half-empty
barnlike room, where they eat potatoes with linseed oil and
a platter of local pickles. Plus a bottle of white wine to make
it seem like more of an occasion. Joachim imitates the people
on the boat, but not unkindly, and she laughs in spite of her
heavy mood. They order espresso and schnapps. He doesn't

mention the past again, doesn't try to continue the conversation they started at the lake.

She knows it's her fault, knows she didn't encourage or help him, even got in the way of his confession. But he shouldn't have let her stop him. It would've been painful but in a necessary way, like the quick sharp hurt of a needle going in, ending your fear. If he'd forced it, things might've turned out differently. If he'd said everything, she would've, too. And then they would've been, at least for the moment, in the same place. But that moment passed without ever happening, and instead of torturing herself about what to say or do, how to finally straighten out this crooked situation, she simply finds herself thinking: *What a shame.*

JOACHIM

Joachim wakes before Helena, wakes even before his own body, lying still next to hers. He opens his eyes. He'd forgotten how young she looks asleep, her mouth slightly parted, her skin pale and smooth as a child's, her expression innocent of anything between them, whether hate or desire. He watches her for a long time without moving. He wants more than anything to lean over and gather her warmth and softness into his arms, bury himself in the intimacy of her sleep, dream one dream with her. But the moment he touches her, the spell will break, and they'll just be two people in bed together, without any enchantments.

He slips off his side of the bed, undresses, and pulls the door of the bathroom gently closed behind him. He takes a long shower, trying to overcome a strange feeling of cold that seems to come from within him rather than the cool tiled floor.

They didn't turn on the stars the night before. Well, the stars were still there, of course; you couldn't turn them off, but they didn't put the light on. Didn't go out of their way to see them. He doesn't even remember seeing them, but they were so tired last night, with that urgent kind of weariness that pushes everything aside on its hurried race to sleep. She drove because he'd had more wine than she had.

But she liked the stars the first night. She even seemed to like the hotel. Not without irony—when was she ever without irony?—but in a real enough way.

He soaps himself thoroughly, washes his hair twice, and holds his face under the water a long time, eyes closed, feeling like there was something he meant to feel now.

Did she have a good time? He can't tell whether the trip is a success or a failure. They came to talk and they didn't. At the same time, he said almost everything he'd been keeping from her, and she didn't seem to care.

Maybe she's right. What's the point of fighting the same fights over and over again? If discussing something will only drive them further apart, why bring it up?

Well, in the interest of honesty. That's what he thought. He lost her the last time by not being honest enough. Who knows, maybe if he'd told her about Ester right away, she wouldn't have left. After all, she stuck around for a few months even after she found out the wrong way.

"I want to believe you," she said at the time, or maybe "I want to trust you." He thought those were just empty words, but maybe she really did want to.

What's different now? For weeks, he's been doing everything right, fixing all the things she used to complain about: taking her out to dinner, taking her for a weekend away, buying her flowers, talking about his feelings, telling her the truth. If it isn't enough, he doesn't know what would be.

The idea of having told her originally has planted itself in his head and he can't get it back out. She would've been angry, or worse, played the martyr, but he would've groveled and doted on her until she forgave him. When Ester came to him about her pregnancy, he could even have asked Helena what she wanted him to do. That would've been marriage; that would've been everything, being able to turn to her in that moment.

But he didn't. He wasn't. He turns off the water and reaches blindly for a towel. The air is thick with steam but there's a chill in him he can't get rid of. He rubs himself dry and steps out to dress.

Helena's still asleep, but she's rolled over onto one side; some noise must've bothered her, the shower running or somebody in the room next door. And just then, for whatever reason, it clicks for him: She isn't the woman she was then. For better or worse. Does it really make sense to do all the things Helena five years ago wanted for Helena now? And if it doesn't, what else is there?

He takes his key, jacket and wallet, and steps out of the room, easing the door shut behind him. Outside the hotel, there's a heavy fog clinging to the ground, and the air has a clammy feel. Maybe that's why he can't get warm.

He walks to the bakery, planning to surprise her with breakfast in bed, but when he gets there, the door is locked. It is Sunday, after all. He'll take her for a nicer breakfast somewhere else, maybe in Cottbus. It's only a fifteen or twenty-minute drive. He carries on down the dirt road they took to the lake, a little at a loss. It's one thing to surprise her with breakfast, another to sit antsily in the room, trying not to breathe too loudly, waiting for her to wake.

He never used to think of things like that, never used to make these little plans. He isn't the same man, either.

The fog cleaves to the houses along the road, distorts them, and it could be any time, any place now. Even any time of day, though he knows it's still early. He knows he must've loved Helena a great deal when they were younger—why else would he have married her?—but when he looks back, all he can remember is the resentment, the petty remarks and the traps they set in conversation, each always trying to catch the other in a moment of weakness. He can't remember ever having felt such gentleness toward her, such an avid desire for her happiness, as he does now. Either he did at the beginning and he's forgotten, or he's learned a new way to love.

"I love Helena." He says it in his thoughts and aloud to the silent gray fog lurking at the edge of the forest, and it feels like saying it for the first time, not just about her, but in his life. Except that this isn't the frantic hormonal frenzy of a first affair; this is something quiet and considered you can only feel for someone you've known a long, long time, at her worst and at her best.

Nor does he feel any of the lightness of adolescent love bearing him back to the hotel; rather, his love is a burden weighing him to the ground. When you're young, anything is possible. Later you realize there are only ever two possibilities: the one that will make you happy, and the one that will make you wretched. And after a certain point, it isn't up to you anymore.

He's surprised to find her in the lobby, sitting in one of the plush chairs with the backpack at her feet. He can't tell whether she only just came down or she's been waiting a long time.

"You're up." He doesn't know what else to say.

"Good morning." She kisses him on the cheek. "I didn't know what the cut-off was so I went ahead and checked us out."

"Did you . . ." he starts to say without knowing what it was he meant to ask. They brought hardly anything with them, certainly nothing irreplaceable, but he has a sudden, gutting fear of having left something of great value in the room.

"What do you want to do for breakfast?" she asks.

"I thought we'd drive into Cottbus," he says. "I wanted to bring you breakfast in bed but nothing's open here." Maybe it was just the room itself, their presence in it. But they're still together now, with or without stars on the ceiling.

Helena offers to drive and he accepts, happy to close his eyes and feel the wind on one side, her warm presence on the other. He reaches over to stroke her wrist as she rests her hand on the clutch, but she shakes him off like a fly.

"I'm driving, Joachim."

They leave the car in the parking lot of the train station and continue on foot, following some tracks on which no tram ever passes. The sound of church bells is coming from two different directions, but maybe it's only an echo. It's a long time before they pass anyone on the street, or anything open for business.

They end up in an imitation of an American chain coffee shop, with an English name and all kinds of elaborate flavored drinks on the menu: salted caramel cappuccino, iced gingerbread hot chocolate, pumpkin spice latte. At least there's a decent crowd.

She orders a muffin and a latte and goes to find them a table. He drops his change while paying and has to scrabble around on the floor to catch the rolling coins. He feels everyone's eyes on his bent back, but when he gets up, no one is looking.

He has to relax. If he keeps looking for a fight, for her displeasure, he'll find it. And that means finding the same old ugly side of himself, the one he's been trying to plaster over with thoughtful gestures and close listening. He doesn't want to see his wife as his enemy, to treat every date as a temporary cease-fire.

She's looking out the window at the empty marketplace and gives him a dazed smile when he sets down their tray. He might as well be a waiter. The chairs are heavy iron with lumpy cushions thrown over them, and the legs scrape ferociously against the floor.

"Thanks," she says.

"You're welcome. Are you having fun?" She looks confused so he adds, "I mean, are you enjoying this trip?"

"Yeah." She sips her latte and licks the foam off her upper lip. "It was a nice weekend."

Was. "We should do this kind of thing more often," he says.

"Mmhmm," she says, or maybe just "Hmm."

Maybe the problem was getting so caught up in the idea of The Talk. Like it was this big monumental obstacle they had to get past. When just showing her a good time was enough. What is there to talk about anyway, three years after the fact? He wants to tell her he loves her again, but then he remembers that she didn't answer the last time. Besides, he shouldn't say it too often. He'll make himself ridiculous.

He didn't quite catch her comment about the hotel but he laughs anyway. They talk about the man at the reception, the Spreewald and the people on their boat yesterday.

"It was nice of you to give some money to that couple," she says, but for some reason, he isn't sure that she really thinks so.

"It just seemed like a stupid thing to fight about. I mean, there are already so many things to be unhappy about without making it harder on yourself." Where was this wisdom when he and Helena were young? He feels like a charlatan.

Then they're done with breakfast and he suggests walking around the city, but she looks at her phone and says something about not wanting to get back too late. They have another round of coffees and head out.

The walk to the train station takes longer than he expects, but the drive is shorter. Having a destination makes all the difference. They keep the radio on but don't sing along this time. When they reach the city limits, he offers to drop her at the apartment while he fills the tank and returns the rental car, but she says, "Don't be silly," and gets out at the nearest S-Bahn station.

She doesn't kiss him goodbye, but then it'll only be an hour or so until he gets home.

• • •

Between one thing and another, it's almost two hours before Joachim gets off the train near his apartment, and he feels exhausted just carrying his backpack up the stairs. They should stay home and watch a movie tonight. Order pizza. Of course she may want to go out, but he can suggest staying in.

The lights are all off and the apartment is silent. She must be taking a nap. He could do with some rest himself. Just slip out of his shoes and lie down beside her.

But when he opens the door to the bedroom, the bed is empty. He checks the sofa again, the bathroom, even the kitchen, as if she might be perched in the one corner he can't see from the living room, watching in silence.

Why would she go out right after she got back? She could've waited for him. He calls her cell phone and listens to it ring four times. He pictures her reluctance, watching the phone ring, then finally forcing herself to pick up. She doesn't say hello, but he can hear her breathing on the other end.

"Helena? Where are you?"

A long pause, her sigh not unlike the way she breathes asleep.

"I'm at home, Joachim. Where are you?"

He looks around the apartment again, and then he understands. Because this is, after all, his home and not hers.

Suddenly, anything he could say is too small to fill the

gaping silence spanning between their two phones. "I thought we could stay in and watch a movie," he finally says. "Do you want to come over?"

"Thanks," she says. "But I think I'm gonna stay here for a while." The way she says "a while" sounds like "forever."

"Helena," he says.

"I know, Joachim, I know. We'll talk later. Bye."

You couldn't, he wants to say, but she's already hung up. You couldn't possibly know.

• • •

It's hard to know what to do with the rest of the day. First he'll go have lunch, read the paper. He could get a drink with Jean and Max in the evening if he's not too tired. Or watch a movie by himself, something stupid to make him laugh. He doesn't want to think any further than that.

The new bakery that opened in the empty store a couple of blocks from his apartment has strung two rows of balloons from the storefront to the branches of a tree—pink and blue and purple. But the bakery is closed.

He walks over to the windows, reaches up and tears loose a string of balloons. They aren't helium balloons, so they just lie on the sidewalk, moving slightly in the breeze. Something slain but still twitching. He steps over to the last balloon on the string and stomps on it. Gunshot sound and then a blue shred of rubber. Purple, pink, blue again, bang, bang, bang. He keeps expecting someone to come running out of the darkened shop or one of the surrounding apartments and stop him. Or call the police. He'd go quietly. But no one does, and when he's through with the first string of balloons, he doesn't have the energy to reach up and pull down the second.

He continues to his usual bakery, asks for a sandwich, a newspaper, and another cup of coffee he knows won't wake him up. Almost all of the tables are empty. He notices that they've put away the cooler for the year. Now that he thinks about it, it was a little cold for ice cream yesterday.

Well, it's her loss.

About the Author

Originally from Virginia, Kat Hausler is a graduate of New York University and holds an M.F.A. in Fiction from Fairleigh Dickinson University, where she was the recipient of a Baumeister Fellowship. Her work has been published by *34th Parallel, Inkspill Magazine, All Things That Matter Press, Rozlyn Press,* and *BlazeVOX.* Her novel *Retrograde,* which will be published by Meerkat Press in September 2017, was long-listed for the Mslexia Novel Competition. She works as a translator in Berlin.

CPSIA information can be obtained
at www.ICGtesting.com
Printed in the USA
LVOW03s0750290817

546751LV00007B/8/P

9 781946 154026